Wait and see, annie lee

Wait and See, Annie Lee

Michelle Curry Wright

WARNER BOOKS

A Time Warner Company

Warner Books, Inc., 1271 Avenue of the Americas, New York, NY 10020

Visit our Web site at www.twbookmark.com

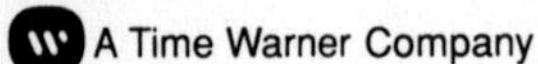

Printed in the United States of America

First Printing: August 2001

10 9 8 7 6 5 4 3 2 1

Library of Congress Cataloging-in-Publication Data
Wright, Michelle Curry.
Wait and see, Annie Lee / Michelle Curry Wright.
p. cm.
ISBN: 0-446-52690-8
1. Waitresses—Fiction. 2. Married women—Fiction. 3. Childlessness—Fiction. 4. Ski resorts—Fiction. 5. Colorado—Fiction. I. Title.

PS3573.R5372 W35 2001
813'.6—dc21 00-060019

Acknowledgments

I gratefully acknowledge the following people: my agent, Liv Blumer, and my editor, Caryn Karmatz Rudy, who are both keen and shrewd and funny; Gary and Celine, my husband and daughter, who make up the warm core of my everyday life; and my restaurant friends (you know who you are) for their delightful and off-center observations.

Most of all, though, I'd like to thank Liz Kurnetz—whose longtime encouragement and action on my behalf have made things leap from the looking glass and into my lap. Everybody should have such a friend.

One

"Poison Control Center, may I help you?"

Annie Lee hesitated on the other end of the line.

When the incident had occurred the night before, no one else had seemed concerned. It had begun with a potted orange tree directly behind table eleven shedding one of its leaves right into a customer's bowl of bouillabaisse.

Annie Lee happened to be at table ten showing the dessert tray when she saw the woman pick out the leaf and then carefully put it on her tongue, in spite of warnings from her friends around the table. "*Rosana, no!*" they cried. "*¿Qué estás haciendo?*" What do you think you're doing?

"*Dios quería que lo tuviera,*" she'd replied with authority, back straight, black suede boots tucked beneath her. "God wanted me to have it." Whereupon, with her male companions silenced, she resumed her animated discourse, occasionally brandishing the soup spoon as a pointer.

Annie Lee had begun to worry then. Rosana seemed to be the sort of person who might do herself some harm eventually, perhaps end up the victim of one too many of her dramatic flourishes. Was she really that sure of things? Of God's hand in them? Of the leaf's innocuousness, at least?

The next morning, while Annie Lee watered the houseplants, she could not help thinking once again of Rosana's unorthodox mouthful. Surely, she told herself, a call to Poison Control would be just the thing to lay the matter to rest.

Poison Control. She found the number where she knew it would be, stuck along with other toll-free numbers to an old Ping-Pong paddle she kept in a desk drawer in the living room, conveniently positioned under the phone book. Her husband thought the paddle and its pasted-on numbers ludicrous. He called his wife alarmist, too emergency-ready. You're practically asking for trouble, Annie Lee, he said.

"A toll-free number is the last true benevolent gesture of our civilization," she'd maintained. "Besides, the fact is that it's simple prudence in a place like Pike to have your telephone list in place." Pike, Colorado, was small as well as remote. Nestled in the southwestern Rockies, high at the dead end of a potholed, serpentine road, it was six hours from Santa Fe and seven from Denver. Oh, there was an airport for those brave enough to fly into it, and helicopters for the occasional emergency transport. But for the most part, people in Pike were, aside from their satellite dishes, modems, and cell phones (which seemed to be multiplying faster than rabbits), cut off from the rest of the world.

Though regular trips to big cities more than remedied Lucas's cabin fever, Annie Lee seemed to need regular, intermittent connections to the outside world. She found toll-free calling straightforward and, for the most part, extremely satisfying.

Until this moment, however, she had never had reason enough to call an emergency number; and after walking up the stairs and into the study with the phone in hand, she'd stood at the window and checked the length of the street to make sure she couldn't see her husband anywhere. He had taken the cat to the vet's for shots and a teeth cleaning and wasn't due back for another half hour, but you never knew. The neighborhood, however, was perfectly quiet and still except for the occasional bird slicing through the summer morning.

Now an older woman from the sound of it—someone kind and eager—was asking Annie Lee if she could help her, and from somewhere deep within, Annie Lee felt herself respond. Yes! Yes, you can! And without the slightest idea that her brain would perform a triple-gainer before landing, she answered:

"Yes. My one-year-old, Sydney, has eaten a leaf from our ornamental orange tree. I'm a little concerned about toxicity." She heard herself say the words, as if the information had been waiting there, cloaked under Rosana like a fairy under a blossom—and then wondered how obvious it was that women who named their children in emergency situations were making them up. Where had the name Sydney come from?

"No harm done." The woman was solicitous and yet matter-of-fact. "Most of it will come out undigested, anyway. But don't let him make a habit of eating houseplants—some of them are quite another story."

"It's a her," Annie Lee corrected, feeling the boldness of the lie grow inside her, sharp and real like a thorny bush. She pressed on: "What if she'd chewed the leaf as thoroughly as a caterpillar would? I mean so I really don't have to worry, not the least little bit."

After a pause the woman replied, "It's not on our list of serious poisons or poisonous plants. Nothing at all under orange. If Sydney starts to show signs of stomach distress, feels dizzy, or actually disgorges, give us a call back. In that case it might have been a spray of some sort. Something on the leaf." Another pause. "Is this your first?"

"Yes," Annie Lee whispered, deeply humiliated and yet smitten now by the idea that she'd really called Poison Control not for the sake of some woman who could more than take care of herself but for the sake of her firstborn child. Someone named Sydney, conceived on the spur of the moment but grown real at once, like a time-lapse image of a budding baby unfurling into a fully clothed human being.

"Well, you did the right thing in calling us. My name is Marietta Lautrec. Don't ever feel you can't call us at the Poison Control Center. That's what we're here for. No matter how unusual the question, how odd the occurrence. Little Sydney's lucky to have such a conscientious mom."

Annie Lee had to ask herself then if she ever would be such a paragon of virtue as that—a caring parent. Shyly, she asked the competent person on the other end if she had children.

"Three children," she chirped. "All grown, all gone away. Still worry about them, though. The worrying never stops, you know."

Annie Lee was nodding. "I could definitely see that," she said. Already she was worried that Sydney would grow up to be the product of an unstable parent, namely herself. That it would affect her for the rest of her life in spite the influences of a rational, loving, and normal father.

"Well . . ." she could not think of any reason to detain the woman longer. "I'll let you go. Thanks again for your help."

"Not at all," said Marietta Lautrec.

After hanging up, Annie Lee felt vindicated. It was just as she'd said: There were kind souls out there, floating in the fiber-optic network, who would listen and understand, night or day, free of charge, no strings attached. All you had to do was reach out.

Shortly thereafter, she called Poison Control again, and then again—she couldn't seem to stop herself. Lorian Parmethia was on duty when little Sydney fired a jet of biodegradable cleaner—the kind you're supposed to dilute ten times—into her mouth. "We're very lucky the spray tip was set on stream." Lorian's approach pushed the limits of empathy; he identified completely with the caller. "We worry more about the eyes in such cases," he said. "We'll have to be sure to recheck those childproofing devices, won't we? In the meantime, let's count our blessings."

It was a woman named Darween Lo who answered Annie Lee's call about Sydney's having eaten a whole packet of Strawberry-Kiwi Kool-Aid. After Darween's initial assessment—her voice was soothing and smoky—she became almost deadpan. "Consider it an immunization against future doses of artificial colors and flavors," she intoned. "Believe me, your little girl will need it. Blue Raspberry alone is a call to arms. Can you tell I have two small children myself?"

Darween. Annie Lee, hearing echoes of Darwin and queen and Halloween, was captivated by the name.

Is this how one came up with a name, she wondered—by lapping evocative syllables together into something greater than the sum of its parts? She hung up rethinking the name Sydney.

Kidney. Australia. The id. The knee. It wasn't bad.

This all seemed harmless enough to Annie Lee, calling people up and asking about possible poisoning. For one thing, her make-believe child, like a mannequin in a simulated crash test, was part of the continuing education of emergency personnel. She was doing them a favor. She, in return, received understanding and respect and reinforcement of this idea that a caring mother was the highest possible life form on earth. It was something to strive for, to hang on to. It was worth bringing up, hashing out, actively pursuing.

Lucas didn't have any idea she'd spoken with complete strangers about herself, himself, and their little Sydney, who was outgrowing shoes and sprouting teeth in a parallel universe. She hadn't wanted to frighten him with her escalating biological needs but at the same time was sad she found it necessary to tiptoe around the issue—what some might consider the core issue of a seven-year marriage.

But then there were men and there were resort-town men, and the latter, notorious Peter Pans, loved their sports and their toys and their freedoms and were infamous for loving women who could not only keep up with them but put up with them. Sometimes these very women were even called upon to rise up and defend the man, whose own family eventually wanted answers. When was he going to grow up, they wanted to know, settle down, move on, rein in that recreation? As if the poor woman had any idea.

Though Annie Lee did not feel at all that Lucas was cut from the same recreational cloth (windproof, rainproof, breathable, and adequate, when layered, to thirty below), she nevertheless was sensitive to the prevailing psychological climate. On the other hand, the underlying assumption in their marriage had always been that they would have children someday. Could she, she started asking herself, have been wrong about something so fundamental?

It was during the peak of fall that year when she had the feeling that she could no longer go on silently weighing issues on her own. An opportunity to say something presented itself one day right around the time the leaves had all turned to shimmering masses of yellows and blazing oranges and were falling and blowing about. This autumn zenith, bittersweetened by northern air flows murmuring of winter, might last one day or three weeks, it was impossible to say. Locals emerged early in the morning and stayed out late, bewitched by the fine half-light of Indian summer.

Annie Lee, inclined to feeling melancholy in the fall no matter how grandiose, sweet, or fleeting it could be, was staring out the front-door window at her husband. As leaves swirled low to the ground near his feet, he fiddled with an extension cord and then dragged his drill across the yard. The old latch on the front gate had once again come loose, and he was about to fix it.

This was not the kind of thing that perpetually single, fancy-free, adrenaline-reliant males did—fix latches on front gates. Annie Lee was sure of it. No, it was something a father did to protect his children from wandering off. It was something a dad did to keep stray dogs from wandering in and biting perfect little dirt-smudged ankles. She could not tell whether this insight sharpened her melancholy or diminished it; but in a moment she found herself standing beside the man.

"What are you doing?"

"Fixing the latch," he said, setting up the drill to bore a new hole into the gatepost. He glanced at her shrewdly. "Isn't it kind of obvious what I'm doing, Annie Lee?"

"The fixing the latch part is obvious," she answered.

"Oh," he said, squeezing the trigger on the drill and initiating a high-pitched squeal lasting four seconds or so. "I see. I'm not just fixing the gate here, am I?" He stopped and looked at her. Lucas was an accomplished reader of her feelings. He was rarely off by much. "I'm securing the barricade. Protecting the nest. Do me a favor, and get me my crossbow so I can go hunting after I'm done with all this piddly stuff. You can do the gathering."

Annie Lee approached the gate and lifted up the broken latch and let it fall and swing. "Do you ever think about what you'd name a child?" she asked, not looking at him while she spoke. Realizing what the question implied, she turned around quickly to clarify.

"Not that I'm pregnant or anything." She saw him close his eyes with relief and hastened, before losing courage, to add, "I'd like to get serious about trying, though, Lucas. I mean, we've been married awhile now. We still love each other, we love our house, we're not deadbeats or anything. Occasionally we say 'to hell with the diaphragm' and it doesn't seem to shock you, the possibilities, I mean. Meanwhile," she squinted at the sun, "I'm thinking of names and you're fixing latches on gates. See what I mean?"

"What you're saying," he said, after his own pause and squint at the sun, "is you think we should let nature take its course."

Annie Lee nodded but bit down on her joy. The worst thing to do with someone like Lucas was to appear too eager.

Miraculously, he continued on. "That we should spend the fast-approaching winter months—productively."

She was smiling now, all traces of melancholy gone like the leaves, which, whirlwinded and spent, had landed in someone else's yard and at someone else's feet.

Lucas lowered his drill to the ground, as if dropping anchor for the night. "Well," he said. "It would be lying to say I hadn't thought about it. The thoughts are weird, sort of like what it feels like to have one of those muscle-stim devices hooked up to you. Your muscle twitches on its own, in an unfamiliar way, and you watch it, sort of fascinated, trying to figure out exactly what it feels like."

Although she was usually comforted by Lucas's scientific references and biological bottom lines, Annie Lee felt the smile fade from her face. There was too much at stake here. After a long pause, he approached her and put his arms around her, kissed her neck, and then held her sweetly, as if to seal their fate together at the edge of some deep, dark, fathomless canyon, traversable only by blind faith.

The wet kiss on her neck made Annie Lee shiver with desire. Desire was one thing she understood.

But it was when their two plaid flannel shirts came together—his in small-check blues, hers in big-check browns—that Annie Lee felt that this just might be as close as people could truly come in life: when, inadvertently, the texture and color of their clothes lay together like a happy stack of dish towels.

Two

The *Farmer's Almanac* that year had predicted a hard winter, but neither Annie Lee nor Lucas had ever seen anything like it. Nor had the elderly Winkleman sisters, who lived right next door and who had seen everything to do with weather in Pike for seventy-some years. With an unprecedented three straight weeks of lows in the minus twenties, gas bills were outrageous and electric bills were far worse. Car batteries had to be cajoled into coming to life in the morning, and so did people.

Lucas was kind enough to concede the weather was great for making babies, but he, like everyone else, was getting that old cabin fever. It was too cold to snow and too cold to ski on what meager amounts had fallen in November and December. The locals were becoming very grumpy, and they weren't the only ones.

Pike, cresting on its recently touted world-class resort status, had hotels full of unhappy people who had come expecting the Colorado sun to be warm as advertised. There was nothing for them to do but eat, drink, and shop, which they all did gorgingly—yet grudgingly, as if they'd been swindled somehow. Annie Lee had been waiting on these people five nights a week for twelve weeks and had begun to lose faith in this whiny, wimpy upper middle class: If they couldn't take a vacation cold snap, how could they be expected to teach the pursuit of excellence, make charitable contributions, or work for the betterment of society?

Ordinarily, she was not inclined to feel this way. Ordinarily, she found a certain simple satisfaction in putting beautiful plates of food in front of hungry people. Who could dispute the meaning of such a job? On good nights she and the other waiters were content to eavesdrop and bandy about the complexities of human nature. During a particularly tough string of nights, though, they theorized on the end of the world and how bad behavior at the dinner table would be the thing that would bring it all down. Such, unfortunately, was the general feeling during the first half of that winter.

It was on Valentine's Day of "the cold year" (as it came to be called) that the weather unaccountably changed. Lucas had raced out the door early, ready to ski at last. He didn't care how mediocre the conditions might be, only that it was warm enough to do it. In his haste, he'd made no mention of cupid nor had he presented Annie Lee with any sort of gift, or card, or comment to seal their status not only as a couple but as a baby-making one on a big, thrilling, sometimes chilling, adventure. Rather than glossing over the fact, as she might have in a more upbeat frame of mind, Annie Lee told herself that this was it, the moment every woman most dreaded—when the man in her life started taking her for granted. At seven years, he was right on schedule.

Annie Lee had wanted to wait to give him her present—a year's membership to the Marinade of the Month Club (for a professional cook, food was at the heart of every gift)—until he'd given her his. But with his quick shower, quick exit, and quick good-bye before work there had hardly been time to respond to his obliviousness of the holiday. There had not even been enough time to shove her gift at him before he'd gone, thus at least getting her digs in.

Several hours later, as she marched to the restaurant, past the rapidly opening and shutting doors of clothing stores, gift shops, and through a thick line of people right outside one of the florists', she had to wonder whether Lucas might not have acted differently had she already managed to get pregnant. Wasn't there some special shelf of things reserved for men shopping for the future mothers of their children? For that matter, Annie Lee had also expected herself to conceive quickly. Instantaneously, in fact. It seemed odd to her that after five months nothing had happened, and perhaps it seemed odd to Lucas, too. And what did you get your wife for Valentine's Day if you thought she might be infertile?

She entered the restaurant and was greeted by a large and unwieldy group of red-and-white helium balloons, all bobbing around, curly ribbons bouncing like the ringlets of so many heads of hair. She batted a fist at them.

February fourteenth had always been one of the biggest days of the year at Restaurant Mathilde, a cozy and popular French restaurant wedged between a sporting goods store and a real estate office. Tonight they were overbooked by four tables at 7:30—which was not usually cause for concern since it was generally assumed that a certain number of people wouldn't show. Tonight, however, people would. With the warmer weather, the smiling hordes were strolling Main Street hatless and with coats unzipped, occasionally wandering into Mathilde to see if they might "get in." And the owner of the place, a charming and accommodating man named Jean-Jacques Janasse—known as Jay—true to form, was packing them in until all hours of the night.

"They're happy, for the first time in a long time," he said

to Annie Lee and to Eddie Stahl, the bartender that night, who were both huddled over the reservations book, trying to decipher the undecipherable. "It's our job to accommodate as many happy people as possible."

With a bevy of customers waiting in the bar and the night about to begin, Constantine Premus, another longtime waiter, the staff know-it-all, and one of Annie Lee's best friends, was expressing his views on love.

"Just can't wait to charge these people exorbitant prices for an overcrowded, noisy, jarring night of love." He adjusted the knot of his tie, which appeared to be an elegant study in navy and white but upon closer scrutiny revealed an intricate maze of tiny male body parts. "Poor dumb suckers, buying into all that Hallmark crap." Con without a boyfriend was a self-propelled aerosol can of pressurized cynicism. Otherwise he was a total sap and everyone knew it.

"But I'll bet Lukey-poo bought you a little something or other, didn't he? Something with a touch of lace but not trashy, right? Perhaps a simple note on expensive bond with his name scrawled across it after the words, 'All my love?' "

She frowned at him. "Where do you get this stuff? Soaps? Ads for fountain pens?"

He ignored her but continued to stare at her unhappy countenance. "You know, when you do that your face changes completely. No more pixie-face-all-freckles-and-high-cheekbones—you gain ten years, giving me that look. It will set your wrinkles earlier, that's what it will do. So he didn't get you anything, huh?"

"None of your business. Like you said, it's all a bunch of crap."

"Until you get the gift," he said. They both laughed.

"Well, ready for death by deuce?" Annie Lee asked him, tying the knot of her red-and-gray rep tie. She was referring to the onslaught of two-person tables—or "two-tops"—which would require far more work of the ditching and darting waiters than an even mix of small, medium, and large parties.

"A slow death by deuce, it looks like," said Con. "They'll want to hear the champagne cork pop, and they'll want to be left alone. They'll want their plates lackadaisically lifted away rather than snatched. And to top everything off, we're foisting lobster on them as a special."

Annie Lee's face dropped. "Lobster," she repeated, horrified. "Are you kidding?" Lobster, a food usually reserved for New Year's or Christmas Eve, would have the sorry effect of slowing things down even further. What was the chef thinking, a food so rich on a night so tightly jammed for time? She was about to ask him but noticed he was having words with Marc, the nasty, brutish, and short French pastry guy.

Jay cut the ribbon on the night at 5:54 and led the first five tables to their seats.

At 6:02, Marc was still spitting under his breath about someone having ordered the wrong chocolate for his famous Lovers' Plate—from which he'd acquired his tongue-thrust-in-cheek handle, "Lover Boy."

"*Espèce de con, ça fait chier. Putain.* (Son of a bitch, pisses me off. Shit.)" Nothing was ever good enough for Marc, who hadn't bothered to learn much English, not even the basic swear words, in fifteen months.

Tonight, even Michel, the chef, had to keep in check his desire to smack Marc with a copper pan. "He's from Paris," he said, shaking his head. "What do you expect?"

The chef was from Alsace and the owner from the south of France. They tended to disdain Parisians, just like Americans with their scapegoat New Yorkers. Besides Marc there were four other cooks—two more non-Parisian French boys and two Americans. The dishwashers were both Mexican. All the front staff—two bartenders, three bussers, five waiters, and an occasional hostess—were American although between them they could communicate fluently with French-, German-, and Spanish-speaking customers. Lately, more and more Euros and South Americans seemed to be discovering Pike.

"Well, you know my mother's Parisian, originally," Annie Lee said to the chef.

"But she's American now," he retorted. "It's not the same. She's not from Paris anymore." He was carting a huge load of bones that had been cooking all day up the stairs to the second kitchen, and Annie Lee tried not to breathe in the stench of the sauce-making material.

"Well, which is worse?" she called out to him.

"That's a good question!" he called back, then said, *Caldo! Caldo! Mucho caldo!* as he passed the dishwasher with the two-ton pot.

Mucho caldo could certainly have been that night's slogan. It was hot in the dining room, and stuffy, and none of the waiters relished racing around madly while trying to appear to be doing things at their leisure. Jay had forgotten that with the warmer weather he'd needed to reset the thermostat, so by eight o'clock the dining room felt like a pizza oven. People were peeling off cardigans and rolling up sleeves, but no one, not even high-ranking royalty, had the bad taste to complain about being too hot anywhere in Pike. Every single table did, however, ask for something special—as if it simply were not Valentine's Day without some *special request*. They wanted olive oil instead of butter. Oil and vinegar instead of the house dressing. Different garnishes, different sides. Meat seared instead of grilled, fish raw instead of cooked. Vegetable substitutions, additions, omissions. The chef miraculously managed to hold it together until he ran out of potatoes mousseline—mashed—which sent him into a tailspin, smoke coming out of his ears like exhaust as he plummeted in a downward spiral. After that, the waiters were careful to spend as little time as possible in the vicinity of the kitchen.

It was about midway through the service (just when Annie Lee thought she would double up in pain if one more fingertip-touching, special-requesting couple was seated) that she found herself at a cool oasis, a refuge, on table thirteen: It was a single, solitary pregnant person, in an elegant Renaissance-red dress, staring at the menu, her eyes glistening with excitement. She ordered enough food for three.

Annie Lee was smitten. "When is your baby due?" She was replenishing the bread basket for the second time.

"In five weeks," the woman said, grinning ear to ear. She had short, wavy blond hair and the kind of wide-open, expectant expression that could draw a crowd. She'd been smiling at staff and customers alike, even as she'd picked up a lamb chop with her fingers to grind off the last bits of meat. Annie Lee was dying to ask where the husband was. What kind of man would let this fetching female take herself out on Valentine's Day?

"Is it your first?" Annie Lee was sure it was.

The woman reached for the butter and, instead of spreading it on the bread, just laid a slab on top. Her nonalcoholic beer prompted a burp, and discreetly the napkin came to her lips. "Is it that obvious?"

Annie Lee nodded. "Yup. You have a look about you." She signaled to a busser to bring the water pitcher. "So, what brings you to Pike?" And whatever it was, Annie Lee wanted to add, why didn't it bring your husband?

"Oh, we just live in Junction," she said, waving, unfazed, to a couple who had raised their glasses to her. Grand Junction was two and a half hours away, in the fruit belt of Colorado. Annie Lee would never have pegged her for a small-town type. "We've wanted to come here for Valentine's dinner for several years. So I made the reservation. Then James, that's my husband, got a call earlier to deliver a baby and had to go. He might still show up for dessert, or he might not. We got a room for the night here in Pike, so he'll be here eventually. I just didn't want to miss dinner, and I don't think the baby did, either!" She raised her napkin to her lips and then patted herself lightly on the sternum, smiling. "What's for dessert?" she asked, as Annie Lee started to clear the plates.

It was the mixed-berry trifle she pointed to on the dessert tray, but not before Jay had indicated that he wanted to be the one to buy it for her. Annie Lee stared at him and asked if he knew her.

"No," he said, looking toward table thirteen and flashing a brief but indulgent smile. "But she seems to be enjoying our food so much; and she's all alone." He shrugged. "I'd go sit with her myself, but it's too busy right now." He bolted off.

Annie Lee was just about to serve the complimentary dessert when a loud burst of applause brought her rushing to see what the commotion was. It appeared James, most certainly an urban refugee from the smart looks of him, had showed after all. Annie Lee got there just in time to hear him tell the entire dining room he'd had a baby to deliver and to watch him plunk down a dozen white roses—in something far superior to the ordinary flower-shop vase—on the table.

The woman was beaming at her husband as only a pregnant woman in love could do. Annie Lee, not a little envious, put down the dessert and noticed when she did that a little white box with a gold ribbon lay in the shade created by the veritable thicket of sweet-smelling roses.

Eventually, the now beloved woman in red pulled out a necklace of pearls and garnets with a tiny silver locket at the bottom and held it up for everyone in the dining room—half of whom were watching anyway—to see. Annie Lee witnessed it all from the waiter station, where she shook her head in amazement. She had never seen anything like it, on Valentine's Day or ever. It was as if true love had walked through the door, and everybody in the place needed a dose of the real thing so badly it froze the cheap imitators solid, made them gawk and then finally surrender. The customers became docile from that moment on; they stopped special ordering, special requesting, special anything. The night was transformed.

James and Arduth Ames (she used her credit card) were the last ones to leave, and even Con smiled as they left. "I would have hated them except for three things," he said at dinner, heaping a pile of buttery red potatoes onto his plate near an odd-shaped piece of salmon tip, "The name James Ames, the hex they put on the dining room, and that stunning vase." He reconsidered his statement. "Somehow it was the vase, though, that clinched it for me. I've never seen a heterosexual take such *care*," he stabbed a piece of the fish and put it in his mouth. "I myself could use a little of that."

"Yeah, well," Annie Lee was watching—out of the corner of one eye—as Marc marched into the small private dining room in which the staff ate every night, "who couldn't?"

Poor Marc was still in the paroxysms of his earlier tantrum. "*C'est de la merde ça*," were his words, thrown out onto the table along with the truffles, the cake, the mousse, and all other vile remnants of the Lovers' Plate. It had all been made with the wrong, the terribly wrong, chocolate. "This is shit."

Well, the rest of the staff were pigs, then, pigs in *merde*. Annie Lee ate enough chocolate to give herself a ring around the mouth and a buggy feeling behind the eyes. The atoms in her brain, charged with sugar and whatever it is that makes chocolate a drug, were popping like bingo balls. On her way home, the scene from table thirteen replayed itself over and over and made it quite plain how badly she wanted to be like the woman in red. Pregnant. Glowing. A lamb chop of a thing to whom complete strangers raised their glasses and sent desserts. Whose husband *ardently* adored her. Ardently. Arduth. She had never heard the name before.

She arrived home thinking of names, the giving of names.

Names led to Marietta and Parmethia and Darween, and that led to Poison Control. Why not? she thought. Lucas wasn't home yet. The radio station had gone off the air. She had a lot of talk in her and she wanted it to be about Sydney—with someone who would understand, someone who would trust that Annie Lee was capable of having children, someone who would assume it was the truth that came out of her mouth. It was late and it was Valentine's Day, but someone would be there, they always were.

She punched in the number carefully, holding down the last digit long enough to reconsider her basic frame of mind, which was vulnerable, lonely, still not pregnant, and prone to romanticizing everything. She released the digit.

"Poison Control Center," it was an androgynous voice that answered politely: "Can I be of assistance?"

"Yes," Annie Lee said, shutting herself in the powder room just off the kitchen, a room she had just started repainting. She had not, she just realized, thought of what question to ask. "I think my child may have swallowed some—paint." She thought of how late it was. "Earlier today, I mean. I didn't think anything of it at the time, but now, well—"

The voice didn't hesitate to interrupt. "What color did he ingest?"

Annie Lee had not even considered this line of questioning. She looked around and stopped at a pot of forced tulips on the toilet tank, with petals the color of a Ticonderoga pencil. "Yellow," she answered, and then thought to clarify that. "Yellow oxide." Some real person might be trying to call in right now with some real emergency. She experienced a pang of guilt.

"Not that it really matters," the voice continued. "In general we worry most about artists' materials from England. Are you using Liquitex paints? My name is Gabriel Salt, by the way, in case we get disconnected." He paused. "Would you mind giving me your name?"

Her name? They'd never asked before. "Annie Lee Fleck," she said, at the same time realizing that once they had her name, they had her. "Yes." She was distracted now, worried for herself, "As a matter of fact, it was Liquitex . . ." Actually, she would be painting with Benjamin Moore house paints. She had painstakingly found the perfect color, then the perfect name to go with it. It wasn't feeling good to lie anymore. Bleakly, she wondered if they monitored calls for quality control.

"You need to keep your paints and pastels away from your child, Ms. Fleck. How old is he, and what were the circumstances of ingestion?" Almost three, she answered, suddenly weary of Sydney's accidents and her own inability to prevent them, and wishing to end the conversation—but finding it more complex now that he knew her by name. The last people on earth she wanted thinking badly of her were the nice people at Poison Control. After all, she was a virtuous person to them, a conscientious mom.

Taking a breath, she extended the lie up a forty-foot ladder. She told Gabriel Salt normally she kept everything under lock and key, but her husband hadn't seen the danger of letting Sydney paint with the artists' paints. Not being an artist, he didn't realize that the brilliance of colors was due to their chemical makeup. "He's a chef," she added, "and doesn't usually go around thinking about beautiful, brilliant things being poisonous." That last statement was true enough.

"No, I see your point. I've always wanted to go to cooking school myself. Imagine that, and here I am at Poison Control." His fragile laugh was crackly and brittle. She imagined his hair was fine like corn silk and very straight and fell over his eyes, eyes of a wet-river-stone color of some sort, watery and sensitive and prone to cataracts in old age.

"Well," she said then, "usually strange logic can be found in everything. Somewhere. If you look hard enough." She didn't believe these words, but they sounded reassuring as she said them.

"By the way, does Marietta still work there?" Suddenly she had a great urge to pry the subject away from herself and her fictitious progeny. It seemed, among other things, an insult to someone like Arduth Ames, whose belly spoke nothing but the truth.

"Marietta Lautrec?" He said the name as if it were the Queen of Sheba's. "Why no, she left some months ago. She's working for a private poisons research center now. In Boston. She broke out of tel-emergency communications and became an authority on exotic ingesta—you know, strange things the average hotline worker might not have answers on. A person scraped by an obscure tropical fish, say, with a certain poison on its fins. Or someone who drank too much pumpkinseed oil. Or managed to ingest a piece of a letter or part of a sponge. A nail-biter who'd started having convulsions because—well, anyway, you get the picture. It's a dream job. You've called here before, evidently, and gotten Marietta . . ."

At this point precisely, with the words "You've called here before, evidently," Annie Lee could no longer deny what she was: She was someone who called emergency numbers for company, and for advice, and worst of all for complicity in her misrepresentations. After thanking Gabriel Salt for his help, and after he'd timidly wished her a happy Valentine's Day, she hung up the phone.

Well, it's obvious why motherhood has taught me nothing, she told herself. Because I'm not a mother. I don't run after my toddler all day. And at night, I don't spend hours putting her to bed and seeing to her when she cries; at night I wait tables. I deal with people for approximately two and a half hours and then they're out of my life. It's possible I'm not even fit for motherhood. Perhaps not even fit to receive a Valentine's gift.

She fell into a fitful, sugar-coma of sleep before Lucas got home, and dreamed, thrashing in the sheets, of having sections again, something they'd done away with years ago at Mathilde. Her section consisted of seven two-tops that were seated simultaneously three times in a row. She made twenty-two dollars after tipping out.

The next morning, exhausted by the long and unprofitable night, she padded downstairs, reminding herself that chocolate had caused her nasty nightmare and that the money had actually been very, very good the night before. Good enough to warrant buying herself a nice little necklace if she felt like it.

Lucas greeted her with a grin and a gift. "Sorry it's late," he said. "But you were asleep when I got home. I had Lina order it from a specialty shop in the neighborhood she grew up in, and it just arrived yesterday." Lina was his boss at Giancarlo, a matronly Italian who devoted herself to all her employees, treated them like family. Annie Lee took the box and smiled weakly. It was the kind of Italian candy, hard with a soft center, that she adored.

"I *love* these," she said, ashamed to have doubted her wonderful husband, the person who was about to put a plate of poached eggs and sourdough toast in front of her. Then she apologized for not having given him his present and said, somewhat sheepishly, that it had slipped her mind. She fetched the brochure and briefly recounted what he could expect in the next year. Marinades for chicken, meats, fish, tofu, and vegetables. Specialty marinades for martini olives and green beans. Even a marinade for fruitcake and one for feta cheese.

"I had no idea you could marinate cheese," he said, staring at the brochure.

"Neither did I," said Annie Lee, feigning incredulity, as she picked out a piece of Italian candy—apricot—bit down on it, and sucked out the sweet gel. Thus was faith in her marriage reaffirmed and all doubts cast aside that morning: with a blue-and-gold box of Italian candy. It remained unwavering until the beginning of summer.

Three

Annie Lee's yearly female exam was set for June twenty-seventh, and it was everything she could do to wait it out patiently until the day arrived. With no bodily changes, she had begun to have doubts again about her fertility: Was she to be singled out, then, as one of those people for whom nature would not take its presumed course?

Dr. Oliver Oram, the town's only gynecologist, happened also to be the designated leader—and driver—of Pike's Pickled Pipers, the biggest bagpipe band in the Four-Corners area, and at Pike's nine thousand feet, the most elevated pipers on earth. Despite the silly name, Annie Lee had always trusted Dr. Oram, the designated driver. Until now. Now he was explicitly warning her, in that warmhearted way of his, not to get too consumed by the baby-making process.

"Maybe you just need to relax a bit about this," he said in the heat of that summer day. Exasperated, she turned a medium-to-medium-rare pink.

"It takes a while for some couples to conceive," he continued. Sensing her anxiety, he removed his glasses and gave her a good gaze, right in the eye. He had cotton-white eyebrows, canopies that moved up and out as he spoke.

She felt like arguing. "It never takes teenage girls very long to conceive."

"My point exactly," was his poised reply. "The last thing they want is to get pregnant, which is why they do. In addition to the fertility and exuberance of youth, of course." He put the glasses—big, square, black-framed things—back on. "You see, feared things are given far too much brain space. And as it becomes harder to conceive, or that being your perception of it, you in particular want it more and more. Which, in my humble opinion, puts it further and further out of reach."

Dr. Oram had the gentlest touch of any gynecologist she'd ever experienced—truly a gifted individual. And when he spoke, Annie Lee had always felt it was not so much as a medical expert, but as some sort of elder counselor from a tribe of advanced beings, dressed up as—of all things—a doctor. Ha! She would have trusted him more in his kilt.

"It's always been my problem with the modern trend of goal setting." He extrapolated now, his ideas in some way illuminated by the heat of the lamp on her inner thighs. "You lose the feel of the process, you miss part of *life*. Well, it's been said many ways. If you do not aim the arrow, you cannot miss the target, and so forth. You are one healthy-looking specimen, young woman."

"So, what you're saying is I shouldn't want to have a child at all in order to have one." It was a frustrating time to be telling her this. "I never really knew what I wanted, besides marrying Lucas, until we decided to try to have kids. I mean, I'm one of those people who wanders around a lot in terms of objectives. You know, goes sideways, even if I think I have a plan. What I'm saying, Doc, is—I rarely have the luxury of knowing what I want. I mean, I came to Pike by accident and it's been over ten years."

He removed the latex gloves with great care, threw them away, and took one of her hands in his. "And what I'm saying is there's no reason why you shouldn't conceive in terms of your cervix, your ovaries, your medical history. The tests show Lucas's sperm count is normal, that's good—not conclusive, but good. But I'm also saying, try not to dwell on it, Annie Lee. Maybe you thought you never knew what you wanted until you had trouble achieving it. Sort of a fascination with what's difficult. Well, this kind of thing can be stressful on a marriage, believe me, I've seen it. In another year, say, let's go one step further. One step at a time. There is ample recourse these days, you know, my dear. Ample recourse."

She should have walked out the door and strolled down Main Street counting her blessings. She was a healthy specimen (according to her doctor) living in paradise (according to the latest glossy advertisements). She should have gone home to her front porch and taken a deep breath of hot, high-altitude summer air full of lavender and the musty smell of window screens. She should have listened to the buzzing of bugs, the occasional cheep of birds, and the high-pitched trills of crickets and then looked up at the towering peaks all around her, put on her hiking shoes, and set out to experience the glory of being alive.

But as she walked home that day, some perverse little voice inside her said, "I never even had an arrow before, let alone a target. And dammit I want a bull's-eye or I'm going to throw a tantrum." After fixing herself a jug of iced tea with mint, she sat down to further refine her strategies, intent on overcoming this difficulty she seemed to be having with something as simple and basic and natural as getting pregnant. With a healthy body like hers there was no earthly reason not to try even harder. To get serious and even scientific about the whole thing.

The next day she purchased $47 worth of ovulation testing kits, basal thermometers, charts, and high-potency vitamins at the Pike Pharmacy—items she immediately hid away in order not to put too much overt pressure on Lucas. Several days after that, she made her way to the lingerie shop (you could not buy plain ordinary panties in Pike, but custom undergarments seemed to be a principal commodity for tourists on vacation) and came back with a blush-wine-colored cellophane bag filled with bikinis, bras, teddies, and even one of those long, slinky nightgowns—in a color delightfully called Mother-of-Peach—which clung, in a vacuum seal, to her body.

She told her husband that it was natural for a woman's sex drive to kick in at her age, and tried not to be too obvious in her frenzy of variegated lovemaking, carefully alternating times of day, states of mind, positions, potions, and types of music. Annie Lee found herself aroused in spite of her clinical approach; and whatever Lucas made of it, he kept his mouth shut and seemed to go along obligingly.

But the bottom line was that despite the comingling of fluids and enough body friction to start a fire, there wasn't any procreative success. No spark of new life, no bodily change. After every monthly menses, she would pick herself up, give herself a little pep talk, and go about researching further possibilities for the advancement of her cause, from the position of the planets to Chinese herbs to the latest vitamin-packed power snacks. Meanwhile, the doctor's profound words (which she began referring to privately as "Oram's Advisory"), murky and distant, continued to play on like a tape at the bottom of some deep, cold, and forgotten ocean.

Finally, there was nothing left for Annie Lee to do but start blaming Lucas.

It was on a drab, dingy-laundry-colored December day, smack in the throes of premenstrual syndrome, that she suggested to Lucas that perhaps his attitude had become halfhearted; that he was not taking the bull by the horns. His flannel shirt in Spanish red may have prompted the comment.

He rolled his eyes, subtly, but she saw it. "I *am* the bull, Annie Lee. And I'm doing what I'm supposed to do: I'm having sex with you, I'm enjoying it. What more do you want?"

"I don't know." They were staring at each other in the bathroom mirror as if speaking to their alter egos instead of each other. She felt and looked normal, she thought, but he looked crooked—that was the thing with mirrors, and, it seemed, with this situation. "I want you to figure out why it's not working," she said. "Because I think I've exhausted my resources. And it's like you haven't made any effort. You haven't even shaved in three days."

He looked up at the ceiling and then blew a small breath out his nose like a—well, like a small bull. "I don't operate the same way you do. Don't ask me to follow your prescribed course of action or it won't be fun anymore." He approached her face, the one in the mirror. "Maybe if you stopped focusing so hard on this one objective, maybe things would happen more naturally, that's all. And what does stubble have to do with anything? You've always liked it . . ."

She wasn't listening. "You don't get it," she put her hands on her hips and, suddenly, as she felt her pelvic bones, wondered if she might not be too thin to get pregnant. "I'm getting older." She flashed on the small, thin peoples of the world fruitfully multiplying. "The statistics on conceiving after prolonged months of failure are not good."

Lucas's previous words finally registered and she was able to ponder this all-too-familiar philosophical inclination. "Did my doctor call you?" she asked him, thinking perhaps Dr. Oram had done so on the sly, talked about her as if she were a child, a simple person in need of something as basic as reverse psychology.

But Lucas didn't know what she was talking about.

"What doctor?" he said, giving her that bewildered look.

* * *

Then, in mid-January, her period was three days late.

The only thing of long-standing and unfailing reliability in Annie Lee's life was her menstrual cycle. Every twenty-seven days since puberty she had marked the passing of time this way. Day twenty-three would herald a short period of dipping everything edible into Nutella; day twenty-five might bring a blemish or a little bustline bloating; and by day twenty-six it was a free-for-all of verbal dysentery. Then, with the onset of bleeding, her life resumed, purged it seemed, and regular. She could count on it, stake bets on it.

Three days late.

She didn't say anything to Lucas, but inside the big party room of her head confetti was flying and streamers were curling down, a Trix-tinted rainbow of congratulatory colors. She started picking out names—Cleo? Georgina? Betty?—and touching her breasts to check for swelling, wondering what breast milk looked like, how it came out, things no book could tell you and you dared not ask another woman. She imagined her face fat and glowing, and saw Lucas helping her down icy steps or through deep snow, leading her belly around like a rare, exotic dinosaur egg.

She allowed herself these expansive thoughts, the fields of tomorrow fertile, as fertile as her pregnant body. She pictured their child sitting at the kitchen table, scribbling with sweetly named crayons. Goldenrod. Bittersweet. Aquamarine. Magenta. She could almost smell the gingerbread houses they would bake while Lucas looked on, the dreamy life soft edged around him. These things filled her mind with a clarity, texture, and color so real she marveled at the world inside her.

Then, as if it were nothing more than a mathematical error made in the kind of pencil easily erased, her period came. Silently, moderately, and without much cramping or fanfare at all. Where had her chocolate cravings been? And what about grease? She had not even eaten one potato chip, goddammit—what was happening?

And she had to wonder then just how she could have been so stupid for the longest three days of her life, how her mind could have played such a cruel slow-motion trick, how she could have sabotaged herself that way. Feeling like an idiot, she tried to get back on track, tried to pretend the whole thing never happened. After all, what had changed? Nothing. She should have been able to convince herself of that, rewind her brain a bit, fit back into her earlier self. But having soared so high, it was impossible to come in for a level landing. From the giddying heights she came crashing down hard, wings dusty and bent like a bird's that has bashed into a window and lies stunned for a time on the ground below before getting up again.

Bewildered by the blow, Annie Lee withdrew—withdrew from socializing, withdrew from activity, and withdrew from sex.

In the last nine weeks, they had not had made love one time.

At first, it was a matter of depression—a lack of desire for anything, really. She didn't want to ski anymore, or skate, or listen to the kind of music that made her happy. Then a couple weeks later, while trying to force fertilizer on her houseplants (which had never required anything more than water to become the famous monsters they were), she made a mental shift and resolutely withdrew from intimate relations as a weapon against her husband. She wanted to make him pay for the situation as well, feel her feelings. Her ploy was not vengeful in the nastiest sense, but it probably came across that way.

Lucas responded by backing off—though, to his credit, more slowly and reluctantly than most men would have. He played it cool and gave her space. Then more space. Eventually, the space became so big he stopped reaching for her belt loops and bra clasps; he stopped visiting her in the bathtub; he stopped even giving her quick pecks on the cheek.

Ultimately, and worst of all, perhaps, was that he quit making them breakfast—a critical meal for couples who work at night, and the Flecks' favorite meal to dawdle over. Breakfast was the place the two of them saw eye to eye on food, despite his role as experimenter and hers as food traditionalist. When it came to breakfast they were in complete agreement about perfection. Eggs. Pancakes. Waffles. Home fries. Ham. Sometimes popovers, crêpes, and fancier stuff. They always said that if they ever opened a restaurant, it would be a breakfast joint: Anything else would test too much the limits of their marriage.

Now, in the morning, Lucas would grab a bagel at the bakery and then commit himself to skiing from the time the lifts opened until the time he had to be at work. Sometimes he would come home after skiing to eat, but not always. Eventually, Annie Lee realized that if you never ate with your spouse, it got harder and harder to call whatever it was a relationship. Plus it got her wondering, *Well, if he's not eating with me, who is he eating with?*

After Lucas went off skiing, Annie Lee would fix herself toast and a soft-boiled egg, which she placed in an eggcup. After whacking off the top she would dip her toast strips into the goo just as she had as a little girl. By cultivating the sick-and-home-from-school mentality, she was more able to justify staying indoors.

It was, in fact, this sense of illness—along with her feeling of now indisputable infertility—that prompted her to pick up the Ping-Pong paddle again one day and consider a call to the people who cared. It was snowing the day she punched in the number, snowing as if it would never stop, and she felt desperate to talk to someone beyond the parameters of a blinding storm, someone from where the visibility was better and the grass greener, even green at all. Denver might well be such a place in March. Maybe she could just ask the appropriate poison-related question and then move beyond that to the real issues of her life. She dialed the number, hoping to get Gabriel Salt, who had, more than any of the other nice people, comforted her.

After two rings, however, it was a man's unfamiliar, overly pragmatic bark that took her by surprise. "Poison Control Center, Denver, Colorado." Its gruffness caused Annie Lee to wonder if they might not be cracking down over there. She felt herself back away, lose her nerve; he was not the savior she'd hoped for. Wait a minute. She had a right to call, to make queries just like anybody else. Who was he to be short with her when she was the victim here?

"Hello, yes," Annie Lee cleared her throat. "Should I talk to you or are you the person who patches me through?" She hoped he might be some kind of newly created receptionist or phone-line bouncer. He wasn't.

"Do you have a question about a possible poisoning, ma'am?" He could have been a retired general from the sound of it.

"Yes. I do," she answered, rising to the challenge. "It's about my child, Sydney." She hadn't meant to resurrect poor Sydney at all. With a kinder voice on the other end, she might have put herself first, focused on her own issues. But this was not the person who would help her cut loose from the land of accident-prone children, bring her gently back to her own truths.

"Age of the victim?" Now he sounded bored, as if his day could only be made more viable by some enigmatic, brink-of-death episode. A stumper. She wanted to tell him there were private research institutions looking for people like him.

"Three," she replied, keeping her voice steady. "But this is her first incident." Oh, now she was lying about Sydney's fabricated past. How low could she stoop?

"And what is your concern?"

"My *concern*," she mimicked his tone of voice, "is that she might have swallowed potting soil while we were doing some indoor gardening. It was—"

"Fertilized?"

Well, at least he was on the ball. "Yes, exactly."

"And what were the circumstances of the ingestion?"

Annie Lee felt a surge of aggression toward the man then, and fancied giving him a run for his money. But what would that do to the memory of Sydney? Her loyalties reined her in. Keep it real, she told herself.

"Well, we were at our potting bench in the basement where I keep all the gardening supplies. Sydney, that's my daughter, has a little makeshift sandbox down there where she likes to pretend she's gardening. I normally don't like to use fertilized potting soil in the winter, but I didn't have anything else, and since I live—well far enough out of the way—I couldn't just run to the store and get some . . ." She paused. "She doesn't seem to be sick right now, you understand, but my concern is that if these little pellets are *timed-release*—that they might kick in when I least expect it."

"Good point, well taken." He was coming to life. "How much soil do you think might have been ingested?"

"I really don't know—" Annie Lee didn't have to feign frustration; she was mad at herself for having been so imprecise. "I looked in her mouth and was surprised to find it so clean of debris—the stuff can't be that easy to swallow. What little dirt I did see I scraped out."

He asked her if she'd rinsed the oral cavity, given the child plenty of milk or water, and induced regurgitation.

"Yes," she answered, and then yes again, and then, "I didn't make her throw up. I didn't want to overreact, didn't want to traumatize her. She's just a child. She's very orderly like her father and doesn't—"

Annie Lee felt the phone being lifted from her hand before she heard the beep of the talk button ending the conversation. Shocked, she whirled around to find her husband, stationary, before her. With one ear pressed vigorously to the phone, she hadn't heard him come in or sensed his presence in any way. He was supposed to have gone straight to work after skiing; that's what he'd said he would do. Yet there he stood, in stocking feet and wet ski clothes, snow dripping onto the floor as he continued to hold the phone up in his hand like People's Exhibit A. Finally, he let it drop, resigned, to his side. "I broke a pole," he said in answer to her unspoken question. "So I came home."

A broken pole!

He replaced the handset and then went about unzipping his coat, pulling it off, and undoing the suspender clasps of his ski bib while Annie Lee watched, mute, awaiting sentencing from the sanest jury in the land.

"You have gone off the deep end here," he obliged her quietly. "I've been standing here for long enough to know—you've taken this too far." He sat down on the ottoman in his long underwear, rested both elbows on his knees, with his hands in front of him. "You don't have a basement, let alone a potting bench, a sandbox, or a child. And me? I'm not that orderly of a person, Annie Lee—that's someone else you made up."

"I realize—" she began, staring at his hands, which seemed lost and confused. "I understand the difference between reality and fantasy, Lucas. I mean, I'm not psychotic." She readjusted the chopstick through her bun, made it tighter, then released a nervously held breath. "It's therapeutic for me to pretend, okay? I work things out that way."

Lucas looked sad underneath the anger. Annie Lee swallowed, terrified of the sadness. "Who are you working it out with, Annie Lee? Just with yourself? With your made-up kid? Who? Because you sure aren't working it out with me." He sat there, bent over, his hands awkward, as if in need of a ball of wax, or some clay, or a piece of wood to whittle. Something he could fashion into what he wanted—solid, comprehensible, and real.

Finally he straightened up and crossed his arms, tucked the idle appendages away. He told her that he had been thinking about it—for several weeks, in fact—and that he'd decided to make the annual trip to his mother's alone this year. They needed some time apart, he said—they both needed to do some thinking. He'd be leaving in four days as planned, but without her. "I'm doing the right thing, Annie Lee," he finally said. "You know how I know it's the right thing?"

She shook her head.

"Because I can't think of anything else to do."

Annie Lee looked down at her feet and listened to him shuffle away. Somewhere, she thought vaguely, a pole is always breaking.

They said very little to each other before his trip. He seemed to want to get a head start on the thinking he needed to do; and Annie Lee, though she might yearn not to be outthought, wasn't thinking clearly at all. She had been caught going off the deep end, and the allegation kept her treading furiously, treading in deep water.

The day before he left, she decided to go skiing, to get out of the house and get some fresh air. Unlike the winter before, this one delivered storm after storm, queued up impatiently behind each other. There were piles of snow everywhere. But as she clunked down the front steps and walked the eight blocks to the lift, she had to ask herself why she had opted out of her regular ski outfit—a black one-piece and black-and-white wool hat—and grabbed instead a purple parka from eight years ago and a turquoise hat she now considered uglier than sin.

The point seemed to be, she realized as none of her neighbors waved to the figure she cut walking down the street, that no one would recognize her. This became clearer as she made her way up three chairlifts to the top of the mountain, right to where she knew Lucas would be skiing. She wanted to see him in his natural state, unfettered, free of the shackles of home life.

Visibility with the falling snow was only about fifteen feet, but she finally spied him at the top of Dunes, a skinny, bumpy gully he was prone to ski in March when tourists would be overcrowding the other black runs. There he was, leaning on his new poles, waiting for his friends to gather. A woman snowboarder, someone Annie Lee didn't recognize, was chatting him up. She wore the latest getup in sky blue, white, and navy; her stocking cap had a flower on it. Lucas laughed at one of her comments, rebuckled his boots, and then headed down the slope with her and two other male skiers.

Annie Lee slid over to where they had been standing and peered down the run. Flower girl was good. She was keeping up with the rest of them. Probably pretty young, Annie Lee thought; snowboarders were from a different generation than she and Lucas.

She watched her husband make a dozen quick turns on the steep terrain and wanted to go after him, to catch up and be part of the group. She wanted to ski past the girl, ski past the men, lead everyone down to the bottom of the run and then turn around and see the look of surprise and admiration on Lucas's face. She wanted to be recognizable to him—that same person he'd skied with for so many years, had such fun with.

But it wouldn't have worked.

For one thing, she'd worn the wrong outfit. How could she suddenly show up in disguise, an ugly, outdated one at that? Secondly, she wasn't in good shape. She would have been the one huffing and puffing down the difficult run, stopping every ten moguls or so to catch her breath and give her legs a break. She couldn't have impressed even a tourist let alone her own tribe.

So instead, she skied off to a different chairlift, one where none of the locals went at all. There, she unaccountably began pretending to be someone else—Caroline Wist from Des Moines—and spent each nine-minute ride up exchanging biographical data with other tourists, refining her character as she went. She was a divorced mother of two boys who were with their father while she got away for a week of self-pampering. (By this time, she'd removed the hat and pulled up the hood of the purple parka.) She wrote manuals she said, training manuals for waiters in restaurants. Oh, yes, it was very profitable—you'd be surprised how many restaurants needed a standard for their front staff. Her boys, Jack and Charlie, were ruled by sports, just like their father. Good kids. No, she was sorry she couldn't meet for drinks later. And she was leaving tomorrow. Nice to have met you, though.

Caroline Wist. Caring. Wistful. Caroling. West. It had just happened that way.

Lucas made himself a Thermos of coffee the morning of his departure and picked up the cat for a final squeeze. Colonel Klink was a sixteen-pound bruiser with ash-gray coloring so intense it seemed to cast the same shade on things around him. Lucas adored the beast and spoiled him rotten. Klink, sensing the imminent departure of his best friend, was rubbing up repeatedly against Lucas's legs, making it hard for him to get to the foyer. Annie Lee followed them slowly to the front door, unable to think of anything to say except, "I'll think hard," which she half called to him after he'd already reached the front gate.

He turned around then, and put his backpack down. "Think about yourself, Annie Lee." His voice was not unkind. "Not about phone people you don't even know, or people you'd like to be. Yourself. And for God's sake, girl," he shook his head, "wear your own clothes next time you go skiing. They suit you better."

* * *

As he drove away to Denver to catch his flight to Seattle, quiet settled upon the house like a heavy drift of snow, or sand, or pure density. Pike, depending on one's state of mind, could either feel like the center of the fun-loving world or its farthest outpost, a place for people cynical about fun, all funned out. Feeling abandoned and cheerless, Annie Lee wondered again how things had come to this. She spent the day cleaning in the frantic way people do whose needling problems have no evident solutions.

At dusk, the skies began to clear. And as random sparkles glinted from the occasional flake, she gave in to her compulsion to call the airlines. After checking on the estimated time of arrival, she asked the clerk, "Will it be a smooth flight, do you think? No severe turbulence or anything?"

"I believe so, ma'am," the voice sounded like it was being patched in from Tunisia.

"Is there anyone in the control tower I can talk to who can actually see the plane taking off?" She wanted to know if the takeoff looked good, what the clouds looked like; she wanted to talk to someone looking at Lucas fly away, because it seemed like an official person might be able to say to her that 99.9 percent of all trips were round-trips. That he would be back, that this plane had a home at the Denver airport and would have to return. That people didn't just fly away for good; statistics could prove that. When they left they either walked out or drove out. They didn't fly.

The clerk had to think about it. "Is this an emergency of some sort, ma'am?" Annie Lee thought she heard the woman cover the receiver with her hand, probably telling someone to trace the call, we got a live one here. So she hung up quickly and looked around her empty house. Of course it wasn't an emergency; he was coming back. He was due back in Denver at 11:52 A.M., in eight days, then with the drive it would be six o'clock before he walked into their house again.

Maybe she would think about Lucas later as he touched down worlds away. She might call his mom's just to make sure he'd gotten there—make light of the situation with his mother before Lucas had a chance to tell her something abbreviated and yet sadly true.

But when the time came, she couldn't do it. Instead, she drank two-thirds of a bottle of red wine on an empty stomach and watched *An Affair to Remember*, with Cary Grant. Despite the cat's discomfort with it, she bawled so hard her sinuses swelled and she had to breathe through her mouth as she lay in bed wondering what Lucas would do if he came back to find her in a wheelchair with a blanket over her knees, uncomplaining, cheerful, and glad to be alive.

Four

Fortunately, Annie Lee would be at work every night but one during her week alone. It was easy to un-swap all the shifts she'd so painstakingly covered before she'd known Lucas would make the trip to Seattle alone. Jay had not been sympathetic to expiring frequent flier miles, not in March, the busiest month of the year, nor had the other waiters, who had only grudgingly agreed to cover for her in the first place because they all owed her for something or other. Now, burned out and ready for off-season, her coworkers were more than happy to get rid of the overload, and Annie Lee was grateful to have somewhere to go at night, something to keep her busy.

She did not ski during the week, nor did she find herself drawn to reading, though the warm and snowy weather might have been conducive to either thing. No, Annie Lee discovered, in Lucas's absence, that she had no desire to go anywhere else, either physically or through the back door of her imagination. From the very first day and then throughout the week, she rerooted herself in her own house, found herself taking it in again as if for the first time. She excavated the nest they'd built together. She let herself drift through time, memories settling on her like the dust motes after their dance in the light. This felt to her like the correct kind of thinking to be doing, a simple meditation on the furnishings of domestic relationships.

It was a fine old house, the last of a dying breed in a town that had recently gone the way of the fashionable resort: from shabby to shiny, shingle-shy to tidy, quaint to cultivated. Buying the property all those years ago—before real estate hit the ceiling—had been one of the shrewdest moves of Lucas's life. Annie Lee had fallen in love, just as he had, with the property's nineteen trees, the cozy seclusion of the small backyard, and the building itself, a vertical white box with a covered front porch, occasional simple ornamentation, and the kind of tall, lonesome windows only historical houses had anymore.

The sweetest thing, though, for Annie Lee, was the fact that Lucas had never really considered it a home until she moved in with him. Only when she arrived with her possessions—two of her mother's paintings, a small Turkish rug, several photo albums, and three duffel bags of everything else she owned—did he begin unpacking all the things he'd collected and stored in the spare bedroom. Thus, they were able to unpack together, as a couple, in spite of the fact that Lucas had already been living in the house for five years as a minimalist—though evidently a phony one.

In time, he admitted to finding it "pleasing" to fill up rooms. Nothing about what it meant that his house had stood empty for so long, or what it was like to have made it through so many days and evenings in the spare and echoing rooms all by himself—just a little comment after they'd begun codesigning on how agreeable it was to fill rooms up at last. And this from someone who'd done behavioral sciences in college. (Well, that's what he said he'd done. Annie Lee couldn't imagine it, though. She pictured a major portion of his higher education spent in the cafeteria improving casseroles or reorganizing the tables so that the light was better at breakfast. He'd already admitted to doing all his studying not at the library but on the steel countertops of the back kitchen.)

For whatever reason, Lucas arrived at the threshold of domestic life with a feel for rooms.

He initiated the process by suggesting to Annie Lee that she be in charge of color, of setting the scene. He needed a starting point, he told her, and since she had been single-handedly responsible for his "desire to furnish," he wanted her to christen each room with color. Not unfamiliar with paints, she accepted, greedily at first, wanting to prove herself to him. It did not take her long to realize, however, that she would in fact be agonizing over each color selection. As if the very foundations of marriage might well be laid along with the paint.

She began by choosing a series of different shades—from magazine photos, scraps of wallpaper, old pieces of artwork, or whatever struck her fancy. She would spend hours narrowing down the choices before finally selecting one. The paint-store computer would match it; and then, with paint bucket pried open, she would begin the process of naming the hue.

To Annie Lee, a color came to life instantly if it had a name to go with it. Catalog companies banked on this simple concept, each year firing up people's imaginations with the fresh colors of their new sweaters. Prune. Cricket. Chamomile. Lagoon. Paint companies had for years been naming their thousands of colors things like Frosted Plum, Jubilant Scarlet, and Misty Morning. Farsighted companies even attempted to name colors after lifestyles or places: Monaco Midnight or Colorado Sagebrush or I'll-See-You-at-the-Polo-Match Maize. For Annie Lee, picking paint colors and naming them was the closest she had ever come to casting spells.

* * *

She'd chosen the upstairs bathroom as her starting place, it had seemed small and manageable enough. The Glass-A-Mar Green went on thick like a layer of sunlit algae and soothed her like a cloth to the forehead. Nevertheless, she didn't know Lucas all that well yet and fretted that he wouldn't like the color, that it might be too bold, too green, that she'd turned the volume up too high—that they would be incompatible as codesigners.

Lucas had trusted, though, and had not shown any doubts at all. His eyes had caressed each of the walls, and then, typically revealing nothing, he had given her a light kiss on the cheek. He'd smiled and pulled flecks of paint out of her hair before returning to his own project, recaulking the outside sills. But that night, he'd cooked up a tropical storm, with fruits and fish and sticky rice tamales. He said she'd inspired him and then after dinner dragged her up to the bedroom before even cleaning up. As he removed her sweatshirt he admitted her green had profoundly excited him. "I'd like to get to know more of your palette," he whispered, smearing the buttons of his jeans into hers, "if I could."

The bathroom had been an auspicious start: Lucas fiddled with the fixtures and dropped a plastic Roman shade down from the ceiling above a small glass-block partition coming up from the floor, to divide the room better. He bought a waterproof radio, and then a waterproof camera. He had twenty-four postcards, all of the ocean, laminated as a poster and stuck it up behind the tub. "Plastic," he concluded, "just went with that green."

Sitting on the closed lid of the toilet, she thought now of Lucas in his faded jeans, the feel of his breath on her neck, in her ear. She saw him in all his happy shades of busy-ness, thinking, sketching, plotting, and realized it had been a long time indeed since he'd puttered happily in their house. When Klink sauntered in and lay down on the small rug (as if sensitive to deep thoughts of his beloved), she decided, an ache in her heart, to run a bath before work and ponder the color green—from palest shoot to deepest ocean and everything in between.

Pewter Platter was the wall color Annie Lee had finally chosen for the kitchen—the room she'd tackled six months after the bathroom, and only after much deliberation. Lucas had asked her how she'd come by it, which was something she had hoped he would do.

"I called up one of the fire stations in Manhattan—Uncle Louis gave me the number for the one in his neighborhood—then I asked to speak with their guy who cooks. Vinnie Vecchio, they said. I told Vinnie I was writing an article on color choices in everyday life and needed to know what color he found conducive to eating. I could hear something sizzling in the background and mentioned it. Shrimp gumbo for nine, he said, then continued on. 'When I cook I don't wanna see bright color on the walls, I wanna see the color in the food.' He paused. 'Pewter,' he said. 'The color of an old pan. Worn looking. Not shiny. That's my personal opinion.' When he asked me what magazine I wrote for, I couldn't think of anything except *Psychology Today*. Then he spelled his last name for me. V-E-C-C-H-I-O. From Staten Island."

And thus the kitchen, done in the color of a warm pan, inspired the baroque and yet industrial look Lucas had given to it. Eventually she realized the kitchen was very much like Lucas, who turned out to be a man spare of words yet curlicue of brain. Today, every part of the kitchen reminded her of him; and though desperate to commemorate the good times and meals they'd had there, all she could really think of was how empty the kitchen felt now. "He's always been happy to feed me," she summarized, heading off to work in his down parka, which enveloped her like a sleeping bag. "And I bit the hand."

* * *

The living room was painted Faded Clay Pot, inspired by an antique postcard from southern Italy. Annie Lee had liked Lucas's comment about the color—that it reminded him of a place he'd never been. And again he honored her with an inspired meal, this one of little rustic pizzas, swordfish, and Calabrian olives. From the tip of the boot, he said, where that color's from. He bought a big old secondhand velvet couch for the room, and found a metal coffee table on junk day, and then filled up the rest of the space with candles. Candelabras, pillars, old lamps, tapers. Nothing perfumed, just light, light, light everywhere. With him gone, the lit candles took on the appearance of church votives, a vigil of prayers all laid out brightly and with hope. Annie Lee found she was pacified most, however, by the *fffft* of the match and by its heat, so close to her fingertips it burned.

She gave the study an entire day of reflection, midway through her week alone. Berrywinkle was the name she'd given to the color of the walls of room number four, kind of a musty mashed berry and forget-me-not color that made you think of Mediterranean blues seen through rose-colored glasses. It was a color that caught the attention of everyone who passed through the snug little room; a restful, vibrant blue that made even the most obdurate personality soften a bit. When the eccentric sisters from next door had come over to inspect the room, just as they did every room, Bea Winkleman had actually shielded her eyes at first sight of the walls, and then slowly, gingerly, removed her hand, as if the walls might snap at her.

"Annie Lee," she'd finally said, plopping herself down in the armchair, eyes round as plates, "you've just made up for all the walls I could never paint anything but white—in one fell swoop. There's no calling this anything but perfection, and that's the living truth. It's as blue as a mountain bluebell at sunset. And I really don't see a bit of harm in it."

Lucas, equally pleased by the turn of the room, had gone so far as to suggest they paint another room the same color.

"That would be ridiculous." Annie Lee had stared at him as though he'd thrown water in her face. "Berrywinkle wouldn't work in any other room."

"How can you even say that word with a straight face?" he'd asked her, shaking his head. "Berrywinkle." He grimaced.

"You can say periwinkle with a straight face. Peri-winkle." She made a sour face. "And Winkle-man." Another face.

"That's different. Periwinkle's a kind of flower and a kind of snail. The Winklemans are real people."

"You seem to have no trouble naming dishes you make up. Bok Choy van Gogh. Franky's Fishcakes. Overture to—"

"That's different, there's etiology there." He had realized how stupid this sounded and added, "Just forget it. Forget I ever said anything. I just think a purist such as yourself would go for the traditional name."

"There's no tradition: I made up the color, I make up the name. And I know one thing," Annie Lee had wanted the last word, "I may not want to tell you the names of my made-up colors anymore." Besides the powder room, there were only three rooms left, and she wondered if she could be as good as her word.

Lucas, though silent at the time, had been hurt by the comment. Had even gone so far as to ask the guys at the paint store if Annie Lee ever revealed the names of paints they'd mixed for her. Later, Lucas had given her a detailed account of a conversation that had amused him, and which, as he recounted it, had very much tickled her fancy as well.

"Hmm?" Marty, the head paint mixer, had said. "Oh, well, actually, she does go on about how a color looks like this or that thing. Kind of rants and raves about it and everything, and then asks me what I think it looks like. I don't know. I mean, if you ask me there's too many colors these days. Just too many damn colors. It's confusing as all hell."

Marty had been working at the Pike paint store for twenty-two years and hated to have even the smallest trace of pigment on him. He had hands as antiseptic as a surgeon's, and beautifully clipped nails, too. Lucas had told Marty that Annie Lee believed all colors should have names, that names were what made the colors real.

"Maybe," Marty had answered, peeling a stubborn remnant of bone white off his thumbnail. "But that's a lot of names. Do you know Jerry Vix came in here the other day wanting to match a piece of a grouse's eggshell on the computer—for a house he's painting? The owners—rich as they come—were bird-watchers, he said. The whole downstairs would be done in grouse's eggshell, complete with speckles. Now the upstairs I think he said would be divided up into different species: some kind of large bird for the master bedroom—now, what was it?"

Lucas had hazarded a guess of Female Bald Eagle Gray.

"Heron Wing Blue," Marty had countered with satisfaction, as if to recall things so formidably useless was as much testing as any brain could take. "The owners flew in periodically on their jet just to check the authenticity of the finish. Can you believe that? I've never heard of people that well-off being bird-watchers, either.

"Anyway, it didn't faze Jerry: He's done that absurd color matching lots of times. The messiest was a piece of banana peel, ripe but not brown. For a breakfast nook in one of the penthouse condos they built right next to the old bank. Fruit-watchers, you think?" He'd shaken his head then, looked at Lucas, and asked earnestly, "Has everybody lost their marbles, or what?"

The next time Lucas went to see Marty Lemon at the paint store, however, he was the one who returned with paint cans.

When Annie Lee saw them, she'd balked. "That's my job," she'd said. "I thought I got to pick wall color." He'd told her he tried to read her mind, that he wanted to do the entire room himself, surprise her. He recounted his trip to the store, just to make her feel a part of the process. He said he told Marty he was embarrassed to be asking for a match on the computer, but that he needed to make a point to his wife. "At least," he'd told Marty, "it's somewhere between white, bone, cream, and antique."

"Did Marty shake his head?"

Lucas had laughed a yes. "He said it was epidemic. '*What we have is an epidemic.*'" He imitated Marty's head shaking. "'*Eggshell or flat?*'"

The only hint Lucas would give her about the room was the name he'd given the color of the paint: Vestige. A good name, Annie Lee had to admit. And what woman couldn't be wooed by having her mind read? Who wouldn't be won over by the idea of a surprise? As it turned out, he had been inspired by an old letter purchased at a flea market, a love letter from a miner to his true love. He began by wrapping up the bedroom in this same old-ivory paper color.

The completed master bedroom had the look of a traveler's or correspondent's lair. A trade-wind theme, with old maps and letters lining the walls, some tacked up as if in haste instead of framed. Annie Lee felt the room spoke volumes, spoke of her life and of his in the middle of a huge sea that was the world and all its stories. In the winter it was a womb. In the summertime, the olives, khakis, and creams of the room, instead of looking overly drab, became forest tones. They would open all the windows at night and drop a circular mosquito net from the ceiling. The net moved with the breezes and cast gauzy shadows on their dreams.

Annie Lee's nights had always been filled with the anxiety of waiter dreams—long tables of hungry people either calling for her or ignoring her, and the momentary paralysis, replayed over and over, of having forgotten someone's special request. But more and more in this house, in that bedroom, she'd dreamed of doors ajar and light-flooded rooms. Of curtains wafting in and out with the very breath of the house. Of filtered morning light grazing the oranges in a big blue bowl. Of clouds benignly casting fast-forward shadows upon the roof. She knew Lucas had similar dreams; he'd said as much.

Yes, it was at night the house worked its magic on them, weaving itself into their netherworld of sleep, wedging itself deeply into the foundation mud of their psyches. Their dream home, odd as it might sound, seemed to be dreaming *them*; and it had been easy, ridiculously easy, to fall helplessly under its spell.

But you had to be in a house to be affected by it. What was Lucas dreaming of at his mother's? She mulled this over every night of her week alone as she slid into the empty bed, slipped under the mosquito net, and stretched her legs over to where Lucas's body had always been until now. She started to worry, on the fourth night, that, given enough time, Lucas's bodily indentation—and what proved he lived there—would, with nothing to hold it down, spring back. From then on she shoved over to his side, committed her weight to the empty half of the bed.

The powder room had originally been done in Klink's Nose, a gray lover's gray with the slightest touch of yellow in it. There had never been anything wrong with the shade, but at some point Annie Lee had run out of rooms. The foyer had already received three coats of Canary in Your House. The attic was done in Ada's Lilac Apron, and the dining room in Dark and Stormy Night blue. She had had to start over, worried, she could admit now, that without rooms to paint, a certain bewitchment of her husband might be lost. So she'd redone the room in a browner shade, Spaded Earth in the Fog, which she'd liked, except that geraniums ended up looking better there than tulips.

Now, however, she wondered if, instead of repainting that room, she shouldn't have come up with the nerve to paint the spare bedroom, the ever-problematic spare bedroom. The room they'd never dared call the nursery out loud. Maybe in bravely painting it, maybe some spell would have been cast by something bigger than her paintbrush. But she'd never been able to come up with anything but a white repaint, a faintly blue-tinged white she'd made a big deal about naming Swan in the Shade. But white nevertheless.

And just as she'd found it impossible to blot it with color, Lucas had little inclination to fill the room up, commit himself to it. Paint cans were stored there neatly, as well as assorted tools and a block of file cabinets. It was kept clean, and occasionally Annie Lee would touch up the walls to see how white felt on the tip of a brush. It never failed to strike her as if she were holding a large container of Wite-out, covering up nicks and scratches, preparing the surface for some final testament of color that was just beyond her grasp.

Now, on Lucas's last day away from home, she sat on a file cabinet surrounded by blank walls, pondering things, perhaps more clearly than she had all week. Oram's Advisory again came to mind, the tape resurfacing from the burbly deep as if in the silence, truth were to be found. How much of recent life had she missed? How much of the complexity of Lucas had she ignored, consumed by her need to get pregnant?

Dr. Oram. She felt desperate to call him now, tell him she was sorry she'd ignored his advice. Why couldn't she just call? It wasn't like he didn't know her, her circumstances, her history. He was real, she was real, there was no fabrication involved. So she fetched the phone and returned to her place on the filing cabinet.

But he wasn't there. The receptionist said Dr. Oram was on vacation, that there was a pipers' gathering in Minneapolis. She mentioned two other doctors coming in for the month who were both capable and gentle. Annie Lee thought she would break down right there on the phone.

"No," she said weakly, "that's okay. I'm sure Dr. Oram deserves a break. Maybe you happen to know if there's an information hotline for infertile women . . ." Without knowing it she must have reserved Oliver Oram as her last hope, someone she could go to in utter despair. She'd counted on him being there when she needed him, and now he was gone.

"Are you okay Ms.—"

"Fleck. Annie Lee."

"Annie Lee. Are you all right? We have quite a list of references for counseling and a veritable library of information on the subject . . ."

"I'm opposed to therapy," she told the nice woman. "I was overtherapized as a child." This was a line she'd stolen from Eddie Stahl, and the moment she uttered it, it fell to the floor like lead.

"Okay, then, dear." The woman was indulgent. "Shall I send you some information on various options for infertile couples?"

"Sure," Annie Lee tried to be polite. "No toll-free numbers, though, huh?" The woman said not that she knew of, then asked if there was anything she could do to help Annie Lee herself.

"No, not really. I just felt comfortable with Dr. Oram. He gave me some good advice I wasn't smart enough to take at the time."

The woman laughed. "Well, dear, that's the story of our lives. You know, we had trouble conceiving, Reed and I. At first. I found myself at this job because of it."

"You did?" Reed? Ah, Reed and Pauline Klimp, now she remembered who she was talking to. He was the small-appliance man in town, the guy with the grape-gum-ball-purple van that said "Klimp's" in bright yellow letters two feet high. The van made you want to hire him to cater a costume party rather than fix a washer.

"Yes, we did. For quite a few years, in fact, we tried and tried and nothing came of it. Seemed like everyone around us was having babies. The whole world, rich and poor."

"Fat and thin," added Annie Lee. "What did you do?"

"Well, we stopped trying. We kind of gave up," she lowered her voice, "even lost interest for a spell, if you know what I mean. Then one day Reed brought home a cat, half dead and bleeding in his arms. You know, beaten up by some other animal, big patches of hair completely gone. A coyote it could have been. And we got so consumed with that poor thing—getting it in to see a vet, surgery, recuperation, and watching its fear of life finally ease into something else—we forgot about . . . other things. Oh, gosh, I remember it like it was yesterday . . ." As Pauline Klimp continued on in her own reverie, Annie Lee listened with interest to her tales of Pike's past before paved streets, before parking problems, before cable, and long before celebrities. Finally, the woman paused, wondering, it seemed, where she was leading herself.

"What color was the cat?" Annie Lee helped her out.

"Orange. Oh, yes, she was orange like the best English marmalade. We named her May Day but called her May. She died years and years ago. But she saw our three children born. Frieda, Grove Jr., and Anne Elise. Frieda moved to Tucson about five years ago . . ." She continued on with the enumeration.

Yes, sure enough, they were real. The only thing that bothered Annie Lee was how Grove Jr. could have come of Reed Sr. "So you're saying you didn't focus so hard on having babies and then you had them."

"Yes, something like that. You need something else to focus on for a spell. Something bigger than you."

Annie Lee thanked her, wondering what that bigger something could be.

"Oh think nothing of it, dear. Life is a great big mystery. And for whatever my opinion is worth, I think lives are written much the *same way* as mysteries, with the most unlikely plots leading to the most logical endings." Annie Lee thought about this as she sat in the nursery, the sun filtered and weak and old as the room itself. She wrote down the words verbatim, thinking to frame them later. She collected such quotes. "Lives are written much the same way . . ." she scribbled.

How did one become an epigrammatist? Of all the jobs in the world, this was the one that tantalized Annie Lee the most. Snippet writer. Deep but pithy thinker. Did twenty thousand words have to be written or spoken before shortening them down to ten or twelve? Or was it like being a caricaturist, all in the skill of making a few lines count?

How would some smarter person, for example, distill Annie Lee's recent bad behavior? She thought of Lucas making love to her, caressing her throat with his lips, uttering—what? She'd been too focused on the motility of his sperm, the potency of her own tadpole-grabbing orgasm. What had he said? He was not one to waste profound sentiments on flowery words. Still, what if he'd said something wonderful and she'd ignored it?

"Have I alienated him completely?" Klink's ears rotated at the question as he lay in the doorway, a wedge of sun trapping him like a ray gun. The massive cat stretched slowly, back arched, and then, with what seemed like a great effort on his part, wandered into the bedroom. Annie Lee felt compelled to follow and found Klink sitting on Lucas's pillow, much as a diamond would sit on a velvet puff. She seated herself on the edge of the bed next to him, vaguely wondering at how pathetic it was that a cat was the closest link she had to her husband.

It was there, however, that she came up with something she

could do, a gesture, to try to move herself back into Lucas's good graces. Relationships were full of such small maneuvers, made, sometimes a bit desperately, to try to equalize the black and white of the chess board. And even though Annie Lee had the uneasy sense that her moves might be too late, or too obvious for Lucas, she could not help herself: She went forward.

All day Friday was spent working on the bedroom's east wall, enlarging that same miner's love letter (which had been tacked up next to an old map of the area) onto the Vestige surface with an overhead projector rented from the library. She transferred the writing to the wall in letters three inches high, first with pencil, and then filling them in using paint whose color matched the ink on the letter. Though Marty at the paint store didn't ask, she told him: "Love-letter Sepia."

"You should tell your husband, not me." Marty's normally placid face contorted, wrinkles forcing themselves around his mouth. "He's the one been askin'."

Annie Lee felt a surge of guilt. "I'll tell him, Marty," she said quietly. "Don't you worry." Marty was writing the recipe for the color on the lid of the can when Annie Lee gently took the permanent marker from him and wrote the name there, too, as if to seal her promise.

Five

At 5:47 P.M. on March twenty-ninth—the day of Lucas's return—the setting sun had begun to cast a golden glow on the western façades of Pike. Lucas had always maintained that ninety-five percent of all real estate was sold during this magical hour, with the sun's eyelashes gently filtering out all the harsher beams of day. Annie Lee simply felt people became weak and vulnerable at this hour, prone to seductions of all kinds.

She herself was stealing a few moments before opening to gaze out of the topmost window at the restaurant, a small, round porthole of a thing, recalling the restaurant's former 1980s surf-and-turf decor. As the sun set, a brief moment of final splendor was given the day. Annie Lee's face relaxed at the freshness of it, the clouds scudding by, picking up tints of cayenne here and radiant lavender there before deepening into their cool evening shades. The false-fronted, brick-veneered buildings of Pike, plunged into the shadows of dusk, were quiet and tiny like tea leaves at the bottom of a huge white cup. Spring winds grazed the tops of the surrounding peaks, bringing up snow like wisps of sand. Below, streetlights plinked on in timed and comforting reassurance.

It was time to put on that bistro apron and get to work. Time to fill her mind with table numbers and wine-list prices and peoples' desperate needs right up until the moment she would go home to her husband. She tied the apron strings too tight and had to loosen them a bit.

At 6:04 P.M., Annie Lee was tilting her head to read the sugar packet as she emptied it into a half cup of strong coffee: "An ounce of prevention is worth a pound of cure." Not one to tempt fate, she prescribed for herself an ibuprofen caplet, Pike's medication of choice and something locally referred to as "skier's popcorn." Rifling through the messy medicine chest, she noted it had not one Band-Aid in it, not one butterfly bandage, not even some sterile gauze. Or superglue for deep cuts. Wasn't this required by law in a place where everyone—staff and customer alike—was using knives?

There ought to be an accident hotline, she thought, someplace you could call for such mishaps. Cuts, abrasions, sprains, and burns. Bruises, contusions, and full-on subcutaneous hematoma. Come to think of it, didn't every single, solitary walk of life need a toll-free number? Half the world's afflictions might be addressed through the simple dialing of 1-800-A-through-Z for information, comfort, and anonymity.

At this point in time, Annie Lee was willing to swear that *any* hotline expert would be more helpful than the one and only psychologist she had had the displeasure to come in contact with, a local celebrity of sorts named Venus Philabaum, whose office alone should have tipped Annie Lee off—with its flat Pepto-persimmon walls and posters of shells and mermaids. For $125 an hour, the author of *Why Cook for Two When It's Only You?* was 180 degrees from her telephone superiors, for she was loath to offer any advice at all. Even her listening was done abstrusely. Instead, she cooed with old-school coercions: "Don't think, just talk. Whatever comes to mind." By the fourth session, Annie Lee had scared herself so badly with her own eruptions of verbal garbage, she'd walked out midsession.

"What are you so afraid of, Anne?" Dr. Venus had thrown the words out fast, like a curve ball thrown against the better wishes of her superego's shortstop.

"You," Annie Lee had had the visceral sense to say in a moment of clarity. "Your color preferences, your handwriting that slants the wrong way, and your book selection. There's not one novel on your shelf."

Venus Philabaum had sent her a bill on melon-colored bond for the twelve minutes the meter was running on that last session, and Annie Lee had sent her $25 in pennies, along with a note that said "A penny for *your* thoughts . . ." Postage had cost her nearly that much, but it had been worth it.

It was 7:13 when Donna, the busser, quite put out, explained that a duck bone had sailed off a plate she was clearing from table two and landed on the arm of a man at table one. She reassured Annie Lee that she had removed the bone and had offered soda water, which he'd refused. "I think he wants the stain to stay there so he can sue me," she said, worried, stretching her neck to scope out the man again.

Annie Lee went to fetch two glasses of champagne before approaching the table.

"We're *very* sorry about the duck bone," she said. "Of course, well pay any cleaning charges or replace the shirt if need be." She searched out the spot, small but greasy enough, and then let her eyes rest on the garment as a whole. A beauty of a thing—linen, the color of a beehive. Or ground almonds. Or sandalwood soap, or very pale sand at dusk. Finely woven, with shell buttons. Easily a $300 item and crisp as any shirt on earth. It made her want to cry both for its beauty—crushing, like the sight of a pale-yellow paisley tie on the first day of spring—and for the blemish.

"Was that what it was?" an impeccable middle-aged face inquired as his equally fabulous button-nosed wife tipped her head with interest. They sipped their champagne and discussed the menu at length. He ended up ordering the duck. And with each slice of the knife, each swipe of the napkin to his mouth, he reaffirmed Annie Lee's faith in humankind. Unflappable man. Where was his expertise? she wondered. In shirts?

At 8:01, a five-top in various shades of ebony, charcoal, indigo, midnight, jet, smoke, flint, and soot was having problems. They were all wearing baseball caps.

"He's a soap-opera star," said Kathryn, the bartender, as Annie Lee marched past her. "I used to watch them. Check out the rock on position two's finger." Kathryn, referred to as "the Magpie" by the rest of the staff, dreamed of the day her husband would spend three months' salary on an anniversary ring, and routinely kept everyone posted on the nightly assortment of baubles and gems. Annie Lee was staring not at rings but at one of the jackets—a soft black bolero with a mahogany sheen—while wondering what to call it. Roasted Chestnut? High-school Hair?

"They don't like their food," the celebrity said to her as he ripped into his own plate of venison chops and began grinding his teeth into the first bite. He seemed amused. Three women and a teenager were holding their plates of salmon out like offerings returned to their place of origin.

"We can't eat this," said the spokeswoman for the group as Annie Lee began receiving the plates. "It's . . . fishy!"

All four plates, untouched except for nicks at the salmon, went by the chef, who was glaring at Annie Lee. "What's the problem??" he said, waiting to take out his frustration on her answer.

"They want the onion soup instead," she told him. "It's fishy fish." She knew better than to elaborate. Just the facts, word for word.

The chef was mad now, tossing sauté pans with abandon, like Frisbees, into the dirty pile. He hated seeing food come back—what chef didn't?

"Bring me a piece. I don't even have to taste it to know it's perfect." Annie Lee brought him a plate, and he broke a fillet in two, examining it before tossing it in his mouth. Shaking his head, he repeated "*It's perfect*" with his mouth full and tipped the plate over with a clang.

"These are stupid people!" he said then, loud enough for them to hear. Annie Lee knew that later she would have to hear the Americans-only-like-halibut-and-tuna lecture from the chef, who was raging now in the tiny kitchen, raging about food being returned, about Americans on power trips, about hat-wearing people who liked dry, tasteless food like turkey. That last part seemed unfair.

"What besides turkey is dry?" The French notoriously hated turkey, could not conceive of a national holiday that paid tribute to the desiccated meat of an overgrown bird.

He gave her a look of incredulity. "The way you cook them? Pork chops." He stuck his thumb up—number one. "Pot roast. Rump roast. Roast beef, et cetera et cetera. You don't believe in sauce in this country, you believe in condiments. Mayonnaise, mustard, ketchup, chutney, mint sauce," he made a face, "and that awful salsa. You cook your meat like cavemen did. Dry. On a stick." He was testing his blade, again, on a piece of paper. "Don't you have work to do?"

Annie Lee yearned to lecture him on the new marinades, but did not have time to do the subject justice.

At 8:13 the lights went down. Every evening between 8:00 and 8:30, Jay would dim the lights and then make a tour of the dining room, floating from table to table to shake hands and occasionally to pick up a plate or empty glass. People loved it and so did he. Only the waiters viewed light dimming with a jaundiced eye, since it invariably screwed up their timing at one table or another.

Annie Lee was not floating at light dimming, she was flitting. She'd gotten four tables simultaneously, an utterly nerve-wracking situation in terms of timing and parroting the same greetings over and over. She heard the chef call her name right after she'd tacked up three of the four new orders.

"What?" she said to him, knowing the kitchen hated getting multiple tickets at once. Maybe she should have staggered them just a teeny bit. "What is it?"

He was jabbing at her tickets as they hung there. "Out of ten people here, eight are ordering the lamb loin."

"So that's good—it's the most expensive thing on the menu."

"No, that's bad, because now I only have two left for the night. We sold a lot last night. So tell people the guinea hen is the chef's special, the specialty of the house. Tell them the chef *highly* recommends—the guinea hen."

"But," she lowered her head as she whispered at him, "the guinea hen is the least popular thing we serve."

"Exactly," he spat back. "We have a lot of them."

But it was too late anyway. Her fourth table ordered two lamb loins, and while she was in the kitchen getting the third degree she didn't have time to tell the other waiters to eighty-six the item. Con came in with two orders and Eddie with one.

The chef got that icy look on his face as he stared at the two male waiters. "We are out of fucking lamb. Con you get one of the two left, Eddie you get the other. Annie Lee you have to go to your table and tell them we're out. Since you took more than your fair share."

"I sold more of the highest priced item on the menu and I'm getting penalized. I don't get it."

"There's nothing to get," the chef was plating another rack of venison, cutting the chops apart with sweeping samurai movements of his freshly de-burred knife. "I'm the chef, I can do what I want."

It was 8:54. An earlier deuce, who had requested the most romantic table in the house, was having the kind of fight meant to be played out for everyone in the dining room. Halfway through the meal, Annie Lee noticed their food—though it had been disgustingly moved around on the plate—remained uneaten. The kitchen is going to have a *fit*, she thought to herself as she moved slowly to the table.

"We're done," the man said not maliciously, but with a certain ceremonial sadness. He touched the side of his plate and moved it imperceptibly away from himself. She inquired, as intimately as she could without removing an article of clothing, if anything was wrong.

"No, no," his woman whispered, hair just as glossy and swishy as the tail of a prize horse. "It was lovely." She looked at him, he looked at her. "But we're having a bad night."

"It's just not going well," he echoed, never losing eye contact.

"I'm sorry," Annie Lee said, aiming her words at the space between them where the focus seemed to be. She went out on a limb at this point and asked if she should just go ahead and bring the check.

"That might be the best thing," he said, while Annie Lee wondered why they seemed out of place and then decided they belonged in a high school cafeteria rather than a real live restaurant. This was teenage stuff. They left twenty-two percent, however, on a Diners Club card, and he had his hand on her derrière by the time they reached the door. Annie Lee sighed, the image of her husband flashing briefly through her mind in the same amount of time it took to remember to refill coffee on table five.

When the chef saw the abominable plates go by, in spite

of Annie Lee's efforts to spare him, he was once again tapping a knife. "Problem?" he said, craning his neck out as Annie Lee walked up the stairs to the landing where the bus tub was.

"No, no problem," she answered, happy for the opportunity to throw him off. "They said they liked the food." That was a lie.

"How could they like the food when they didn't eat any of it?"

"They were having a fight."

"A fight," he repeated, reconsidering his position. "About what?" He made it sound as if the subject of the fight had a direct relationship to how he would view the catastrophic plates of food.

Annie Lee bit her lip. Her answer would have to be good. "I didn't hear all of it," she said. "But something about having to visit his mother. She didn't want him to go, to miss her birthday."

The chef thought about this. "A mother comes first," he said yanking down a ticket from the line and calling another waiter at the top of his lungs. "Was the mother sick?" he crossed his arms as he faced her.

"Yes, I think she was."

"Was the woman beautiful?"

"Most men would say so."

"Okay," he said. "The woman was manipulative and didn't care about her food. The man was hungry but lost his appetite in the face of an ultimatum involving his mother, the poor guy. *Le pauvre mec*."

"Well," she told him, walking away and feeling she must stand up for womankind even in this particular embodiment, "the mother could have been the most manipulative one of all. Did you ever think of that?"

"It doesn't matter," she heard him toss the words after her and could swear she heard his shoulders shrug. "It's his mother."

The rest of the night went by smoothly except that now, thanks to the mock fighters—who were probably already in the steam shower soaping each other up—Annie Lee couldn't stop thinking of her husband. She couldn't recall what it felt like to be kissed on the lips and experienced a moment of pure, existential panic: It was as if everything—marriage, memory, happiness even—was as featherlike as their lips touching, and just as fleeting.

She hoped there would be something good for dinner—something to occupy her, ground her, and cheer her up—and headed upstairs to the private dining room where the staff had gathered with their beers and their glasses of wine.

Six

Anywhere between 10:30 and 11:15, the staff dined and debriefed together like an old-fashioned family, the bickering, bantering kind. Tonight, Jay wanted a recap of the incident that had cost him a cleaning bill, two glasses of good champagne, and his personal apologies. Not to mention the embarrassment of food flying through the air in his establishment.

Annie Lee furnished the flight plan of the duck bone and concluded by saying the customer responded well to treatment with alcohol. "As a matter of fact," she continued, "that guy responded well to life. A one-in-a-billion customer—rich, handsome, and easygoing. Born and raised on the right side of the bed." She took a bite of quiche Lorraine. "In general, you should never assume people are going to be nice. Then, if they are, you can be surprised."

Jay didn't agree, and he put down his wineglass. "In general," he said, "people *are* nice."

"The two things are not mutually exclusive," Con interjected. "Annie Lee is simply operating on the basis of a well-known restaurant theorem: Sauce is predisposed to land on those least likely to be charmed by it." Though Con and Annie Lee pitted themselves against each other regularly to pass the time, it was equally easy for them to bolster each other's American positions in a ferociously French environment.

"Hmpph," said the owner. "I have a hard time with sauce being *predisposed* at all. People are predisposed. Not sauce."

"It's too metaphysical for the French." Annie Lee shrugged at Con, who was nodding in agreement.

Meanwhile Kathryn, in the middle of her nightly gem recap, didn't seem to mind that no one was listening to her rattle on about the pitfalls of something called a European-cut diamond. Eddie, who'd filled in for one of the waiters, was talking cleavage, his favorite subject, which launched Jay into a diatribe against the American fixation on breasts. Annie Lee seemed to be having a paradoxical moment of concurrently missing her husband and disliking all men except for that sweetheart on table one.

She made a quick, contemptuous comment regarding the opposite sex, and then, to clear her mind, focused on the leftover dessert for the evening—*île flottante*. Just what she needed. A succulent association of frothy egg white topped with crunchy caramel and bathed in *crème anglaise*. Sometimes Annie Lee used those exact words to describe it. Sometimes she said "soft meringue mounds adrift in a sweet cream sauce," and other times it was just simply "classic floating island."

Her reveries were interrupted by Eddie, who wanted to know if he was just dreaming, or was it her time of the month. Before she could lash out, Con interjected.

"She misses her husband, you insensitive blockhead." He put his arm around Annie Lee's shoulders. "And everything that smacks of men and their habits, well, it reminds her that you can't live with 'em and you can't live without 'em. I know I can't. When's he coming back anyway?" Con had changed into a turtleneck for dinner, forest green, which altered his looks.

He was one of those people who looked best in some kind of uniform—any kind, it didn't matter. Policeman. Butler. Fireman. Waiter. Pizza guy. Regular clothes always made Annie Lee stare at him and wonder if she really knew him at all. The green turtleneck made her want to top him off with a classic-car cap and a herringbone jacket and pipe. Then she'd know who she was dealing with.

"He's back, he got back tonight," she said. "No more questions will be entertained. It's my own private business, and even though I know you discuss my marriage behind my back, you're not getting one word out of me." But, meanwhile, she was worried. What if Lucas didn't want to start fresh? What if his own pacing was different and he needed more than a week apart, or worse yet, realized he felt better away from his own home than in it? It was a miracle marriages survived in any other state than perfect stasis: There were just too many variables. No, two people had to be in a sort of arrested development, each holding the same how-to manual, in order to proceed.

Dinner was over when all the floating islands were gone. Con vacuumed and found a pair of women's cashmere-lined calfskin gloves under a chair at table eight. The gloves fit all the women perfectly. They drew toothpicks, Kathryn won, and immediately asked Jay if she couldn't just wear them while she waited for the thirty-day lost-and-found rule to be up.

"Absolutely not," he said, while the other women shook their heads in concurrence.

It took Annie Lee roughly ten minutes to get home—about the time it took to walk anywhere in Pike. Avoiding Main Street's core of ten blocks—a wall-to-wall string of shops, restaurants, bars, and real estate offices ("for those," she liked to say, "unfortunately deciding to stay")—she negotiated the alleys, past the backs of restaurants and bars whose bottles were being emptied into recycle bins. She and Lucas had always loved the alleys of Pike. And these days, it seemed as though the alleys were all that remained of the original town. Blessedly unpaved, they were studded with stones and ruts, were murderously icy in winter and mucky in spring. You could still get lost in the alleys, feel the ghosts of Pike's past flutter by, with no interference from present-day sport-utility vehicles or $3,000 bicycles or people waving their wallets around like magic wands.

Annie Lee breathed deeply. The bracing black air—what would you call the color of space at night in Pike? Blackuum? Deep Dark Space?—slowly filled her lungs. The air whispered, its breath moist and seductive, of the coming spring. Suddenly, Annie Lee ached for the next season to be here. For new beginnings, buds on her trees, shoes you could run in, a softening and warming of everything, the melting of icy hearts.

She turned north on Spring Street and marched uphill for three and a half blocks until she came to the familiar gate. She looked at her house, dwarfed by the dark sky, and felt her stomach sink. She'd expected lights to be on, but there were no signs of life coming from anywhere within. Only the tiniest tinkle of a wind chime from the Winkleman sisters' porch next door greeted her. For a moment she thought maybe Lucas hadn't returned, but there was the truck, back in the driveway: He was home but he'd gone to bed. Her anticipation shrank like a salted slug.

As she crossed the threshold, however, familiar kitchen smells assaulted her, caught her off guard, lured her in. She turned on the tiny halogen light near the stove and then opened the refrigerator for confirmation of her husband's return. She spied some fresh leftover containers and tipped them up to see what was inside.

Before their falling-out, Lucas's habit had always been to label everything in the refrigerator with grease pencil. On any given day she would have neat packages at her disposal, a smorgasbord to choose from: "Oatmeal/Raisins." "Marinated Tofu."

"Bolognese Sauce/Spaghettini." "Steak Tidbits/Peppercorns." "Egg Salad/Green Olives." "Tiramisu from Restaurant." "Two Slices Parma Ham."

Like all trained cooks, her husband showed little inclination to waste anything. Nonwaste had always been a form of domestic worship for him; the liturgy of the worship service came in the form of leftover banquets planned for lunch midweek, little tea parties that would stump him as he puzzled over what kind of wine you could serve with a Thai soup, chicken salad, and two slices of focaccia.

Yes, Lucas was the leftovers genius. He would always know what to do with six vegetables and a stale loaf of bread. And while he made do, joyfully, elegantly, frugally, Annie Lee would be happy to watch and clean up a bit behind him, an acolyte with a whisk broom and dustpan, doing her devotional acts.

Ultimately his creation would find its way to a plastic container. "Tuscan Salad," he would mark it. Then it would appeal to Annie Lee, once it had gone from the chaos of random ingredients to something more apparent, labeled, and with a name. Without fail, she would remember the dish and ask him to make it again, having already committed it to memory. He would look puzzled, not recalling. It would drive her crazy that he couldn't do it again, give her that same pleasure; but by that time he would already be on to his next act, completely fresh and impromptu: different ingredients, different name.

When they vacationed, usually in some urban environment or other, Annie Lee was prone to finding the best deli counters and the best coffee shops. She'd go for some simple thing like an outstanding tuna melt, the perfect pickle at its side. Or a tub of fresh mozzarella salad and a crusty loaf of bread she could tuck under her arm. She'd want to return the next day for the same calculable pleasure, overlapping the layers of pleasure and memory into a sort of sandwich of reminiscence.

Lucas, on the other hand, liked to pore over the menus

tacked up outside restaurants, where he stood reading how each item was described. Since this happened on vacation, she usually had her camera with her; and having nothing to do while she stood there waiting for him, she would take pictures. Eventually, she devoted an entire photo album to these pictures of Lucas standing next to the doors of hundreds of restaurants, contentedly reading menus. He took copious mental notes at each stop; but even when someone from inside asked if they could be of assistance, he would shake his head politely, smile, and say, "Just reading your nice menu."

In San Francisco, not that long ago, he had finally been invited inside an almost painfully elegant Italian place whose arched door was framed with ivy. Annie Lee, unnoticed by the man in whites doing the inviting, had waited patiently outside for fifteen minutes before Lucas had exited, a little flushed, she thought, and hustled her down the street. Over coffee, she asked him, as nonchalantly as possible, what he'd done to be given the tour.

"I said I was a cook myself, that's all, and that I was enjoying reading their menu."

"Did it make you want to leave Pike and work in a place like that?"

"No, absolutely not," he said, staring at her with disbelief. "Chefs in those kinds of places remind me too much of my father. They're all egomaniacs. It's bad enough in Pike, and it's getting worse all the time."

"That guy back there seemed nice enough."

"He was just the pasta guy. And I think he might have been on the make."

Lucas loved splendid, elegant, imaginative cooking; he liked to cook it and he liked to eat it, but he didn't necessarily like the people that went with it. Though his skills had lured him to frilly dinners, more and more his personality lured him away from them. Cooking and entertaining at home had become his way of reassuring himself that fancy food and good people could go together, though in real life—professional life, at least—many times they did not.

Annie Lee had not seen leftover tubs in many weeks.

She thought of how many such tubs there had been over the course of their marriage—how many choices she'd always been given—and wished she could decipher what the two inscrutable plastic containers meant, that she could know what a week away had done to Lucas's state of mind based on the words "Chicken Breast/Sage Leaves" and "Jasmine Rice." Yes, it was true the lights were out and he'd gone to bed without greeting her. And yet, she was cheered (almost absurdly so!) by the sight of something as simple as that familiar black writing on the reinstated plastic tubs.

At this point, however, fridge door still open, she realized that a full larder might have looked better, from Lucas's point of view, than an empty one. A teeming refrigerator would have indicated that she'd taken better care of herself, been more self-sufficient, that she hadn't played the victim by starving herself. She should have proven to him she could do leftovers, too. That left to her own devices, she could adapt! She could change! That would have made him wonder about her, wonder if he hadn't underestimated her all these years.

Annie Lee knew deep down she would never have been able to pull off such a trick, not without help of some kind, a leftover hotline, say—a number to dial where the words "I have some bologna, hard-cooked eggs, celery, carrots, and cream in my refrigerator. Can you help?" would be met with the enthusiastic response of an ingredients genius, perhaps some burned-out chef who'd gone the way of books and research:

"There's an old country dish from Yugoslavia," he would say, staring at his computer screen and the database he'd painstakingly put together, "where chopped egg and cream are combined in a saucepan and seasoned with salt and pepper. Parboiled vegetables—any ones you happen to have on hand—are then added to the mixture, which is simmered and reduced and then served, hot, over egg noodles. You do have egg noodles, don't you?"

"Of course," she would answer. "Everyone has egg noodles."

"And get rid of the bologna," he would add. "You don't need bologna, nobody does."

The sad truth was Annie Lee hadn't filled the refrigerator, she'd gone out for six lunches and one dinner.

While Klink stared stoically at the just-closed door of the refrigerator, Annie Lee made her way to the powder room, where she brushed her teeth, washed her face, and then massaged her right thumb joint, sore from uncorking wine, with Arnica cream. She took off her clothes in the living room and left them on the couch. Finally, she made her way up the dark staircase, tiptoed into the bedroom, and then slid noiselessly into bed next to Lucas, the smell of her peppermint toothpaste strong enough, she thought, to wake the dead.

After lying there, boardlike, for several minutes, she readjusted to sharing the mattress by mincing her movements, abbreviating them. Lucas shifted only after she'd fiddled with her pillows, wedging one between her legs as she always did. From the deep cave of sleep, he sighed and moaned and seemed on the verge of snoring. Before she could think better of it, she nudged him—gave him a shove, actually—just to let him know he had company.

Lucas was a heavy sleeper. "Hn-n-n-n," he groaned.

She answered with the impunity of the desperate—frustrated that he'd cheated her of any kind of greeting whatsoever. "You're snoring, Luke," she said. "Turn on your side."

Still asleep, he shifted and molded himself into a childlike curl with his back to her, and mumbled something, something close enough to a greeting for Annie Lee, who did not hesitate to prop herself up carefully on one elbow to reply. She whispered her answer to the sleeping mound who could not hear her, filling him in on her week alone. She told him how much she'd netted in five nights, described the new grilled tempeh sandwich from the deli on West Currant, and admitted to having called Dr. Oram's office. Briefly, she recapped the weather, for no account of Pike was complete without it.

Finally, she lowered herself back onto the pillow and fell asleep, grateful to have expressed herself to him, however one-sided the exchange.

Seven

The next morning, Annie Lee woke up hungry for breakfast. She discovered herself alone in the bed, on Lucas's side, in fact, and wondered if she had tried to grope him or had merely taken over the space she'd committed herself to keeping both warm and indented over the course of the week.

From downstairs she could hear the clangor of wooden spoons and whisks against steel mixing bowls. Throwing an old V-neck sweater over her lacy nightgown, she padded downstairs in the socks she slept in, anxious to see him, but nervous about setting things right. On the way down, she saw the morning sky flash at her from the window in the study: a high-pressure day, as they called them in Pike, and what would amount to a sky so blue you had to shield your eyes from it, a syrupy cerulean that stuck in your throat, melted snow, and reflected itself in everyone's expensive sunglasses. As a crow sailed by sideways, she readjusted her prognosis: With gusts like that another storm could not be far behind.

What Lucas saw was a vision in sea-foam green, lilac, and bright red: Annie Lee, a disorderly braid down her back, eyes slightly puffy from deep sleep, had the hint of a tentative smile cutting through an otherwise wary face.

"So," he said quietly, handing her a mug, a chunky old thing the color of powdered mustard. "Here's your starter cup." He gave her a quick glance and then asked her how she'd been but did not wait for her to reply. "I forgot I'd invited the sisters to breakfast this morning weeks ago, so they'll be over at nine for crumpets. Bea called to confirm last night and said she'd bring over some of that wild-raspberry jam."

"You mean you told her she didn't have to bring anything, hoping she'd bring jam," said Annie Lee, and then added, "I'm fine." They hadn't had the sisters over for months: why now? She squinted at him, noted his unwillingness to say anything more personal. Where was the reunion scene hiding? Where was the part where he sees she's changed, then looks her up and down and they get on with their lives? "I'm cheerful now," she wanted to testify, "I'm uncomplaining!" Had he seen the wall?

"How are *you?*" She stared at him as he turned around to work at the stove, whipping this, flipping that. He always looked fresh in the morning, unlike a lot of other people who worked at night. He took care in putting himself together—shoulder-length dishwater-blond hair combed, white sleeves rolled up, clean jeans, chef's clogs, apron already on. Fresh like a white-feathered bird, watertight, strokeable—you wanted to follow him around.

The first time Annie Lee had ever kissed Lucas she had wanted to smear herself all over him like jam on bread. It was their second date, and he had again invited her for dinner at his house. Moroccan food, eaten with the fingers. After figs and dates and mint tea for dessert, he'd brushed up against her as he took her plate away, and she'd gotten the first faint intoxicating whiff of him. She had followed him to the sink and looked into his eyes and said, "I'll wash the dishes." His eyes, she'd noted, were an oddly combined grayish green. Not Smoky Jungle—far too hot. Not Foggy Seas—too cold and wet.

Side by side and silently, they'd washed the dishes.

It was with a soapy platter in her hand that she felt Lucas's breath on her neck. Carefully, in a moment that seemed to span both time and space, she put the platter back in the water. He turned her around and touched her lips with his fingers, then with his mouth. She felt an electric shock of familiarity in his skin and his smell. She thought about sleeping with someone she could call her friend and had feelings, she concluded, that bordered on incestuous.

He seemed to feel the same way. Often, he'd peppered their day-to-day life with old-fashioned yet intimate gestures. He might brush her hair in the morning, and then braid it. Or dress her from underwear to jeans and sweater. Tie her shoes. Most men were good at undressing women, but how many could dress them, or wanted to? How many men—besides hairdressers—could comb a woman's hair? Annie Lee thought she'd found the only man on earth who could make her want to rip off her clothes with an innocent gesture such as putting in a hair tie or picking a piece of basil off her tooth.

In time and with these familiar gestures, they'd eased each other into the stories of their lives, familiarizing themselves with the similar landscapes and markings of their pasts. One day, early in the relationship, Lucas had asked her if she'd ever written a story. They were playing a full hour of Crusaders on Radio Pike, and Lucas seemed hypnotized by the music. Nope, she told him, never knew where to start. You? Without another word, he'd retrieved an old spiral notebook from someplace upstairs (she never did find out where) and read from it to her, his fifteen-year-old coming through like a timpani solo in the symphony of the self.

The story involved a group of brown bears who steal him from his bed at night and take him to their den where he sits, a mere human boy, listening to the great ursine wisdom of the ages. He is able to feel their feelings and learns, much to his surprise, a visceral yet complex language of growls, murmurs, and grunts. He learns empathy and fierceness and deep communion with the earth. He begins to feel a profound calm inside. After many months, his heart full and his step sure, the adolescent human is told he is ready to go into the world and fulfill his fate: He will be the emissary to the world of humans, the elucidator of bear wisdom. They are depending on him to bridge the worlds of relatively silent fauna and overly verbal man. The boy feels powerful and proud.

But on the very day he is sent into the world, a bear tooth hanging from his neck, he meets—in a clap of thunder, a lightning bolt through his heart—the new girl at school. Someone with eager, darting eyes, a pencil perpetually forgotten behind her ear; and with every thought of her, every fleeting burst of pheromone and longing, he remembers less and less of what the bears have taught him. At the climactic moment of their first kiss, just as their lips touch, the last bit of bear training slips away; and thinking somehow she has stolen his bear wisdom with the kiss, he is forever doomed to pursue her, only half conscious of his fate.

"I've never read anyone that story," he'd told her afterward. "I must have been listening to a lot of Crusaders back then, or something. Haven't thought about it in years."

Annie Lee had gotten excited. "It's a perfect adolescent story!"

"Well," he said, "it was the story of my *life* at that age. Once I fell for Nora Clare—the real new girl—it was as if someone pulled the plug on my power. I thought I could do anything until then—anything I set my mind to."

"Until hormones kicked in."

He shrugged. "They rule the male life. It's a miracle I ever started cooking, or doing anything for that matter. At first I even took home ec because of this one girl. Then, once I actually started chopping, mixing, sautéing, it was like I was recovering information or something from a dim past. I had an inkling of lost bear wisdom, even if it was just omelettes and apple crisp.

Pretty soon it became *pâte à choux* and chocolate soufflés. Now I think I'm reverting to omelettes and apple crisp."

Annie Lee had asked for the name of the girl in home ec. Over the years, she would learn the names of every significant person in Lucas Fleck's adolescence, and, like a litany, could recite them along with any distinguishing traits or important moments.

"Anna Tompkins."

"Was she the one you lost your virginity to?"

"No. That wasn't Anna. That was Cindy Sherman."

"Cindy Sherman—like the photographer! What was she like?"

Lucas had thought hard before answering, as if he had been asked to stir the soupy past with the wrong spoon. "She was the kind of girl every guy wanted. I couldn't believe she was interested in me. I hitched a ride to her house every day after school for three months, desperate to peer inside her blouse, lift up her pleated cheerleader skirt. Her mother owned a dress shop and was never home. Her father ran the biggest GMC dealership in Seattle. She was an only child, so we had the house to ourselves. Her room smelled like hair spray and nylon shag carpet; and she had her own TV, which she liked to have on while we rolled around on the bed."

Annie Lee had been jealous of the girls of Lucas's youth; and he'd seemed equally covetous of her earlier years. It was as if they discovered that in order to be a couple, their adolescent selves had to meet each other. From this, everything about their updated, adult selves could be understood.

Except what was happening today. Today was adrift, cut off, floating not in the past nor the future but in a stifling present where neither of them seemed to know the other. Without bearings, Annie Lee scanned the room for an anchor, anything concrete upon which to base a conversation. An old *New Yorker* magazine that lay on the counter caught her eye and, struggling for control, she asked Lucas where he'd gotten it.

"Someone who must have not known my mother well gave her a stack of magazines the day I was born. You know, with my birthday as the date of issue. For sentimental reasons. A copy of *Fish Weekly*, or whatever it's called, would have been more appropriate. I'm surprised she even kept them—maybe she's just never made the effort to clean out the attic since Dad died. Now, all of a sudden she's cleaning out the attic." Lucas's father, an eminent surgeon, had died of a heart attack over a decade ago.

"I liked the illustration, for obvious reasons. I thought I'd have it framed." Annie Lee approached the counter to study the cover more closely. It showed an old, boxy house, front porch sagging, a look almost identical to theirs right down to the peeling white paint and lopsided window boxes, closed gate and open front door. The likeness was uncanny. Though she said nothing, she was buoyed by his having brought the relic back. He was saying their home still had meaning, that he still had faith in it, wasn't he? Or was he merely reacting to the remarkable coincidence of living in a house identical to the one on the cover of a magazine bearing his date of birth?

As if hearing her thoughts, he returned to more mundane matters. "Okay, I did mention I'd love a spoonful of some of their jam. Bea made one of those lip-smacking sounds and said she'd see what she had. And added that Eudora always noticed when the jam jars disappeared. They can't help being themselves."

"Eudora notices everything down to the dust motes. But it must be nice having someone to lay the blame on all the time," she said. "It'd be like me saying, 'Let me check with myself and I'll get back to you.'"

"You do that already, Annie Lee." He caught her eye briefly and then returned to pouring just the right amount of batter into the rings. Colonel Klink had located himself on the counter next to the stove and was watching Lucas's movements with rapt infatuation, head moving as the crumpets flipped.

"It looks like the cat missed you." Annie Lee could not help tossing the words out like a wobbly dart, her own projected feelings flying in their wake.

Lucas was silent a moment. "Klink is a male cat. Neutered at that." He was staring at the bubbles forming in the batter. "We understand each other."

Annie Lee was stung by the nastiness of the words. "You know, Lucas, maybe you could stop flipping and turn around. Maybe we could say hello, even, instead of doing this—this awful thing we're doing."

"Okay," he said putting down the utensils and crossing his arms as he turned to face her. "Hello, Annie Lee. You say you're fine." A blank stare punctuated his sentiments. "Who knows what that means today. You're still not pregnant. And I'm unsure if we'll ever try to get you pregnant again, since failing seems to destroy you. I don't know how to act around you. I don't even feel like a man—"

"Well . . ." She was threatened by the comment. "I don't feel like a woman. I can't conceive and I can't make my husband want to tear off my clothes anymore—"

"Wait a minute. Don't fob that off on me. You haven't encouraged advances in weeks and weeks and—"

"You haven't exactly made them. Maybe I'd change my mind if you showed some real enthusiasm." She pointed grudgingly at the stove to remind him to turn around and pour and flip and also to give herself a break from scrutiny.

"And why is that, Annie Lee?" he continued. "Everything is stilted. You don't want to be disappointed every month, but you harass me for not making you feel desired. And you think kids will solve everything. Falling into that old trap. You're putting all your eggs in one basket because you need a baby in your life. Sometimes it doesn't work like that, you know."

"All what eggs—" Annie Lee couldn't help herself.

"Don't play the martyr, girl. You're healthy. My mother says we really ought to reconsider in vitro if we're serious about children."

Inwardly, Annie Lee rolled her eyes. "Your mother would. She spends all day studying fish eggs under a microscope. She doesn't study the happiness of fish. Or their pleasures." Margaret Fleck, a marine biologist, did independent research for the State Fisheries Department on spawning practices of wild salmon. "It costs thousands of dollars, remember? Where are we supposed to get that kind of money? Sell the house?" It was a comment meant to get a rise out of him, not an option she ever seriously considered. She felt herself losing all the ground she'd gained during her week alone.

"I'm never selling this house."

"Well, there you go then. Your house is more important to you than having children."

"Annie Lee," he looked as if he were about to shake her, "you're acting like a crazy person. The house is all we have—our only material possession that's worth anything. So say we sell the house to have the baby. Then the baby has no house if we do conceive. And we don't have a house if we don't. We can't sell the house. My birth date on the magazine reinforces that notion."

A loud rap at the door interrupted them. It sounded very much like a jar of jam hitting old wood. Even the door's window rattled.

"Coming!" Annie Lee yelled as she faced her husband one last time before hustling off to get dressed. "I thought so much about this house and our life when you were gone . . ." She willed herself to say the right thing—what was it? She hadn't meant to say she'd ever sell the house; and now he thought that's what she meant!

Lucas turned toward the front door. Out of the corner of her eye, Annie Lee saw him wiping his hands on his apron as he went to receive the guests. He was wiping them hard.

Eight

I brought you our last jar of wild raspberry since you made it plain you had no preserves of any kind," Eudora put the mason jar on the counter with a thud and scanned the room for messes, intruders, or anything at all out of the ordinary. Annie Lee had not gone up the stairs completely, opting instead for a surveillance perch halfway up.

"Where's Annie Lee?" Eudora approached Lucas, who busied himself setting the table.

"She's getting dressed. She'll be down in a minute." Frustration trimmed the graciousness off his sentences.

"Your house hardly looks lived in. Was Annie Lee gone, too?" Eudora, shuffling the books on the coffee table, was straining for a glimpse of their titles. "She didn't visit us while you were gone. We thought surely she'd decided to go along, but Bea swore you got in your pickup alone. Who's reading *Robinson Crusoe?* I used to teach that in the upper levels."

"Annie Lee reads it whenever she's depressed. She says it cheers her up."

"Hmmm, I didn't know that. Well, I never did like Crusoe

much: too chipper for someone so bad off." Going back to the coffee table, she sifted through books again. "Doesn't she usually go with you on your trips back home?"

"Yes, she does."

"You're being nosy, Eudora." Bea's warning words didn't register.

"So are you two having marital difficulties, then?" Eudora was reading the jacket copy on a book whose cover showed a man with sun-blistered skin in an inflatable boat.

"Yes." Lucas didn't look at them as he spoke, so he didn't see the long gaze pass between the two women, one of whom had her arms crossed. "My wife is going crazy because she can't get pregnant. But she won't even try anymore because she doesn't want to be disappointed. Sort of a catch-22 situation. She doesn't believe in fertility drugs because she doesn't want quadruplets. She says she wants to sell the house to be able to afford in vitro fertilization. That's our story."

"Oh . . ." Bea's attention had been snagged. "You can't sell the house. That would be a *big* mistake."

"You don't have to tell me that." Lucas faced them and ran a hand through his hair, pulling at the roots just slightly.

"No, but you see," Bea said, "this house is special; I thought maybe you'd sensed that. It's different from most houses." The two of them crowded around him like sorceresses.

The sisters—Eudora and Beatrice Winkleman—lived next door to the Flecks in a cavernous powder-puff pink Victorian, the only house in town with a widow's walk—an eight-foot-square perch covered entirely with bird feeders, like antennae on a mountaintop. Every jay, chicadee, grosbeak, blackbird, nuthatch, and finch within miles frequented the Winkleman roof, a post from which they could gaze down on the cats below to mock the lowly life of hunting and sleeping while they, the superior winged creatures, snacked and sang and observed the world instead.

To some degree, the sisters were very much like their rooftop flocks. Born in the pink house, neither of them ever married or even considered marriage an option from what anyone could tell. Eudora had taught high-school English and geography all her life until retirement. Bea had started the town library in the fifties and before that had been a records clerk at the courthouse. Though they'd begun Pike's oral history project and were codirectors of the Pike Historical Society (to which they'd appointed Lucas an honorary subcodirector), they were essentially private people who guarded history as well as preserved it. They refused, for example, to provide the museum with a single one of their vintage photos despite a large and nearly scholarly stash, scrupulously organized by year and kept in the living room in an old trunk.

"We're not dead yet," Bea was fond of saying. "When we're dead, we'll give the museum everything Lucas doesn't want." Lucas had learned most of the town's history—mining and otherwise—from the sisters and their photos; he stared at the pictures, Annie Lee thought, like a man yearning to pierce the images and enter them. The sisters saw this in him, too.

In public, the Winklemans walked everywhere arm in arm, like lawn mowers on a mission to tread over whatever stood in their way. Despite their cohesive formation, however, their lines of reasoning were for the most part diametrically opposed. Eudora, the dour and practical one, spoke of the minutiae of life as if her calling was to pile up tiny facts into a big and incontrovertible pile. She was never at a loss for the quotidian advice everyone else needed to make their lives more efficient, more sanitary, or more orderly—counsel usually delivered via a third party like Annie Lee.

"Tell her she needs to use white vinegar in her rinse cycle to get these things to stop smelling like old socks," Eudora would say, sneaking a sniff at someone's dish towel while drying cups and saucers.

Or, "They need to feed their roses once a year if they want anything to come of those runty bushes. Like blooms, for instance."

Or, "If she really wants that lemon pie to look good, she shouldn't skimp on egg whites. You need lots of egg whites, more than any cookbook ever says. Why doesn't anyone ever just come out and say that instead of pretending the number of whites exactly matches the number of yolks?"

Bea, on the other hand, though adequately conversant in the mundane, had predilections toward the big picture. "In a world gone crazy with mate finding, soul searching, politics, and gossip, we will be a part of none of it," she'd recently said, when the city manager had asked them to head up the next Fourth of July parade. As if a parade by definition signified all of the above. The refusal had, to their astonishment, made the front page of the local weekly. "Sisters Say No!" the headline said, above a picture of the city manager at their doorstep, and Eudora and Bea looking dismayed at having their picture taken.

The Flecks considered themselves fortunate to have such neighbors as friends. Certainly, they spent more time with the Winklemans than anyone else did, accepted their jam in summer and soup in winter, took their advice like the dutiful children they'd never been with their own parents. Besides physical proximity, why were they singled out by the formidable duo? Both of them felt it had to do with the fact that they'd left their house alone, hadn't remodeled with a full basement, three extra bedrooms, two more decks, and a hot tub like everyone else in town had. They hadn't tampered with history. No, they couldn't afford it, but by the same token, they fiercely loved the house just as it was. This was obvious to the sisters, and Annie Lee felt certain it explained their strong reaction to Lucas's comment about selling the house.

Annie Lee returned in olive drab wool pants and a deep rose red silk chemise that had been thrown on in haste.

"I was just saying that this was our last jar of jam." Eudora approached her after giving Lucas a long, hard look in the eye. "But then you have to be willing to pay for fresh crumpets. Hmm," she added, surveying Annie Lee from head to toe, "Nice combination of colors. You don't look at all like a Christmas tree—which is what usually happens with red and green."

"Thank you," Annie Lee was grateful for the compliment and smiled her first genuine smile of the morning. "Chinese red. Historically, the color of life, of opulence, and of special charms. As for the jam, we just need enough for these crumpets," Annie Lee assured her. "Then you can take the rest of it home with extra crumpets for yourselves."

"That would constitute Indian giving." Beatrice's lips and chin were pursed like a closed-up string bag. "And I won't be any part of that kind of behavior. It bespeaks a bigger tendency toward niggardliness. Fraudulent comportment." She paused for a moment. "I realize I'm not supposed to say that—'Indian giving'—which, historically, is way off base anyway. But what do you call it when someone gives and then takes back? You could more correctly call it U.S. government giving, couldn't you? Anyway, you get my drift."

"We do, Bea," said Eudora. "Now let's take our coats off and stay awhile."

Underneath the identical anoraks, reminiscent with their hoods and heavy metal zippers of the Alaskan frontier, each dressed according to her personality. Eudora wore a pink oxford shirt, pressed to perfection, gunmetal gray slacks, and a bolo with a big chunk of silver and turquoise at the neck. Bea had on flowered leggings, loose over her bony legs, and a long peach sweatshirt that said "Haste Makes Waste" in elegant nut-brown script.

"You haven't told us about your trip," Bea said to Lucas, as she patted the tops of her loopy white curls to test their spring. "How was it? Was your mother happy to see you?" Bea adored Lucas, doted on him. She loved that he cooked, that he conversed, and that he'd decorated the house. He represented the epitome of the natural man to her, and she was, even at her advanced age, attracted to that.

Lucas answered after some thought. "It was fine. I cleaned out the gutters. I painted the pantry."

"Hospital White I bet," Annie Lee could not keep the words from coming out.

"Beeswax was the color I chose." He shot her a glance, and Annie Lee noticed that this morning he was a little puffy around the eyes, too. She hadn't noticed it before.

Lucas redirected his comments to Bea. "I threw away the piles of junk she'd managed to dislodge from the attic but was not capable then of getting out of the garage. And I cooked her real food for a change, which she ate like someone who'd been in solitary confinement for months. Even though she could easily afford to hire people to clean for her and cook for her, she treats her house like base camp and lives at work. Maybe people take care of her there; I don't know."

"She must be happy to have her son back home from time to time," Bea said with an adoring look.

Lucas just shrugged. "Hard to say what's going on with my mother."

Lucas admitted freely to never having understood either of his parents. He contended they'd arrived in the world as full-grown adults of the species—people perpetually mystified by infants, babies, and children of all ages. When he was growing up, he said, they seemed to be constantly consulting a master checklist on the generic child. At some point it was time for him to get braces. To join the Boy Scouts. One year they inquired why he hadn't signed up for track and field, as if he ought to have known by then what to do. His father made sure from that point on that Lucas took all the proper science and math classes, the understanding being that only when he became a doctor would his father stop treating him like an "undercooked three-minute egg."

It came as a great surprise to Lucas that during his junior year in high school, Kelly Fleck, who had never mentioned his son's predilections before, hired him to cater their dinner parties. This pleased Lucas, bolstered him enormously, and for the first time in his life, he felt useful, understood, a part of the family. Eventually, however, he realized that his father meant only to pass Lucas off as a boy genius tapping in to hobby number one, the kind of kid headed for a brilliant career, who needed to entertain himself with things like fine cuisine and chess and growing orchids and opera and scuba diving. Dr. Fleck was showing off his son—and saving a few bucks in the process.

Lucas, however hurt, continued to cater the parties. He learned how to order food, hire people and train them, how to rent supplies—china, champagne glasses, tents for outside parties, even musicians. By the time he was eighteen, he'd made enough connections in Seattle to start a successful business. It seemed he'd gained the respect of everyone but his father. Of course.

So, he took his father's money and went back East to college. Annie Lee couldn't believe he would opt out of such an easy career choice, something staring him right in the face. He told her that even though he had no idea what to study in college, he liked the idea of reading books on someone else's tab. And, he said, it was never his intention for one minute to become a doctor or play chess or go to the opera.

For her part, Margaret Fleck had always worshiped Kelly and had been unable to come to grips with what had gone on—or never gone on—in their life as a family. For the past decade, she had chosen to live with fish instead of people, as if, with mankind's best representative gone for good, it made no sense to have anything to do with small-time stand-ins. Her only son's presence was welcomed in that it gave her a chance to reminisce with someone who could at least follow along and know better than to muddy the clear, viscous fluid in which she had chosen to immortalize her husband.

Annie Lee had always served as sort of a buffer between them—Margaret vaguely acknowledged her son's wife as some present-day smoke screen obfuscating her own clear view of the past. Someone who had never had Kelly's approval—or disapproval—and therefore didn't quite exist. Much of Margaret's life depressed Annie Lee, but not nearly as much as it depressed Lucas, who had a hard time dissimulating to the contrary.

"Well," Bea concluded, seeing Lucas unsettled by his thoughts, "you're a good boy to see to your mother. If she can't appreciate it, the devil take her, poor thing! I for one give you credit where credit is due." She looked around to see what kind of response she would get.

Eudora was giving her sister a disapproving sort of look that said "cool it, sister," which cheered Annie Lee immeasurably. It looked as if Bea was about to get a lecture to go along with the look, but then Eudora saw the old *New Yorker* and, genuinely excited, went over to it.

"Look at the likeness to your house!" she said, and as she picked the magazine up to get a better look, something fell out from between the pages. It fluttered to the floor next to Annie Lee, who bent over to retrieve whatever it was. That was when she found herself staring at a Polaroid picture of her husband and a blond woman sitting at Margaret's dining-room table, chairs scooted side by side, smiling into the camera.

"Who's this?" she said as nonchalantly as she could before feeling the blood pump inside her chest, course through her veins, and then gush up into her face.

Nine

Lucas actually reddened as he saw what she was holding up. He stood facing all three women, who were waiting for an answer. Annie Lee felt her own blood shift into reverse and drain from her face. She thought she might actually faint. Instead she bit her lip, hard, until she felt a trickle of blood in her mouth and tasted salt.

"Cindy Sherman," he said, after what seemed an eternity to Annie Lee, and then continued on quickly. "My mother must have shoved it in that magazine for me to take home. I didn't even know she owned a camera—she said she bought it to take pictures of valuables. That Dad had told her to, and ten years later she'd finally gotten around to it."

He looked at the sisters. "My first girlfriend. From high school."

He looked back at Annie Lee. "Mom ran into her at the supermarket and somehow recognized her. Then—without telling me about it—she invited Cindy over for dinner one night while I was there. You know how I've said Mom remembers everything that happened before Dad died and nothing afterward?"

"That's Cindy Sherman?" Annie Lee stared hard at the picture she'd snatched. "You said she was skinny and had freckles."

"Well, she did. Fifteen years ago."

Annie Lee could not help but observe two large and sweater-stretching breasts. Not fake. Eddie Stahl's cleavage discourses had taught her that much.

"Is she married?" She was thinking Cindy was too eagerly inclined toward Lucas to be part of her own happy couple.

"Divorced. After ten years. He was a Mercedes-Benz dealer."

"I suppose she has kids, too . . ."

"Two girls."

"Well, you look pretty cozy." It was a struggle just to get the words out without shrieking them and jumping up and down and stomping her feet. Shallow breaths were robbing her air supply. "Why did your mother do this?"

Lucas started fiddling with silverware. "I guess she felt bad that we spent every other night reading our respective books in our respective chairs after our dinnertime chat. She's not that comfortable with me—it's like I'll reveal more than she needs to know about who I am. Cindy, on the other hand, represents a time period Mom comprehends." He dropped a fork onto the floor. "Search me, Annie Lee. My mother is completely incomprehensible to me."

"So she invited your first love over for dinner just to ease the boredom of home life. Thanks, Margaret. Appreciate it. On your son's first trip back home without his wife. At least she was aware I was gone; or maybe it never really registered I was ever there. What did you cook for them?"

"Come on, Annie Lee, this isn't exactly appropriate."

"'Appropriate,' funny you should come up with that word. I mean, I thought I had problems three minutes ago—when all

I was was a little bit infertile and slightly estranged from my husband. I'm waiting to hear what kind of dinner you threw together: Tell me it wasn't barbecued trout . . ." She turned to the sisters, feeling craziness burble inside her. "That's what he fed me on our first date. Barbecued trout with little piles of grilled vegetables all tied together in bundles with leek ropes. And a risotto with wild mushrooms he'd foraged himself."

The two Winklemans, riveted by the dialogue, weren't moving at all, in spite of Eudora's habit of tinkering purposefully with things, straightening them, wiping them off, examining them.

Annie Lee, who was shaking her head, hardly noticed that Lucas had taken her firmly by the hand and was leading her into the foyer, excusing them to the sisters as they went. Annie Lee continued on even as he dragged her. "Well, I'm never speaking to your mother again. Not that she'd ever notice if I didn't."

"Mom did ask about you, Annie Lee. Remember I said her advice was to reconsider in vitro."

"If we were serious about children. That's what you said. If. Of course how could you ever be serious about someone like me, someone without a résumé, someone hardly *there at all?*" For the moment it was easier to get raging mad at Margaret Fleck than at her husband, who had not yet denied the thing everyone seemed to be presuming. Had the two months of abstaining turned him into some kind of strike-anywhere match, ready to do it wherever he could with whomever made herself available? Or was it closer to revenge?

Annie Lee finally seemed to realize she'd been moved. "No wonder you don't want to sell the house. You want me to move out. Cindy Sherman's moving in. With her two kids, and her two breasts, her two big, fat ovaries—"

Lucas actually put his hand over his wife's mouth, a gesture so out of character it stunned both of them. "Stop, okay?" he said, setting his jaw. "I don't know why my mother invited her over or took our picture; she's never been that predictable. I mean she'd be the same for months or years, then she'd do something radical. Take up jiujitsu. Have all the hedges turned into topiaries of fish. Buy a tepee for the backyard. The Cindy Sherman thing was totally unexpected. We had dinner. We talked about old times. We were asked to be in a picture. I don't know why." Garbled sounds came from behind his hand. "We said good-bye. I came home."

"Well," Annie Lee said, free from the hand at last and making up for lost time in raised tone and volume, "I feel creepy about this. Creepy about you and your hand over my mouth. Creepy about that *New Yorker* cover and that mysterious picture falling out just like that. For whatever reason, Lucas," she rubbed her mouth, "I seem to be assuming the worst." She felt numbness setting in.

Lucas attempted to keep his voice down but was only partially successful; his words came out flinty from between his teeth. "You think whatever the hell you want, Annie Lee, because at this point my thoughts are irrelevant to you, they have been for months. You are the vortex, everything gets sucked into your storm. The rest of us don't have lives, or thoughts, or feelings. Or needs. Everything is you, Annie Lee. You, you . . ." He shocked her by kicking the wall with his foot, "YOU!"

Self-conscious now, Annie Lee turned in the direction of the dining room, where, sure enough, the sisters were peering at them from around the corner. Clearly, they'd eavesdropped on a good portion—if not all—of the encounter. She smiled weakly, to indicate that the blow had not been directed at her, and was about to run blindly up the stairs to lock herself in the bathroom when another loud interruption—from the door this time—caused her instinctively to leap as quickly as she could to answer it. Lucas headed back to the dining room, while

Annie Lee, humiliated by the outburst, tried—the words "you, you, YOU" still ringing in her ears—to focus.

She had indeed labeled herself a raving lunatic, hell-bent and monomaniacal. She had been about to tell Lucas as much when everything about the reunion scene changed. And now everything was turned around. Was he, she summoned enough logic to wonder, deflecting some of the attention from himself onto her?

From the middle of the hall, she could see thirteen-year-old Megan Doyle's face looking through the front-door's lace curtains and, reaching the threshold, realized, looking down, that Jimmy Jr. was there as well, gripping his stuffed polar bear with all his might. There were three other Doyle children from the tangerine-colored house on the Fleck's other side, another rampant-remodel type that boasted hardly a remnant of its former small and charming self. It was Megan's face, however, that was the most familiar to Annie Lee, for the girl spent half her life at the Flecks': she came for company, escape, advice, and the kind of cookies her mother never bought.

And, size of the Doyle house aside, Annie Lee felt privileged that in a town that lacked for both seniors and large families they were wedged between both. Every Sunday when she saw the Doyles troop off to St. Cecilia's, parted hair plastered down, belts in belt loops, and bows in hair, she felt herself go with them in spirit, even though she hadn't set foot in a church since her own twelfth-grade graduation mass. The Doyle family, with their clubs and volunteer work, their barbecues and ongoing domestic projects, represented order, right down to the way Jim Sr. packed a vacation-bound vehicle. Flawlessly, effortlessly, and magnificently he did it, like a spatial genius assembling a giant mess kit. And as she would watch him from one of the second-floor windows, wedging the bags together, fitting rolled sleeping bags into the final slots, triumphant, gloating almost, Annie Lee would think everything in life should be so orderly. But it rarely was.

"Hi, Megan, hi, Jimmy." Annie Lee composed herself and opened the door for the two of them to come in. She studied Megan's worried face. Saturday was the only day of the week Jim and Judy let their kids watch cartoons, and none of them ever missed the chance. Something was happening at the Doyle household. "What's up?"

Megan, looking uncharacteristically self-conscious, picked up Jimmy and came inside, kicking off her shoes and pulling off his. "Mom wanted to know if we could hang out here for an hour or so. Harold went to the climbing wall. Ollie and Helena are with Mrs. Bupke." She handed Jimmy to Annie Lee, who took him, feeling his warm head against her cheek.

"Mom and Dad want to *talk*." Megan wouldn't look up at Annie Lee.

"Well, come in the dining room," Annie Lee said. "Have some crumpets. We made extra." Annie Lee had never heard of the Doyles wanting privacy before. Jim and Judy marshaling the kids out of the house on a Saturday morning sounded utterly earthshaking. What was happening to everyone? She found she could think almost clearly if she repeated the words "Cindy Sherman, Cindy Sherman, Cindy Sherman" to herself in the breaks between other thoughts. She seemed to be able to diffuse her own hysteria this way even if it was always there, right underneath the skin, like blistering sores about to erupt all over. "The sisters are here," she said.

"Right now?" Megan whispered. Megan swore she wasn't afraid of the sisters, but she was ill at ease with them and their summoning her to her best behavior, her finest Catholic foot forward.

"Come on," said Annie Lee, nudging her and piloting Jimmy and his bear, Popsie, into the next room. "Think of them as characters in a movie." Megan visibly relaxed but still kept her hands behind her back. "Believe me," Annie Lee added, "we're all characters in a movie. *(Cindy Sherman, Cindy Sherman, Cindy Sherman)*."

"These two are over here on loan for an hour," Annie Lee said by way of explaining the situation. "I told them they were in luck. We don't have crumpets very often."

"Kwumpets," Jimmy repeated, making a beeline for Lucas, who scooped him onto his lap as Colonel Klink begrudgingly took his cue to jump down. "I love jam!" the pie-faced and pink-cheeked boy said, spying the jar on the table.

"Yes, young man," Eudora interjected in her schoolmarm's voice. "It's very special jam that you may taste. You must promise to use your best table manners. Do you know what that means?" Jimmy nodded a toddler's most solemn oath and set about tying a napkin around Popsie's neck.

"Your jam is really good." Lucas had taken a small spoonful, all by itself, and placed it on his tongue.

"Just jam," Eudora answered, but it was spread thickly on her crumpet. "We make it in years the raspberries are particularly plentiful. You have to get off your posteriors and pick the little suckers, you see. Find 'em, then reach through those brambles and pick 'em. It takes some time, and it takes recalling how good the jam is to persist. Of course, we add something extra special to the recipe. Our secret ingredient."

"Something flowery," Lucas said. "Rose petals, it tastes like. Something like that."

Eudora, astonished, stared at him. "No one has ever figured that one out," she said, her hand involuntarily coming up to catch the gasp from her mouth. She looked at Lucas as if he were now capable of something surprising and crazy, something that came out of nowhere. Lucas responded by eagerly initiating a discourse on great jams he'd tasted and where and when: He managed to fully engage both Megan and Jimmy for ten minutes. Finally, the other adults joined in, and there the four of them sat for another hour, talking with the two children about everything except the matter on their minds.

Finally, Judy called to ask if Megan and Jimmy were all right, which angered Annie Lee and made her all the more determined to find out what was going on in these other people's lives. If she can't thank us instead of checking up on her kids, she's got a problem, Annie Lee thought. Then she thought to add, Hmmm, maybe she really does have a problem, a notion that consoled her.

When Megan Doyle finally took her brother home, the sisters slid their chairs out and excused themselves as well, but on the way to the door, Eudora tapped the *New Yorker* magazine and said it reminded her of the pictures they had of the Fleck house. She asked if they'd ever looked at them closely. Lucas was shaking his head, Annie Lee said she didn't think she'd ever seen the pictures. They were both staring at the magazine with all their might, like two people separated by the miles but under the same moon.

"Well," Eudora declared, "I think you-all should have a look at the pictures of the house as it was years ago."

"Orna Vitale's house," Bea said, "We've mentioned her, I think, over the years. Lucas, you remember her."

He nodded, eager to reroot himself in his house. "She wanted to know my intentions. Would I remodel? Would I turn over the property once it quadrupled in value? What did I do for a living? Her eyes were small and beady and very blue. Finally, I just told her I'd fallen in love with the place from his first step through the door. She asked why, in ten words or less, and I answered, "Because it feels like home. I can't explain it. That's nine."

He glanced at Annie Lee, who lowered her eyes. He'd made the speech for her benefit.

"Orna was smart as a whip," Eudora pulled a Kleenex out

of her sleeve to dab at a leaky nostril. "She ran a bookkeeping business from her home and sold moonshine, too, all without the help of a man."

"She made beer, Eudora. Well, malt liquor, actually, but it was not moonshine. Landsakes, sister." But when Eudora said they'd bring the photos by later for the two of them to see what they could see, Bea added cryptically that surely Lucas and Annie Lee would find clues to the present in photos from the past. After the door slammed shut, the only sound was that of Klink making mournful demands.

"Your cat needs water," Annie Lee said, her voice as dead as she could make it. She was scooping up plates from the table, trying to load all six settings on one arm without moving any of the silver. She wished the staggered pile—Margaret Fleck's set of one-of-a-kind antique dinner plates—would all come crashing down and break. But it didn't. Of course not. Lifting and stacking plates was what Annie Lee did best in life.

"Don't jump to conclusions, Annie Lee," Lucas said, as he gathered his ski clothes together like a fireman at the sound of an alarm. "You tend to do that."

"Well, would you tell me if you'd slept with her?" she said as she unloaded the dishes next to the sink.

"No, probably not. But neither would you tell me if I asked you if you'd slept with someone."

"Well," she said, with some resignation as she watched him put his sunglasses on and turn to go, "there you go then." She was fingering a tea bag tag, something she'd pocketed earlier in the week. She'd wanted tea for breakfast but upon reading the quotation on the tag could not make herself imbibe a liquid steeped in such thoughts. Now, as she headed upstairs, she pulled out the small tag and read it again on her way to the study: "Consider the little mouse, how sagacious an animal it is which never entrusts its life to one hole only." Attributed to

Plautus—some Roman. Obviously, an enemy to woman and a friend to man.

She settled herself in the Berrywinkle study, her most reliable refuge. In a sunny corner sat the most comfortable overstuffed chair on earth, whose slipcovers she had dyed Skylac, another heady blue shade. While the entire south wall was consumed by built-in bookcases and the computer, the opposite wall was the home of Annie Lee's dozens upon dozens of framed quotation artifacts. Epigrams, advertising slogans, fortunes from cookies, bubble-gum wrappers, and standard issue great proclamations. In times of trouble, she read her walls like a rosary—the quotations were beads of time, each one delivered to her at the most synchronistic of moments. During this meditative exercise, she would strive to push other thoughts aside in order perhaps to see a bit more clearly or less clearly, whatever was required in the present moment.

It was almost impossible to do today, partly because Plautus's one-liner, though apt, brought everything back, back, and back again. Men simply were not monogamous creatures. Who had slipped the renegade quote into the Earl Grey package for her to discover at such a vulnerable moment?

She could think of nothing that would make her feel better, that would shed light, solve anything. She twiddled her thumbs, badly, like broken spindles, and then considered a quick call to Poison Control. After all, what did it matter now? Who cared what anyone thought? She yearned to un-shroud herself, get down to the nitty-gritty and talk about the vast world of poisoning with some highly evolved person on the other end. About ocular poisoning, aural poisoning, epidermal poisoning, and the most complex and pervasive of all, emotional poisoning.

For at this time, Annie Lee felt her own emotions were indeed poisoning her, that the hurt and anger and helplessness inside had transmuted themselves into chemicals coursing through her veins. But she lacked the wherewithal, the expertise to extricate herself, give herself the correct antidote.

Was it a cold shower she needed? Four hours of exercise?

Unsure of how to proceed, she reached for the book she'd been reading and pulled out the bookmark. *The Life and Times of Shana Rae Obley* chronicled an Appalachian widow and mother of ten who'd met every misfortune, every horrifying privation of her life with the grace of a poet and the grit of a pioneer. Shana Rae had not only survived her ordeal, but had gone on to become a bestselling author. The author photo showed her happy, smiling, teeth beautifully straightened and whitened. This, above all, touched Annie Lee, for she knew Shana Rae's malnutrition had caused many of her teeth to rot. After all the woman had been through, after living it and writing about it and then waiting patiently for her ship to come in—after all that, she'd opted for the further tortures of oral surgery. As if a defective smile was simply not good enough to get her kind of happiness across.

Temporarily distracted by a life less fortunate than her own, Annie Lee made her way to the health club, where she took what was no doubt, the longest shower ever recorded there. The attendant asked several times, right outside the stall, if everything was all right, and Annie Lee assured her—torrents of hot water beating down on her back and head—that it was. Finally, Annie Lee turned the water off and headed, her body red with heat and still under the mute and anxious look of the attendant, for the sauna. It was her intention to scorch the wet furies right out of herself.

Ten

Hello, everybody," Annie Lee said as she entered the restaurant that night, waving falsely cheerful fingers to the owner, chef, cooks, and bartender. Her husband had gone straight to work after skiing, something she feared he might do. Having finished the story of Shana Rae, she told herself it was probably better to have an unfaithful husband than a dead one, but by the time she arrived at work her resolve on the matter had weakened in spite of the shower, the sauna, and an entire bar of Swiss chocolate. She found herself somewhat heartened by her job, by the prospect of other lives laid out to anesthetize her own.

"You seem very upbeat tonight." Jay's tone was accusatory as he looked up from the reservations book. He had probably just gotten a confirmation or two for the overbooked midsection of the evening.

"No, as a matter of fact," said Annie Lee quickly, "I have every reason to be clinically depressed. Is that better?" She glanced at the reservations as she always did, to get a handle on numbers, configurations, actual names. Tonight, she noted, a startlingly discernable culinary theme had begun presenting itself. The Lavenders were coming in at 7:30, and at 8:15 some people called Turnipseed. Con would have insisted the names were made up; but weren't the chances of several people making up names much more remote than the names actually existing?

"What's up?" Annie Lee said to the chef before initiating all her prep work—the butters, silverware, salt and peppers, candles.

He shrugged. "Not too many big tables. Nothing after nine o'clock." He returned to his *mise-en-place* after yelling up to the afternoon prep guy to peel twelve more potatoes.

The special of the night, an irregular, misdelivered sport fish called snook, accompanied by a bacon-studded sauce, was going to be a problem; Annie Lee knew it already. It didn't come with pasta, and the vegetables had not been decided upon. She pointed that out.

"Why do they have to know every vegetable on the plate?" the chef was now hammering out a multicolored brunoise of vegetables that arranged themselves like tiny dice. "Tell them the vegetables are unspecified. They may be unspecified for the rest of the night—maybe for the rest of the season." He was already irritated. Even though Annie Lee knew his resolve would weaken, the question was when—in two minutes? In two weeks?

"Well, what exactly is snook?" she queried delicately, knowing the customers would plague her with the same question throughout the service. "I mean, is it—"

"It's good. That's all they have to know."

"Then let's just call it 'good fish with a bacon sauce,'" Con suggested. "It sounds more Chinese than French, but certainly nothing sounds worse than *snook*."

"Why do they have to know everything about everything on the fucking plate?" The chef slammed down his knife, inadvertently sending a carrot morsel onto his cheek. "I don't care what you call the fish." His nostrils flared. "Tell them it's Mediterranean blue snapper for all I care. Whatever name you think will work. Just sell it, because I have twenty."

"Better put pasta on it, then," said Con, undaunted by the chef's tizzy.

"Fuck off," said the chef, which Annie Lee figured was the signal to start the shift.

By the fifth table of the evening they were serving pasta with the fish—at which point it started selling, especially after they'd learned it was coming with haricots verts. People had nothing against buttery green beans, like they had against cabbage, for instance, or Swiss chard.

Annie Lee's first table, a couple from Ohio, wanted steak and kept staring at the menu for more beef options. Annie Lee told them that the filet on the menu was wonderful and that there were no additional beef specials.

"Well, we know about steak," said the middle-aged woman dressed in a tight-fitting tailored suit of bright cerise jersey, gold buttons straining against the weight of flesh pressing against it. There's that damned cleavage again, thought Annie Lee, trying not to look down from the woman's face.

"I'll take the tenders," the man said as he handed Annie Lee the menu, "cooked well done, no sauce. Skip the veggies. Substitute more taters for all that other stuff. Neither of us wants 'tizers," he continued. Annie Lee felt she'd walked into a language funhouse full of shortcuts and weird curves. Her eyebrows went up involuntarily.

"And I'll have exactly the same thing!" chirped the large, pink woman, who reminded Annie Lee of a bird without a beak. She liked them. "Oh, and my husband hates to ask, but if you have any A-1, we'd sure appreciate it!" A snowmobiling brochure lay on their table next to a brand-new $500 cowboy hat and a bottle of generic aspirin.

"Well done on both of these," Annie Lee said to the chef as she hung the ticket up. "No sauce, no vegetables, double *pommes de terre*. Just tenders and taters," she laughed. "And no 'tizers." Shep, the American sous-chef, was staring at her and then at the ticket for clarification.

"'Taters,' what is that?" The chef ripped the ticket off the line and brought it closer to his face.

"Forgive them," Annie Lee said. "They're cave people. You know, dry meat on a stick. They actually asked for A-1."

"Jesus, Annie Lee," said Shep. He looked up at her and then went back to nimbly arranging baby beets, both red and white, in an asymmetrical pattern on the plate. His fingers were red, which caused Annie Lee to wonder if Cindy Sherman's hands were in that Polaroid. Had she worn nail polish? Was it something Lucas was secretly drawn to? The thought was an intrusion, and she turned her back on it, eagerly returning to the bustling dining room.

In the course of her shift, Annie Lee waited on a just-married couple from Albuquerque, ten relentlessly demanding tequila drinkers from Rio de Janeiro, four local businesswomen who tipped eight percent, a single man writing everything down with a roller-ball pen in some sort of small Day-Timer, and four orthopedists from Chicago.

The doctors were all staring down at one of the bussers' knees as he stood there explaining—hands in a T-formation—about the mechanical effects of skiing hard one hundred twenty days a year. She would have marched over to shoo Mikey away, but Con was already there, handing him a pile of plates he'd had to clear himself and then not exactly whispering to him that this was a dining room not a doctor's office.

When Annie Lee approached them, the first thing they did

was ask her name. She cringed. When people asked for a name it generally meant they would use it, over and over again like an irresistible magic word. She was about to whisper her name to them, thinking that might prompt them to call her in the same subtle way, when something else came out of her mouth instead: "Cindy Sherman," she said, and then tagged on a smile by stretching her mouth to the appropriate points on her face.

"Now there's something I've never heard before," said one of the four, a beefy man with short gray hair who looked like Aaron Burr. "The full name of a waitress."

"Well," said Annie Lee, considering her inspiration, "I—I just got divorced. I was trying out my maiden name again."

"Fascinating," said a younger, dark-skinned man named Carlos, whose neatly filed and buffed nails had sent chills of desire down Annie Lee's spine.

Annie Lee harbored a hand fetish, something she had never told anyone. Well, hands were sexy. They didn't brag or overdo it, they were natural—quiet or busy. Hands tied bulky knots on boats, and picked up big rocks to build with. They cradled fountain pens, scalpels, and paintbrushes. They dropped tree balls into the earth, moved chess pieces, and floured pieces of chicken. Lucas's hands could make her knees weak in the way they spoke their own language—in the kitchen, in the garden, in the bedroom. His hands were wide, knotty, relaxed, and coated with delicate blond hairs. Like his mind, they had always been politely curious, inquiring, eager for new knowledge. *Lucas again.*

She refocused on the hands before her. Was she capable of an affair? Is this how it started? With something as simple as a heart squeezed by circumstance followed by a glance at an attractive appendage?

"We'll have the Riesling to start, Cindy," said Carlos. "You don't look like a Cindy. Actually, you do look like *someone* . . ."

Annie Lee prepared herself for what she knew was coming:

that she looked like one of two movie stars. Something she couldn't see, but evidently other people did, and regularly.

"Mia Farrow!" he said. "That's who. You look like Mia Farrow. Prettier, though."

"No, she doesn't," said the nerd of the bunch, the virtual surgeon. "She looks a lot more like Sissy Spacek."

Bingo, thought Annie Lee. And the first time any one table had hit both movie stars in one fell swoop. "Uh-huh," she said, reaching for an empty beer bottle. But Con bumped her from behind and sent her, chest first, into Carlos's upper arm.

"Sorry, Annie Lee," she heard Con mumble as she felt her face get hot and tried to tell her breasts to ignore the caress, that it was an accident, completely unintentional. Her nipples hardened.

"Excuse me," she said to Carlos, and then, realizing Con had called her by her real name, added, "Annie Lee is another name people call me."

"You have a lot of names," he said, staring at her chest area. Or was he? What was happening to her? She was blatantly lying—he was blatantly staring.

On her way to the waiter station, face still flushed, she was told she had a phone call—which was unheard of and very much frowned upon in the middle of a busy night, of any night. She raced to the bar, thinking maybe one of her parents had died, or that one had finally killed the other even though they'd been divorced for ten years.

"It's your mother!" Jay said, mentioning that she'd actually spoken French to him, as if Annie Lee had been misrepresenting her heritage all this time.

"Mom, what are you doing calling me here? Did Dad call you or something? Is he sick?" Annie Lee, the only one of the three daughters to take her mother's side after the divorce, still did not communicate with her father. She still believed someone had had to take Isabelle's side just to keep her from looking ridiculous. They cultivated their relationship by way of regular and frequent phone calls. But never at work.

Her mother ignored the questions. "Didn't you tell them I was French? The man acted surprised." Even her indignation sounded French to Annie Lee. It was so obvious.

"Yes, of course I did. They *know*. What is it? What's the problem? I mean, I'm serving people food here!"

"I wanted to tell you I discovered something . . ."

Annie Lee was silent. "Does it have to do with food or wine or anything I need to know about my tables? Is it emergency information of some kind? This is a busy place, Ma—"

"I've discovered the color that made your father leave me. Not that I care about him coming back anymore, but it was a color that did it. And I discovered it. After all these years." She sounded flushed. "I feel—relieved, Annie Lee. I had to tell someone. And who but you could possibly understand such a statement?"

"What are you saying?" Annie Lee did not want to hear about her father, did not want him dredged up at this particular time—in between serving desserts to one table and adding up a check on another. Nevertheless, how could she not be interested in good reasons for cheating, or her mother's perceptions about reasons for cheating? Now was the time to be interested in this particular subject.

"I was cleaning out my closet and found a dress I hadn't even seen since—well, since before the divorce. It was a lilac dress, the color of faded wallpaper hyacinths; I'd bought it at Ann Taylor. Your father stared at the dress a long time the first time I put it on and finally said it didn't look like me. He crossed his arms when he said it, and he wasn't an arm-crosser, *chérie*. That was the beginning of the end, I'm sure of it. If I didn't look like myself, perhaps I came across as someone else."

Annie Lee was walking down a surreal road. "Everyone seems to be cleaning out closets these days," she said, thinking of Margaret Fleck. "Listen, Mom, I gotta go. Really. I'm having a bit of a snag in my own life."

"Oh?"

"I can't talk, Ma!"

"Call me tomorrow, Annie Lee. I mean it. Or I'll call you."

In all those years and all those phone calls, Isabelle had never interrupted Annie Lee at work. Not to tell her she'd gotten a commission for her first portrait. Not to tell her an agent had offered to represent her. Not to tell her she'd been approached by a New York gallery owner.

While Annie Lee raced from the bar, worried that everything would be screwed up because of the time lapse, she considered—with an involuntary tightening of the stomach—the talk they would have about her father. And then about her husband. Could a color really be so culpable? Probably. Could men be understood if not forgiven? Questionable.

The only way to control the table of crazy Brazilians was to keep the drinks coming, nod a lot, and fuss over them obsequiously like a little maid, which Annie Lee didn't mind doing since she'd already decided to add a nice tip onto the bill.

Having corralled Claire for help removing appetizer plates, she noticed a lull in the Latin din and at the same time caught a glimpse of Claire stacking the plates way too high behind a very round man with a handlebar mustache. First one fork fell to the ground. Then a crust of bread and a lamb bone. Terrified that everything would come crashing down in the momentary silence, Annie Lee cleared her throat and said, rather loudly, the first thing that came to mind:

"So. Those gentlemen over there," and she pointed grandly to the orthopedists, "have wagered that you will agree with them on which movie stars I look like. They'd like to buy you a round of drinks if you can come up with both names. Sort of embarrassing, really . . . but, well I told them I'd relay the wager."

All of the Brazilians spoke English well, and at the mention of a drinking wager, began talking in Portuguese like athletes in a huddle. There were a lot of rich South American tourists in Pike these days, and they always seemed to know more about popular American culture than most Americans. Annie Lee thought she heard the name "Mia" but said nothing.

"Well, we are not sure," said a woman whose face reminded Annie Lee a lot of the early Cher. "But we do go to the American movies quite often—" She was interrupted then by a beautiful man with long, straight black hair that lay in an ebony sheet halfway down his back. He blurted out the two correct names, much to the amazement of Annie Lee, who smiled in triumph. "Unbelievable," she said. "Really remarkable."

The Brazilians were all craning to get a reaction from the orthopedists, who, of course, had no idea what was going on. When the four of them turned around to see ten bronzed faces attentive to their every movement, they looked at Annie Lee. who had come over to clue them in. "They told me I looked like Mia and Sissy. I told them you'd just said the same thing. Now they want to do shots with you."

"Oh," said Aaron Burr, nodding at them as if they spoke only Japanese. Nodding and smiling, smiling and nodding.

"Well, buy them their shots . . . What are they drinking?" he said without opening his mouth very far, still smiling.

"Tequila," said Annie Lee. "Very good tequila."

"Is there such a thing?" Mr. Burr wanted to know.

She ordered fourteen shots of very good ten-dollar-per tequila from Eddie, while Jay, the owner, lingered at table fourteen, entertaining the four local businesswomen. Eddie thought the shots were for the entire staff and poured them in rocks glasses to make them look more normal. "When are we gonna do these, Annie Lee? I'm ready now . . ."

"These aren't for us, you idiot. We don't even have fourteen employees. It's kind of a joke between the orthopedists over there and the Brazilians. They're doing shots because I look like Mia Farrow and Sissy Spacek. Although God knows I seem to be acting more like Claudette Colbert."

"Huh?" said Eddie, pouring himself just a little nip.

Con came in at that moment. "Hey, what's going on here?" he said, miffed at being left out of any illicit activities.

Annie Lee, gathering up the fourteen shots, checked the dining room to make sure the owner had his back to her and headed out. Not that she had technically done anything wrong. But uniting the entire dining room in a farce wasn't something that happened on a regular basis.

By the time the Brazilians did those shots, they were so drunk and so delighted with the little game, they started making the same wager to other tables via every available floor person.

Con, happy to oblige on a night when the seriousness of the establishment was being questioned, ran up twenty-three extra shots. He was making the Brazilians pay even if the rest of the people's answers were wrong. One table actually said Annie Lee looked like a young Rosalynn Carter, and did that count?

At the bar, the owner interrogated her. "It's a long story," she began.

"But the short of it," Con quipped, "is that you sold an extra forty-seven shots of alcohol tonight on account of our actress look-alike here, Miss Annie Lee Thing."

"What are you talking about?" Jay was nodding to the four local women, who kept looking around for someone to fill them in. He motioned to them he was coming, which he hastened to do, looking around the dining room as he approached them.

When he came back into the bar he ordered four of "whatever poison the rest of the dining room is drinking. And put it on the Brazilians' tab."

Annie Lee took a deep breath. She was tired of the whole charade and rolled up her sleeves in anticipation of the end of the night. On her way to the reservations book to see if it was in fact over, she found herself staring into the faces of Judy Doyle and Sheila Bupke, seated inconspicuously at the bar and as close to the door as possible.

"Oh, hi," she said, unused to seeing Judy without Jim in a restaurant setting. Sheila Bupke, however, was another story. One that could partially be told now by the six olives on two toothpicks that lay on her square napkin, the washed-up debris from a free-flowing river of vodka.

Judy Doyle looked somber as she sipped her tall drink with a lime wedge in it. "Thanks for watching Megan and Jimmy Jr. this morning," she said quietly. "We really appreciated it."

Annie Lee was taken aback with the seriousness of it all. "Are you kidding?" she said. "I love to have Megan over, you know that. She's like a daughter to me, except that her advice is usually more insightful than mine. She's promised to teach me quilting, you know. And Jimmy, well, the sisters just ate him up. As a matter of fact, so did Lucas. You'd think he liked kids or something. Ha!" She laughed. "Send 'em over anytime."

Judy looked like she was about to cry. Something was going on. Her eyes did in fact fill up, and two of the biggest tears Annie Lee had ever seen spilled onto her flushed, round cheeks. Much to Annie Lee's surprise, Eddie materialized a clean cotton handkerchief and handed it to her without a word.

"It's okay," Sheila Bupke said to Annie Lee. "She'll be fine, won't you Judy. You must have work to get back to . . ."

The four local women were, in fact, signaling her. On her way to their table, Carlos of Chicago grabbed her hand and slipped her an extra twenty. "A little something for you. My personal apologies for having to put up with us." His hands were cool yet strong. She felt the paper money in her palm like part of someone else's more exciting intrigue and looked at him, wishing for a Learjet and a terrace somewhere in Montreal, say, or Florence, Italy.

"Do me a favor," she said, suddenly weary of certain tiresome personages. "Wave at that group of women over there staring at me, trying to get my attention. Not now, wait till it looks normal." Annie Lee smiled. "It's all part of a plan to hopelessly confuse them. They deserve it."

Carlos looked at her and smiled. "You're much more attractive than either of those pale-faced actresses, much more vibrant. It was a pleasure to meet you Cindy Lee Sherman. Maybe we'll see you again."

"Never know," Annie Lee blushed, wondering if the real Cindy Sherman had come on to Lucas like this. Like gangbusters. She had the curious feeling that reality had shifted, that her vision was blurred. That what used to be clear was now curled with smoke.

The local women were no longer staring at her as she approached them but at Carlos, the dark, handsome stranger who'd waved at them in recognition as he'd exited the restaurant.

"Who was that man?" said the one who pretended not to know Annie Lee in the restaurant but then tried to be nice on the street. "He looked familiar." Annie Lee had hit her mark.

"He said the same thing about you, actually. Said you looked like someone from where he'd grown up in New Jersey." The woman was nodding wildly. "I grew up in Teaneck, New Jersey! Did you tell him my name? Why did he run off?"

"I don't know your name." Annie Lee lied her biggest lie of the night: She knew Eleanor Easley's name and her hometown just by virtue of living in the same small town as Eleanor. "Evidently they were very tired from a long day of heli-skiing.

Orthopedists from Chicago. They were the ones, along with the Brazilians over there, who started all the drinking wagers."

"Yeah, what was that about?" said one of the other women, Pat, who was putting on lipstick, peering into the tiniest mirror Annie Lee had ever seen, one so small you had to hold it back two feet to see anything in it, and then the chances were good you'd find someone else's lips, someone at some other table in the distance.

"Oh," said Annie Lee, the gall floating up inside her like a big balloon, "it was a silly thing having to do with which two movie stars I look like." She ignored the blank stares from around the table. "The Brazilians got it; they guessed the names," she continued as she laid down the check, "and then they wanted to make the same wager with other tables."

"Wait a minute," said Eleanor, "which two movie stars *you* look like?"

"That's right," said Annie Lee. "Can I get anyone more coffee?"

They ignored the question. "Did the man who waved happen to mention where he was staying?" Eleanor Easley was staring toward the door.

"Carlos?" queried Annie Lee. "No, but I think their reservation had 'Hotel' written next to it." There was only one really huge full-service hotel in town, and everyone called it the Hotel. All the other hotels went by their names. Eleanor smiled sweetly. "I think I remember a Carlos in high school," she said. "Thank you," she added, not in gratitude, but in dismissal.

In the bar, Annie Lee asked Con if he'd ever shot anyone in the head before and would he mind doing it as a personal favor for her—just blow that lady at table eleven off the face of the earth.

"Didn't like her, huh?" Con was straining to see Eleanor. "Oh, her," he added. "Not worth your trouble. Did she hurt your feewings? I'll snap that bitch in two if she did." Annie

Lee laughed and noticed Mikey over at the table doing the same T-shape explanation of his knee for the women, who seemed happy enough to be looking at his beautiful young face, admittedly a triumphant collaboration of storm-blue eyes and tanned skin, topped by bleached-blond hair. They were the last ones in the restaurant.

"Night's over," said Annie Lee, like a judge with a gavel. "Let's get 'em outa here so I can go home and be miserable with my husband." Was Lucas even going straight home? "On the other hand, Conny . . ." she wavered, thinking how awful it would be to get home first and have to wait for her husband. "Let's go out tonight!"

"You wanna go *out?*" Con stopped dead in his tracks. Annie Lee rarely joined them in their late-night revelries anymore. "Hmmm," he began to nod his head slowly, "that might work for me."

On her way out, Eleanor Easley asked to see the owner, to which Eddie replied in the spirit of the night, "He went home early to catch *Star Trek*. Can we leave him a message?" Actually, he was in the basement restocking wines. What was happening to everyone, had they no shame?

"Just tell him thank you," she breathed, trying to read the reservations book for Carlos's last name. "For everything."

"Uh-huh," said Eddie, racking glasses furiously. "Sure will. Thanks. For everything. Good night now."

Eleven

By the time she sat down to staff dinner, there was no wind left in Annie Lee's sails.

It might have been better to keep her mind going, keep up the banter, pluck out the shift's notable details like M&Ms out of trail mix. But she was too tired. And with her defenses down, her mind swerved off into enemy territory. Images she had repressed all day settled on her, quiet and big like snowflakes after the fury of wind and in colors so bright they seemed chemically infused. Bad TV Orange. Computer Screen Green. Oil-spill Blue. She had no control.

Cindy Sherman, a Day-Glo blond, was coming into focus. She was being mauled, piece by piece, by an overly animated opalescent-toothed Lucas, who fumbled frantically—his hands normally so agile—with her sweater buttons. She, a tigress with claws of Radioactive Strawberry, was unsnapping the first button of her skintight jeans, eager to play a part in the stripfest. Her Syrup-pink push-up bra popped off of its own accord, casting a partylike if grotesque inevitability over the scene.

Sick with jealousy, Annie Lee found it necessary to freeze-frame Cindy and Lucas midway to their cartoonlike moment of consummation. Her eyeballs ached now, as if someone were pressing on them with their thumbs.

The sound of Con's voice interrupted her, shifted her focus back to the plate she had been staring at for—how long? A pile of green vegetables lay before her. She stabbed at one and then, thinking better of it, reached for one of six small cherry tartlets that could not be served tomorrow. Custard on the bottom flavored with vanilla beans—she could see the black specks. Medium-sour cherries all lined up and topped with a light glaze. She brought a bite to her mouth.

Con, whose seventh sense alerted him to dessert diminishment, grabbed a tart without ever turning his head away from his monologue. It was something about his table two, a single, fur-coated woman, and why she couldn't have joined Annie Lee's single, notebook-toting man so that they wouldn't have been overbooked by that one critical table.

Annie Lee gratefully tuned in.

"Those two people," Con went on, "the Turnipseeds—did anyone actually *see* that name on a credit card?—had to wait in the bar for forty-five minutes—"

"No," Jay interrupted. "It was twenty-five minutes at the most. They had a good dinner . . . they left happy. I bought them drinks. Twenty-five minutes. At the most. He introduced himself as Eli Turnipseed."

Con rolled his eyes. "Whatever," he said, sawing at his salad greens crossways, shredding the lovely pile, "they had to wait. Meanwhile, the two single people were both thoroughly miserable human beings who should have stayed home. He kept asking me to get his server—you, Annie Lee. And the nasty madam with a fur coat the size of a bear pelt could under no circumstances be begged, cajoled, stroked, or bought enough drinks to have a good time, because we didn't have Clamato juice for her bloody Bloody Caesar. Gee-zus. I doubled her shot of tequila and noticed she forced it down. Anyway, the two of them together could have canceled each other out so beautifully. And with any luck, Annie Lee would have had to wait on them both. Only Annie Lee was too busy on some project of her own."

He glared at her while jamming some unspecified meat into his mouth. "Why were they calling you Cindy anyway?"

Annie Lee flashed on Carlos waving at Eleanor, and the Brazilians toasting Sissy/Mia, and a smile punched through her face. In spite of everything.

"Hey, Annie Lee," Jay interrupted her, waving his hand in front of her face, "what do you think, you can grin away after a long silence and nobody's going to want to know why?"

"Oh," she said, clearing her throat. "People are strange, as Jim Morrison would say. That's all."

"People are people." He was quick in his response. "Life is strange. Besides, the line is 'People are strange when you're a stranger.' Which is different." Annie Lee had long ago come to the conclusion that the French were required in the course of their education to take a class in making short and snappy remarks. Because they all knew how to do it, make that final thrust home in one line. Her French extraction might explain her own penchant for aphorisms.

"I stand corrected," she said. "Your truism beats mine in both technical and artistic merit. Life is strange. Now, that's deep." She pushed out her chair and went to fetch the vacuum.

Vacuuming was everybody's least favorite job. It required the picking up of chairs, the occasional moving of tables, it was loud, and it took twenty-five minutes. But tonight Annie Lee did it with abandon, yanking at chairs and going over some spots three, four, even five times. She found a sprig of thyme and one of rosemary—fallen from plates—to vacuum over, and leaned her nose this way and that for a whiff. She put her free hand on her hip for a while, then switched vacuuming hands altogether to give her left arm a workout but couldn't get the same gusto going and switched back.

In the first half of the dining room she picked up four swizzle sticks, a sugar cube, a spoon, a napkin, and several peas that she was tempted to suck up but then stooped to gather at the last moment. It occurred to her then that Lucas was probably already done at his restaurant (Giancarlo was about three blocks down from Mathilde, and across the street), and she wondered whether he would go home or go out. He always went right home. But tonight? Tonight *he* was different and might therefore start doing everything differently. The thought frightened her.

She put two hands on the vacuum and very nearly swabbed the deck with the loud machine, back and forth, back and forth, sucking at the floor as if wishing that everything in life could be vacuumed up as neatly as bread crumbs.

She was maneuvering the thing around Rosana's famous orange tree now, thinking of poisons again, the poison of an overactive imagination and the poison of jealousy, which she had never truly experienced regarding Lucas. Until now. With her defenses down, jealousy returned in full force. Greedily it snaked through her veins, the color of antifreeze, on a campaign to sting every cell and then claim Annie Lee as its prisoner.

As she neared the tree, and at the height of what could be called an emotional panic, she caught a glint of something out of the corner of her eye. A shiny twinkle, like an SOS signal from a mirror, snagged her attention. Within a split second of the flash, the industrial-strength chrome vacuum cleaner crunched onto something solid and as large as a pebble from the sound of it. It was another split second before Annie Lee connected the timing of the sound with the fragmented glint and hastened to shut off the machine.

Mere seconds later, she was elbow-deep in the vacuum cleaner bag. Dust backfired around her like a cloud. Her beech-wood colored hair, out of its hair tie, lay in tangled ripples down her back. The tails of her untucked man's white shirt brushed the floor where she knelt, and her after-shift red tennis shoes, unlaced, were half off at the heels. She was too busy digging to look up, digging furiously, as if her life depended on it.

"The bag break again?" Con, a wad of bills in his hand, was still counting the money and dividing it up for the night. He wanted to get everything done quickly so that they could go out on the town, which he'd mentioned again to her just as she had plugged in the vacuum's cord.

When Annie Lee didn't respond, he came over to her. "It's pretty easy to change, pumpkin. When it gets heavy, you *unzip* the back of the pouch, you *take* it out carefully . . ." Con, a mood swinger, was back on track after those two tarts and a little lemon ice cream he'd helped himself to in the empty kitchen.

"Oh, be quiet," Annie Lee's face was furrowed. "I think I ran over a *diamond*!" Staring into space, focusing every feeling into her fingertips, she searched the bagged restaurant debris in a backwash of greasy dust.

"Oh, sure, Annie Lee," Con returned to his cash disbursements. "If wishes were horses, then waiters would ride. They'd ride bareback. They'd gallop like Comanches. They'd be circus performers. They'd . . ." his voice trailed off as he headed back toward the bar.

It took her several minutes after Con had gone, but finally she thought she felt something angular and hard and retracted her arm carefully, even though there was no reason to be careful since her whole arm would without a doubt be coated with the dirty, grimy dust she felt sticking to her like tiny feathers on tar.

But there, sure enough, at the end of her right hand, between the tips of fingers whose nails looked more like a machinist's than a food server's, was a diamond the size of a pea. Not any high-altitude pea, either, but a big, sea-level Miracle-Gro pea. It was colossal.

She blinked a couple of times at it, as if it were a foreign object beamed down from another planet. "Oh, my God!" The words erupted from her mouth as she sat there, cross-legged on the restaurant floor, fresh table linen at chin level making a white blur of everything around her.

The thing she noticed first of all was that the diamond had not one speck of dust, dirt, or grime on it even though it had traveled through the bowels of a vacuum and was wedged between the scummiest thumb and forefinger on earth. It was pristine. She could see what it was Kathryn went on and on about, sparkle being an actual term, and so on. Its brilliance wasn't in any way diminished by the late-night lighting of the restaurant. It spewed out a full-spectrum of flash and twinkle, white and colored, as much at ease in her pepper-and-cocoa-colored hands as it might have been on black velvet. And as she stared at it, rotating it with her Statue-of-Liberty arm and rotating her head at the same time, she fell under its spell.

Holding the diamond in that brief crack of time, she saw herself differently. Free. Free of every cloud in her sky. Above it all. Safe, secure, taken care of. She'd stuck in her thumb and pulled out—a plum! How long had it been there? Days? Weeks? Did the thirty-day rule still apply? There was no doubt it was the real thing, its gleam was too great for anything remotely synthetic. How much was it worth?

Even if she had to hold on to it for years, many years, wouldn't the thought of just having it change her? To know there would always be financial recourse. That, as a last resort, she would always have money for in vitro and a bird's-eye maple crib. Money for a new roof and the kind of rugs people stared at. Money to open a restaurant with. Money fixed problems;

everybody knew that. People argued about it, but when the money came, it was obvious—it could help.

She could feel strength returning to her, like a sick person, fever broken, sipping a bowl of broth. She felt power in her shoulders where it had not been for a long time and let the force flow through her veins. So what about Cindy Sherman? Annie Lee could have her dogged by some private detective, someone infinitely smarter than she. He would do brilliantly annoying things until Cindy realized that she was no match for Annie Lee Fleck, rightful wife of the man in question. Charged with the electricity of the spheres, buoyant in the presence of luck, and with her eyes practically straining against their sockets, Annie Lee was at this point—interrupted. Not by the staff, who had all gathered at the bar and were peering in on her, like a still-life tableau. Not by any solitary pin of reality sharp enough to burst her bubble. And not by any doubt that what she was holding was anything but the real thing. But by a ferocious wind that threw open the French doors in the middle of the dining room and blasted her with a storm-portending gust, warm and wild.

She could hear the tips of towering aspen trees whipping onto rooftops, could feel the wetness in the air, and looking up, saw not only those co-workers staring at her in silence, but a woman who'd come in at the same time as the wind, through the front door, though, aiming herself at Annie Lee like a runaway truck. None of the staff saw her until she'd passed by them, fur coat flapping, Chanel purse trailing from a long chain. A bat out of hell, it seemed to Annie Lee, who was having the vaguest of premonitions about the red-lipped face, framed at this moment by a heap of mussed hair, a few twigs strewn in it by the approaching storm.

The image burned itself into her brain and reconnected her to that night's clientele. It was Con's Clamato woman, the same one who could not be begged or cajoled, or however he'd put it, to have a good time. Annie Lee, shrinking back from the woman, wondered for a moment why no one at the bar was coming out to save her, to ask the customer what she wanted, why she'd come back.

But it was all happening too fast.

Tripping the woman as she passed by them might have been the best of all possible maneuvers, but no one was able to think of that in time. So what the staff saw as they stared was this figure in a floor-length white fur pitch by and go straight to Annie Lee, stare down at dirty fingers for a moment, and snatch the diamond out of her hand as if it were some gum ball and Annie Lee a snot-nosed kid.

"Mine!" she easily could have said to make the moment true.

Instead, she paused for just a fraction of a second. "Oh, thank God!" she said before turning around, whirling away, oblivious, through the French doors. She disappeared into the garden and then into the night, giving the impression that she'd had an escape route all picked out. No one ever figured out how she managed not to fall and break her neck, posting through the cratered snow with those heels on.

Annie Lee was staring down at her hand. It exhibited the red after-marks of someone having slapped it or yanked or scratched it. She couldn't recall the woman actually scratching her, but her hand told a different story. She felt her eyes fill up.

Con was the first to speak as he walked toward Annie Lee. "Let's get you cleaned up, dearie." He was helping her to her feet but couldn't bring himself to touch her right forearm, a loglike appendage coated with muck from the elbow down.

Annie Lee, stunned, allowed herself to be led back to the bar, where Eddie had already started figuring things out.

"How the hell did she know to go through the French doors instead of come back out the way she came in?" He was pouring Annie Lee a stiff cocktail of some kind. "Let's see what her name was . . ." he opened the reservations book and began scanning for an eight o'clock single as he kept the patter going. "Wolverton. Party of one. Well, isn't *that* fitting . . . ? Here you go Annie Lee, drink this. My father calls it 'hair of the puppy.' It has tequila in it, but other things, too."

Annie Lee obediently took a sip—only later finding out that the fizz in the drink came from half an Alka-Seltzer—and then realized Jay was vacuuming the rest of the dining room for her, something he'd never done before for anyone.

Claire and Mikey, arms around each other like earthquake victims, were staring at Annie Lee with pity. Claire never let a good excuse to rub up against Mikey pass her by. Con was going through the credit-card slips to check out the woman's full name, and Eddie evidently was calling another restaurant, Elmira's, to find out if she'd been there and what they knew about her.

"Libby Wolverton," said Con, holding the slip to the light. "Big loops, but sharp points on her *v*'s and *w*'s. Odd combination. Tip? On a tab of $46.23, tipped to equal $55.00 even. A tip of . . . $8.77. Which is about eighteen percent." He had a calculator in front of him.

"Yeah," Eddie was saying to his friend Margo, who ran the bar over at Elmo's, as they called it. "She did . . . ? Where's she staying? . . . Uh-huh . . . Uh-huh . . . Okay. Well, thanks a lot." He hung up the phone and raised his eyebrows.

"She's all alone here, at the Hotel for a week. She's been to every restaurant in town, according to Rolf, who waited on her last night and struck up a conversation with her. She's from New York. They went out to buy Clamato juice for her. Evidently she spent some years in Toronto, the clam cocktail capital of the world."

"Oh, perfect," said Con. "They fetched for her. How many more days does she have in town, did he say?"

"According to Rolf, Libby the Wolverine named off at least five restaurants—so you figure she doesn't have too many days left." Eddie was thinking; you could tell by the way he still had his hand on the phone even though he'd put back the receiver. Like another call had to be made—but to whom, and for what purpose? Finally, he spoke. "What're we going to do to make her life just a little more interesting before she goes back to life in the city?"

Annie Lee ignored him and thanked Jay, who had returned from vacuuming and positioned himself at the reservations book to study the next night. She felt empty inside, and feeling empty left her vulnerable—exceedingly sensitive—to human kindness.

"I didn't find any more diamonds," he said to her, and then looked up. "But Annie Lee, come on. What if you'd gotten attached to it, a big jewel like that? The owner would have eventually come back for it, right?"

Annie Lee shrugged, and slumped on one of the bar stools. "I don't know," she said. "I thought I might have had something for a minute there. I mean I had the thing in my hand. I was in the middle of something important. A feeling of limitlessness and of power. Of opportunity. I needed that feeling of hope, and she took it away, snatched it . . ." Her eyes were filling up. "Right out of my hands. Didn't even see me, didn't look into my face, didn't acknowledge my arm dredging for her stupid stone . . ." She reached up to her forehead with a trembling hand.

"No, she didn't." Con had his arm around her, while Eddie and Jay just stared. They'd never seen Annie Lee cry before, not even a little bit. Annie Lee, feeling the floodgate of tears about to burst, looked up at the ceiling, vainly trying to contain the water in her eyes.

"Everything is falling apart in my life," her voice quavered. "Everything. This was a sign!"

"That fucking bitch," said Eddie, shaking his head.

Twelve

Con was helping Annie Lee with her coat, zipping it up for her as if she were three years old. "You're still going out, Annie Lee," he said, pulling the mitten lumps out of her pockets and holding them open for her. "What you need is plain, ordinary diversion. Something to get your mind off—everything. And I saw someone I liked in the dining room."

From her own private stupor, Annie Lee duly registered Con's ulterior motive in pushing for a night on the town: He wanted to bump into someone, someone in particular, purposely yet accidentally. And in Pike, chances were good given the limited number of entertainment outposts that if you ran into someone somewhere, you would run into them again somewhere else. Tourists knew each other by sight after a few days of circulating. Waiters bumped into people they'd waited on the night before. So Con wasn't being overly hopeful in thinking he might at the very least bump into Mr. Right if he headed out with his eyes open. Annie Lee wondered who it might be.

Eddie said to count him in, and even Jay said he'd tag along, that vacuuming had stimulated him and he needed to wind down. Annie Lee, fully aware that they were trying to form a posse, told them she had suggested an outing in an entirely different state of mind, and now she wasn't so sure. "I'd have to leave my clothes outside when I got home," she complained. "The smoke smell seeps into the cracks of my house. It's awful."

"It's just smoke," said Jay. "It goes away. Your house doesn't mind. Your washing machine takes care of the rest."

"My cat pees on things that smell foreign, including smoky clothing. Even underwear, which I can't take off outside. It's a risk. Besides, you French people defend cigarettes, of course you're going to defend smoke."

Jay was locking the outside door of Mathilde as the group—Con, Eddie, and Annie Lee—filed out. "Look," he said, "if you're going to let a cat dictate your life—"

"Or a crazy hag with a family of foxes on her back—" Con added as they all leaned into the wind. Annie Lee knew that Con knew that the diamond did not reflect the sum of her problems, that things were not good at home. He knew by sheer omission—they talked about most things but had not touched upon recent developments between her and Lucas—that her problems must be big ones. "Life is theatrical, dear. And theater is distracting. Ergo, let's go have a drink."

"Come on Annie Lee," Eddie took her by the arm. "Just think, if we're lucky we'll run into some of tonight's—or any other night's—characters. We can spill drinks on them by accident and stuff like that. It'll be fun."

"Which bar should we go to?" Con jammed his hands into his pockets and started jingling change. "How about the Hole in the Wall? Wouldn't that be the perfect bar for a night like tonight? I could have something really seedy like a Jack and Coke. Maybe I'll even have a cigarette—blow the top of my head right off!"

The Hole was the oldest remnant of a once-vintage town. It was big and loud and had pockmarked floors, hammered tin ceilings, and enough smoke circulating to create its own weather patterns. You could practically see the specters of gamblers and miners drinking their full-sized glasses of whiskey, feet on the brass rail. Neither Lucas nor Annie Lee spent much time at the Hole anymore, like they had in their earlier restaurant years; but occasionally it did seem to break up the monotony of the primmer, better-lit establishments.

"Okay, okay," she said, wondering briefly if she could catch anything from the glasses there. "The Hole in the Wall. What have I got to lose?"

The last time she'd been to the Hole in the Wall had been in July four years ago, for Guillermo Valdevino's green-card party. Guillermo, whom everyone called Val, was one of the cooks at Giancarlo as well as Lucas's best friend. He had worked his way up from diving (dishwashing) to prepping vegetables to pasta guy, then finally to sauté. In the course of his years there, he had fallen in love with the pastry chef, married her, and received permanent resident status—the elusive green card. Lucas loved Val like a brother. He always said he never met anyone so ready to say yes to opportunity, bad or good; so when Val became legal, it was Lucas who organized the big fiesta.

It was at the green-card blowout, with every restaurant and bar employee in town there to wish him well, that Val told the world that he'd legally changed his name to Billy Vinegar. He wanted to say good-bye to all wine references in his last name and to every man in the Valdevino family who had drunk too much in his lifetime. This would be his first act of loyalty to America and to sobriety. His wife, a sweet but no-nonsense horsewoman named Jessica Mars, laughed out loud—used to Val's eccentricities, no doubt—and commented it was a good thing he was not a sommelier somewhere with a name like that.

Val—Billy Vinegar—had been the only sober one at his

party. The rest of the revelers did not leave until they'd done serious damage to themselves.

"I've never seen you dance like that before, Annie Lee," Lucas had said four or five days after the party, summing up the complexity of his emotions in one sentence that he delivered while putting a cold beer can up to the back of his neck. This was something Annie Lee had never seen a man do before or since.

"I blacked out," she had countered. "I wasn't myself."

"Yeah, well, who were you exactly? Do I know the person you were?"

"I don't know who I was. Mescal is a hallucinogen—I was out of my body." When she'd related to him how painful the hangover was now that she was back in her body, he had softened a bit. "Yes," he had said then, a smile creeping up, "you do seem as if you are paying a price."

She noted his lovemaking changed after that incident. He became a bit more zealous and more possessive, too. She heard the words "my wife" more often—as if they were a family unit now, something not to be tampered with. Ultimately, Annie Lee concluded that the episode in the bar was what had left Lucas open to the possibilities of making love without protection—that somehow it had kick-started his biological clock, set it ticking in time with the words "provider-protector-progenitor." Nothing was articulated until that fall day he fixed the latch, but things had actually started for him that night she danced on a bar top.

It had been an important episode for Annie Lee as well. In addition to what she had seen in her husband—the need to rein her in, claim her—she had learned some things about herself: She could dance on bar tops, was secretly attracted to Latin men, and couldn't hold her liquor. This had seemed shallow even then, but it was all worth remembering now.

* * *

Upon entering the bar, what assaulted them first were the odors of beer and smoke merged together into a single smell that never left the premises but merely dwindled and then rekindled itself at 3:30 opening, sort of like sourdough starter. The establishment was clinking with activity, three bartenders working as fast as they could with their speed-pourers, soda guns, and beer cappers to satisfy the needs of thirsty people standing two deep and throwing their money down on the bar. The crumpled bills lay like bets on the names and initials carved into the bar top by patrons of another age.

Eddie hooked his arm through Annie Lee's again and was dragging her toward the bar. Instead of focusing, she relaxed her eyeballs, too tired to have to wonder what was going on around her, to have to recognize people and respond to them in any way.

As they reached the pool tables in the rear, however, a familiar sort of movement, glimpsed obliquely, caused Annie Lee to look hard toward the exit. Someone had just pushed open the bar door and had one foot out. Clogs. A hat of light-blue-and-white Norwegian wool, unavailable anywhere west of Oslo, where Annie Lee's mother had purchased it. For her son-in-law. It was Lucas, leaving. Lucas was leaving.

What was he doing at the Hole?

If he was going to have a beer, he usually went to the Miners' Union, a smaller place and closer to home, and someplace the tourists hardly ever went. The Hole was a place people went to be seen and get crazy, and tonight he'd chosen it. Had he then had second thoughts?

She was almost sure he hadn't seen her, but it was possible he'd caught a glimpse of some of her co-workers and, thinking she might be there too, had fled. She thought of him trudging home, greeting the cat, and finding an otherwise empty house. Relieved not to have to face her? Relieved to have a cat to come home to? Not relieved at all, in any way, by any thing?

Frankly, she could not come up with a scenario that heartened her or made it clear why she should be running home to him. She hurt inside; there was a painful feeling of bodily estrangement—as if her feet held no direction, her abdomen no core of certainty, her chest no breath of freedom. Paralysis.

"Order me a half shot of mescal," she screamed into Eddie's ear, wanting nothing more than a temporary loosening of the straitjacket. She got a wide-eyed look of fear from him and could only think of one way to reassure him: "It's what I drank here last time!"

Eddie passed on the order to Jay, who glanced at her, worried, before buying the first round. Con raised his glass to her—it sure enough looked like Coke—and grinned at her, appearing as ready for action as he'd indicated. He had on one of those Greek fisherman's caps.

Annie Lee closed her eyes and took a little tiny sip from the shot glass before remembering how objectionable the stuff was. Rather than shoot it back, she closed her eyes and took several small sips. Gasoline mixed with tequila: She remembered it well.

When she opened her eyes she found herself staring at none other than Carlos the orthopedist, who was smiling at her, glass up, from across the room. He was surrounded by the Eleanor Easley group. Oh-oh. She averted her eyes, scanning the rest of the bar and recognizing most of the faces, just as she knew she would. The Brazilians were playing pool at the far table, betting, it looked like, that their guy would win over some Norte Americano. Near the big window were some folks from Elmo's and a Giancarlo group, Val and Jessica among them. Off at a corner table were Sheila Bupke and Judy Doyle, Judy still looking sad and Sheila still pounding the drinks, checking out the men around her even as she consoled her friend.

Midway through her survey, Annie Lee was startled by a tap on her shoulder and might have jumped out of her sneakers except that they seemed stuck to the floor. Converse low-tops could not offer enough protection against spit, gum, chaw, spilled drinks, ashes and butts, sticky garbage, and anything else at ankle level. This bar was disgusting, there was no doubt about it. Boots might be necessary for snow in Pike, but it seemed they were even more critical for barhopping.

It was Jay handing her another shot. "*Tiens*," he said. "Here you go. *Chin-chin*. The bartender just handed this to me. For you. It's from that guy over there with the mustache. The one staring right at you. Wasn't he having dinner earlier?"

Annie Lee stared at the drink and then at Carlos. She thought of her husband, who—though innocent until proven promiscuous—had done the wrong thing in not coming home after skiing. And then the wrong thing again in fleeing the scene here and now. It didn't look good, not good at all. Jealousy, that nasty thing, tailed her thoughts and then overtook them, a blinding, burning, and obliterating green. The color of whirlpools, deep and fast. The only antidote within reach seemed to be a shot of something so vile it hurt going down, but it didn't matter. Annie Lee brought the little glass to her mouth, threw the liquid back, and felt the clutch of jealousy immediately loosen as the floor shifted slightly beneath her feet.

She walked toward the man Carlos, and the group of women he was ignoring, and authorized her own hand to touch his upper arm in greeting. It was almost a caress. Another expensive shirt, she thought, the cuffs rolled up just enough to make me weak in the knees. Lavender Haze. Pale Amethyst. Columbine Innuendo. The color of distant mountains, of clouds' underpants, of 300-count cotton sheets. Oh, God.

"Cindy Lee . . ." he said, staring for some reason at her shoes. "I'm so glad you're here. I was just telling these women we had mutual family to discuss. Now, if you'll excuse me," he said to them, and she felt herself again being taken by the arm and led away. His grip on her forearm was firm, unambivalent. They passed Val, who raised his Pellegrino to her. "*Chica!*" he said. "Jessie and I haven't seen you here since—"

"No need to go into that," she said, smiling at Jessica.

Val was giving Carlos the once, twice, thrice over. "Funny thing is, Lukey was just here. You just missed him."

"Did I?" She tried to sound on an even keel.

"Yeah," Val said, "we couldn't believe he wanted to come to the Hole with us. Seemed kind of depressed—are you guys having, you know, like, problems between you?" Another long stare at Carlos.

Jessica nudged him. "Val," she said, aiming her voice below the belt, "that's none of your business."

"No, it's not," he held up his index finger. "But since when is that an issue? Are you a friend of Annie Lee's?" He turned to Carlos who was confused about the name change.

"Is that her name?" Carlos said, tipping himself back to stare at her.

"Oh, so you're just on the make. *El lobo*—" He stared at Carlos's shoes, his pants, his shirt, and then started speaking Spanish to him, some sort of tirade that sounded like a poem to Annie Lee, gushing and full of fire. Carlos acted amused but was not amused and responded in equally hot syllables, then turned to her.

"She is a big girl, whatever her name is. I invited her for a drink, not a trip to my hotel room."

"What should I tell Lucas then, Annie Lee?" Val had the look of a matador, all pomp and strut.

"You tell him nothing. You don't know what's going on, Val," Annie Lee said, seeking out Jessica's understanding, which was delivered via a nod of the head.

"I know a guy who's in love with his wife," he said, back to staring at Carlos. "And not too many of us are."

"Yeah, well," Annie Lee was kicking at an empty Junior

Mints box on the floor, "like I said, you don't know everything."

"I know what Mexican booze can do to you, *chica*. The evil agave."

Unfortunately, the comment got Carlos's attention. Annie Lee tried to ignore this as she attempted an exit, but when she heard them revert to Spanish, she did not appreciate the tone of voice of either of the men and felt she must stay.

"So what *is* your name?" Carlos moved closer to her, as Val huffed away, looking over his shoulder.

Annie Lee sighed. "My name is mud," she said. Val, introducing her husband's undying love into the skit like a Greek chorus, had made it impossible for Annie Lee to continue on whatever course she'd set. "Do you love your wife?" she asked Carlos point-blank, staring at him.

He got very serious. "Yes. I do."

Men were so full of shit! "Then why do you cheat on her?" The alcohol had gone to Annie Lee's head. She really wasn't much of a drinker anymore, had for the most part given it up in hopes of healthier and better attempts at pregnancy.

"Who says I cheat on her?" He spoke with a mixture of pride and indignation.

"Cut the crap for just a second, okay?" she motioned for Con, her only ally, to order her another shot, feeling that out of pity for her he might acquiesce to being bossed around. "You cheat on your wife just like my husband—no, I'm not really divorced—cheated on me." Boldness was snowballing. "For what? To feel powerful again or something? Is that it?" She looked to Carlos for a comment.

He shrugged. "If a woman takes a man's power away, he looks to another woman to give it back."

"Uh-huh." Annie Lee didn't like the turn of the logic but couldn't think straight enough to straighten it out.

"Now," he said, caressing her cheekbone, "why so serious, little Mia Farrow? Why not just go with the flow?"

Just then Con arrived with the shot and a comment about how he was only being Annie Lee's errand boy in order to see her dance on the bar again. Something he hadn't known about.

She was horrified. "Who told you that?"

Con retrieved a cigarette from his shirt pocket and held it up reverently, like she'd held the diamond up earlier. "Not important who said what about whom. Big people talk about ideas. Little people talk about other people. Bottoms up." Con was showing off, and Annie Lee wondered again, for whom?

"Of course, women have needs, too," Carlos added, brazenly reevaluating Annie Lee's body as if she'd just turned into a potential go-go dancer in a cage. He retrieved a lighter from his pocket for Con, whom Annie Lee swore was blushing as he tipped his head to it.

"Not all women surrender to them, though," she said, feeling now he'd presumed too much in terms of her willingness. This made him distinctly less attractive. "Sometimes, you know," she said, straightening her spine, "there's a *right* thing to do and a *wrong*—"

"Annie Lee!" Eddie interrupted from behind, gripping her arm again—she might as well have a handle there for all the use it was getting. "Listen, you gotta come with me right away," he said, weaving her through the crowd, having people make way as if he'd had a former life as a bodyguard. "We've got business to attend to." He motioned to the far comer of the L-shaped bar. "Look," he said. "Our dreams have come true."

Annie Lee's eyes were lazy in their focus, and it took her a moment of squinting through the sting of the haze to recognize her. *Her.* Sitting at the bar under her family of foxes.

"Oh my God, Eddie."

"Isn't it beautiful?" he crowed. "What should we do? Should

we douse her? Follow her home and scare the bejeezus out of her? What?"

All Annie Lee could think of was to go over and say something. Tell the woman her actions had brought a certain waitress—a fellow human being—to tears. And then perhaps slap her, hard, across the face to draw the matter to a close. To Eddie, she suggested they approach the woman, for the sake of preliminary surveillance.

Ms. Wolverton herself was beyond noticing much except the bartender. "She switches to clear alcohol after dinner, evidently," whispered Eddie to Annie Lee, whose chief hankering was to pull all the stray twigs from the woman's hair.

"It's rude to stare," she heard Eddie say to her, and she looked at him to make sure he was joking. As she did so, she noticed that Jim Doyle had arrived and was crouched over Judy, had his hand under the crook of her arm. Sheila Bupke, certainly drunk enough to be belligerent, had the look of a dog who swallows its bark and goes right in for the attack. Annie Lee, momentarily diverted, watched for Judy's reaction to Jim. She wouldn't look at him, even as he whispered something in her ear. Sheila Bupke's mouth was moving in big *O*'s and *E*'s, her teeth bared, but she seemed to be playacting. Finally, Jim gave up and, without answering Sheila's grimaces, went to the door of the bar where he turned one last time to stare at his wife, who sat still, gripping the tall, tubular glass as if she were arm wrestling with it. It still looked serious.

"I've got it," Eddie said to her. "We wait until she's ready to leave. We follow her discreetly back to her hotel, along with Con and Jay. Right as she's opening the front door, we pelt her with snowballs. Ambush her with big, soft wet ones, some a little harder, a little more painful. I could go make a stockpile right now—"

Annie Lee didn't like the idea. Though they talked endlessly about getting revenge on rude customers, they never actually did anything about it. Chances were if she or any other waiter bumped into the same nasty person they'd waited on the night before—at the Chinese place, or the bakery, or the bookstore—she would simply run the other way. She made a face at Eddie, eager to call his bluff, and returned her stare to Libby Wolverton and her cocktail.

The martini glass, half full, held no garnish, which led Annie Lee to believe that for all her fuss about a Bloody Caesar with celery garnish, this bare-bones drink was more in keeping with her current state of mind, and that it better represented what kind of fluid was coursing through those veins. Clamato was too sanguine. Vodka or gin was pale and constricting and cold and turned blood the color of the bluer veins in her hand. Varicose Violet.

She caught a glimpse of Con in the big bar mirror, smoking, and lost her topographical balance. Where was he? No one in the mirror looked familiar. Con was talking and laughing with that virtual surgeon, who appeared to be enjoying himself as well. Both were taking puffs in the elegant way nonsmokers smoke, tipping their heads up. So Carlos's friend was the mystery man!

Annie Lee longed for a breath of fresh air, to be outside, walking, walking toward somewhere not home, where her head could rest in peace and quiet, where someone would take her clothes for her and wash them. Hand her a fresh pair of flannel pajamas and lead her to the refuge of a safe couch, a wool blanket laid on top of her like a leaden shield. She couldn't very well show up at the sisters' at this hour, though it was tempting.

Libby Wolverton shifted then, and moved her glass just a fraction of an inch on the bar. Annie Lee noted it sparkled, flashed her just as she'd been flashed earlier while vacuuming. She stared at the glass, focusing with all her might, and then nudged Eddie hard enough to hear him say "Ow."

"Eddie!" she whispered, "Look what's in the bottom of that glass!" It was the Miracle-Gro diamond, sitting at the bottom of the V, cradled by the angle, and immersed in the closest thing the woman could find to an antiseptic. She was cleaning it after its earlier ordeal, its ramble through the viscera of common household machinery.

"Jesus," she heard him say. "It's huge."

Annie Lee felt a crazy click in her brain. Like a sleepwalker she slipped into the motions of some preordained plot, and walked the length of the bar, where she ordered a vodka martini, no fruit. When it was handed to her, she drank the first half inch, matching the level to that of the liquid in the other woman's glass. Then she slunk back to Eddie's post and ever-so-smoothly wedged herself, back first, next to Libby Wolverton, right at the bar.

"Distract her for a minute," she said to Eddie. "If she's got the nerve to come here and do a dumb thing like that, she deserves what she's about to get." Eddie gave her that half-crazed look—like all of a sudden he couldn't go through with it, someone else would have to. Not surprising from the likes of Eddie.

"Do it," she said, implying his reputation would be forever sullied if he didn't.

Hesitantly, he inched in and then pretended to stumble, creating a heavy disturbance near the brass rail of the bar, close to the woman's calves. At the sound of her flustered exclamations, Annie Lee gently put her glass down next to the look-alike, faked a coughing spasm, and then picked up the glass with the diamond in it, unsteadily, as if truly inebriated. It wasn't hard to do. Once the glass was in her hand, she turned and muddled her way to the pool tables, wondering what to do next, giddy with the maneuver.

It was obvious she had to drink the martini. She checked the glass's rim for a clean part of the circumference and tipped the bottom up. The diamond clinked against one of her left molars—she couldn't tell which one—and she used her tongue to manipulate it off her teeth. Putting the empty glass on the floor under one of the tables, she then stood up, careful not to look toward Eddie or the bar, or to call any attention to her trail.

It seemed like a good idea to leave now, get the heck out of Dodge—casually, though, and without looking guilty. Jay had gone home. Con was socializing with a vengeance. She would bet her life that Eddie had taken off, knowing him, ready to forget everything if questioned. "What diamond?" he would say. "I was too drunk to recollect anything that actually went on that night."

She felt someone take her elbow and thought if it was Carlos, she would nudge him away, get the riffraff out. But it was Val; and as she felt him put his arm around her shoulders, she was grateful it was someone connected to Lucas, someone safe.

"What do you think you're doing, Annie Lee, with all these drinks and shit? You're not a drinker, girl. You wanna talk to me?"

She did, actually. Right now, she wanted nothing more than to talk to one of Lucas's best friends, rehash his transgression, get an incestuous point of view. She started to say, "Yes, Right after we get out of here," but the gemstone knocked around in her mouth and, in an effort to shove it in a cheek like the pit of a fruit or a piece of hard candy, missed the mark and felt it roll toward her epiglottis.

She was about to choke.

Panic put her life on the verge of flashing before her eyes, and she did the first thing her body told her to do: she swallowed. The gem was big enough to hurt and to surprise her, and in a blinding moment of confusion, she grabbed Val's soda water and washed the lump down, her eyes tearing in the two-second crisis. An alarm went off inside as she wondered obscurely what the punishment was for people who not only stole but swallowed.

"You okay?" Val said to her.

She shook her head. "Uh-uh. I'm in trouble. I need a phone." The emergency was real this time. Who knew what a billion facets etched into the hardest surface on earth could do to one's esophagus? Not to mention the further reaches of one's insides.

He pulled her, arm still around her shoulders, to the back of the bar and then into a little alcove she never knew existed. "What's up?" he said.

"It's a long story but I've got to get out of here without being noticed." She could swear she heard the shrill voice of discovery, Libby Wolverton's, and had the wherewithal to give Val instructions: "Go get the martini glass from under the pool table—act natural—and put it in your coat." At least they could get that glass out of the way, make it look like there was only one glass to begin with. Even if it did have her fingerprints on it. With one glass, no one would ever figure a switch had been made.

The beautiful thing about Val was that he was a man of action and took care of things without asking questions. When he returned, he ushered her through the office and out a back door, another feature of the bar unfamiliar to her. As she let herself be led, she felt surely there must be a whole world of escape hatches unbeknownst to her, a subculture of tunnels, places to duck into, the veritable true pathways of life. It was the literal and figurative equivalent of being streetwise, being able to cut and run, slip around an obscure corner, blend into the scenery instead of always insisting on the course most evident.

They walked briskly and silently to Val's. He kept his arm around her shoulders, and she let herself lean into him, happy for the warmth of his body and the sober feel of his walk.

Jessica had come home a few minutes earlier and was watching a show on sunken treasure when the two of them showed up. Quickly, she turned off the TV and came over to greet them. There was mayonnaise on her lips from what appeared to be a very late night snack, the thought of which made Annie Lee close her eyes. She swayed on the spot and saw the color of beaten egg yolks behind her eyelids.

"Annie Lee needs to use the phone," Val told his wife as he wiped her face with his shirt sleeve. Jessica suggested Annie Lee's wet tennis shoes come off if she didn't want to catch pneumonia, and Val handed her the cordless handset.

Annie Lee punched in an eleven-digit number. "Hello, Poison Control?" her hosts heard her say as they stared at each other in disbelief.

Thirteen

Annie Lee focused on the hard feel of the phone in her hand and the curative smell of toast in Val and Jessica's house.

"Yes, I have a question about ingesting a large gemstone. I mean I did ingest one. A three- maybe four-carat diamond." She cleared her throat.

"Clearly, there is adequate air exchange," said the courteously mournful voice that Annie Lee instantly recognized as that of Gabriel Salt. It seemed both unlikely and inevitable that he should answer the phone, and, unfazed by the nature of the ingestion, he jumped right into the particulars.

"No discomfort in the esophagus?" She could almost feel his polite fingers palpating her throat. There seemed little chance he would remember her with so many voices filing by him day by day. The fact was, she didn't want to be remembered, because at this point she would be unable to conjure up the requisite imaginary child, keep the mythology alive, and extend that lie again. There were other lies that might suit her better now, it seemed.

"I have a residual feeling," she said running her fingers down her neck, "like swallowing an ice cube whole. Could it cut me on the way down?"

He paused, and Annie Lee wondered if he was retrieving some sort of book, flipping through the thin pages of a ten-pound tome on the varieties of swallowed objects. "I suppose it's possible. Unlikely, however. If it did, the tiny fistula, the kind we're talking about, would probably heal itself quickly enough. Especially since the gem seems to have gone down like a large pill."

He continued on. "Assuming you want the piece back, you want to minimize the pain of expulsion. There are two ways to go. One, you should eat lots of fiber. Psyllium seed husks—Metamucil or something similar. This will serve to bulk up your intestines, making elimination more frequent. You will have to examine the stools carefully, however, in order to retrieve the object." He made it sound as if people regularly ingested things that hurt on the way out.

"Two, you do just the opposite. You drink lots of fluids. You buy one of those disposable enemas, or you let the object pass on its own. Chances are you will feel it come out—I don't think it will be all that dangerous—and you will have less searching to do. Momentary discomfort, that's all. Either way would work. I used to swallow coins as a small child—almost obsessively, according to my mother. There was never any worry about them eventually finding their way out. *Now* I can't imagine swallowing such a filthy object, and a choking hazard at that."

Annie Lee absorbed his words like paper towels on a messy spill. "So, there's no chance of it staying in my stomach, never coming out?"

"Oh, there's a chance, yes. If it becomes systemic, you'd need to get X rays to determine its exact location. Then they'd proceed from there."

"Meaning?"

"Meaning surgical removal, I suppose. Not much chance of that happening, though."

"How do you know?" Her voice became serious, quiet.

"Sheer numbers, Ms.—" He had sensed fear and was trained to massage, to soothe, to smooth out. Modulation of the voice was key.

She wanted to lie. She was desperate to be someone else, but she simply could not cross that line this time. It seemed utterly inexcusable to tell a fib. "Fleck," she half mumbled. "Annie L."

He was silent. "Have we spoken?" It was a discreet inquiry, meant to wheedle the involuntary information out. "That combination of names is singular. Very singular: I've heard it before."

Would he remember her? It didn't matter, she had to tell the truth now; this was a real situation. "I've called before, yes. It was some time ago. Hard to believe you'd remember my name, though."

"Well," he answered, "many people swallow foreign objects Ms. Fleck. Mostly children, but a good many adults, too. Nearly all, based on records of surgical procedures, come out the other end, so to speak. I think you'll be just fine. Is there anything else I can help you with?"

"Well . . ." she was hesitant. He *was* asking.

"Yes?"

"I know this is an emergency line, but would you mind answering a tangential question for me? Semipersonal. Your input would be—highly valued."

He didn't cough or sputter or act surprised, he simply paused again, that pause of review or orderly thought. "I may have to hang up the phone or put you on hold if something comes up," he said soberly. "But—well, I'd be happy to help if I can."

Annie Lee thought she heard a trace of eagerness there, beyond the obligatory employee mindfulness, and it was impossible to resist it. Here was someone whose focus was fixed upon her like a floodlight. There were so many questions to ask in the world, and so few people attentive to them in this way. She dove in. "Okay, it's on the abstract side; but it's application isn't. Power is what it's about. What do you think it is—power, I mean? What does it all boil down to?"

"Power," he said softly. "Big question. One presumably inextricably connected to other questions, one fraught with antecedent situations I know nothing of. But I'll take a stab." The pregnant pause. "Power is control, I guess. Taking control, having control, and sometimes even handing over the reins to a higher power. I suppose real power ultimately involves understanding the nature of power itself. Whence it springs, et cetera."

"Yes." Annie Lee, infatuated with his syntax, felt a pang of love for this man. "It's Gabriel, isn't it?" she asked. "I just realized I recognize your voice from the last time. Gabriel Salt."

"Why, yes," he said, the surprise warm in his voice. "I'm flattered. I always think that even though I give my name on a call, I'm pretty much anonymous. Goes with the territory."

"No, no. I certainly remember you," Annie Lee felt a headache coming on—as well as nausea—from all the alcohol, "and your kindness." She closed her eyes again and saw Indoor-pool Blue.

"When you called about your daughter ingesting paint?"

This stunned her, popped her eyes open again. "How . . . did you remember that?"

'Well, I didn't have to." She thought she heard him sniff with satisfaction. "Because we keep records of calls. A database, actually, something I initiated some years ago and have seen to fruition. I wouldn't have used it at all if you'd seemed hesitant or unwilling to give me your name. Although I *could* have pulled you up with Caller ID alone. How is your—little girl, wasn't it? Sydney."

Annie Lee felt her stomach say hello to her throat. "I—"

she began, and then sighed, deeply, and surrendered. She sighed again. "There is no little girl," she said quickly and then stopped, waiting for him to hang up on her, give up on her, send her back to the land of the loonies who have no one to turn to. But nothing happened. He was waiting.

"I'm a little bit crazy, I think," she obliged. "Or was. I've had a pretty bad case of baby envy, you see. At certain times, I've needed to pretend everything was different. In the process, I've lied to myself and to you, and hogged this—this emergency hotline. I swore I'd never call you again under false pretenses, and I swear I'm not lying to you now. I've ingested exotic material. And, as it happens, the diamond is just the tip of the iceberg."

She glanced around at Jessie and Val, sitting there on the couch, staring at her as if she were the TV, and decided it wasn't worth trying to hide anything anymore. And that what Gabriel needed at this point was a little background. Some antecedents.

"You see . . ." she began, and then plopped herself down on a carved wooden bench that might have been an old Mexican church pew. "I swallowed a diamond that belonged to someone else. I'd vacuumed it up at the restaurant I work at, and its owner had snatched it out of my hand just as I'd retrieved it from the vacuum bag. The snatching woman had the diamond in her martini at a bar later on, and I switched drinks and slugged down the thing, not really intending to swallow it. I just wanted to play with her, get some of my personal power back. I think. I didn't really know what I was doing, I was kind of drunk, which I still am, but not in a good way. When I found the diamond originally, I figured it could magically extract me from the current state of affairs—which is that I'm infertile and have driven my husband to having an affair with an old high school sweetheart.

"In the bar I contemplated cheating on my husband with

an orthopedist named Carlos, who had his own superficial views on power." Annie Lee surprised even herself with the articulated synopsis of her life. She paused while Gabriel Salt silently connected the dots as they were enumerated to him, then continued. "So what do you think: If a man feels he's lost power, well, how does he regain it?"

Gabriel was coming to life. "Hmmm. More difficult still, since men are prone to not understanding power once in its throes. It's heady stuff, addictive, blinding. But ultimately, getting away from feeling victimized by exterior circumstance is of primary importance. The power is there, you simply have to reconnect with it. You can't give someone power, they have to reclaim it for themselves. And that includes men."

"Is that what you do?" Gabriel's answers were making Annie Lee curious about him.

"Hah!" The laugh came barking out, and then he corrected himself. "I'm good at telling other people what to do, possibly instilling confidence. My own confidence is a different story . . ."

"Well," Annie Lee wished she could see the man, "how would you change your life? You said before you had aspirations toward cooking . . ."

He was silent a moment. "You remember that?"

Annie Lee smiled. "Well, yes. I live with a cook. I work in a restaurant. When people say they want to get involved in that life, I wonder if they know what they're wishing for. So?"

"Honestly, I'm too solitary a person to work with others well. Let's be realistic. I'm bookish; I'm shy. I've been thinking in terms of a cookbook."

"Uh-huh," Annie Lee nodded cautiously. "Always good if you've got a great idea—what kind of cookbook?" Lucas collected cookbooks: everything from antique and Amish to name-brand cookbooks, like Jell-O and Libby's, to classics. They had cookbooks by the yard, all lined up neatly like the family encyclopedias.

"Well, that's the thing," said Gabriel, "I know it would have to be different. And since my avocation is psychology, well, I was thinking—and don't laugh—about a cookbook of sorts that begins with a personality test. You find out what kind of cook you are, with the following choices: egomaniacal/experimental; recipe-bound/traditional; refrigerator oriented/practical; and shopping oriented/craving.

"Then for each type, I compile a reference list of great works as well as an abbreviated anthology—certain recipes sure to please the individual. It's kind of self-discovery and personality testing through cooking. What do you think?" He asked the question in a whisper. Annie Lee smiled again. Only Gabriel Salt had been able to distract her tonight. For that, she owed him her full support.

"I like it! My husband would *love* that idea. Love it."

"He would?" Gabriel's voice cracked.

"Yeah, I could even mention it to him if we're ever on speaking terms again. He has an actual background in psychology, believe it or not. Not that that means anything, but occasionally it's interesting to discover that schooling might have a direct bearing on life."

This elicited a stifled giggle from Gabriel Salt, who asked her what she'd studied in school; when she told him English lit, he virtually guffawed. Comparative lit, he announced back as if anteing up and raising her one. German and French. He'd written his undergraduate thesis on *Buddenbrooks*, by Thomas Mann, the subject of which he could not recall. Knowledge of world literatures had helped him get this job, he said, and when she earnestly asked how, he said with a heavy German accent: "I'm just kidding *Frau* Fleck."

Self-deprecation sealed her bond with the man. "Tell me, Gabriel, what do you think I should do?"

"About what?"

"Everything. Everything I've just told you. What do I do? Say I recover the diamond. Then what?"

She heard him whistle that you-got-yourself-a-big-problem ditty.

"Well, it seems to me you need to apply the whole discussion of power to yourself first. Un-victimize yourself. Don't be a victim of infertility, just be infertile. Seek help if it's available. Let your husband deal with his own problems; let him explain himself in his own time; don't harangue him. If you love him, that is. If not, just slap his face and move on. Find yourself not guilty in terms of the diamond and tell the woman it was an utter accident and that you almost died because of it. Did she suspect foul play?"

"Who knows? She was inebriated like everyone else at the bar."

"You'll have to return the diamond, Annie Lee. It has to go back to its owner no matter how horrid she is."

"But why?" Annie Lee had begun to think that with the diamond safely inside, in a strange way yet inarguably, it belonged to her. That perhaps it would sit there indefinitely, never coming out, never causing pain. Just sitting at the bottom of her stomach in much the same way it had rested in the bottom of the martini glass. Helping her see things differently. A source of power, of confidence.

"For you to keep it makes you a criminal and its prisoner—it becomes a bad-luck charm. You don't want that. But you may want to get as much out of its power over its owner as you can while you have it in—and I do mean *in*—your personal possession. I think it will all turn out okay for you. I really do."

"You do?" She liked people who told her it would all turn out for the best. "How do you figure?"

There was a longer pause. "Like I said, other people's lives make a lot of sense. It's almost frightening how much sense other people's lives make in contrast to your own."

"Oh, Gabriel, I could not agree more!" Annie Lee cried. They sat in quiet contemplation, each on their own end of the line. Realizing that she was once again monopolizing emergency hotline time, Annie Lee then thanked Gabriel quickly but sincerely and hung up the phone.

Jessica and Val had politely turned the TV back on during her conversation with Gabriel Salt in order to give her the illusion of privacy. But by the time she was through, they were staring at her so hard she was the one whose eyes shifted to the simulation of some sinking ship, tipping up on one end and then going down like a toy. She watched just to avoid making eye contact with either of them.

"You swallowed that fur-coat lady's diamond?" Val got up off the couch and started pacing, while Annie Lee wondered if he had a photographic memory for fur coats, or women, or whether he simply always knew who the players were around him. "It's in your stomach?"

Annie Lee nodded and swore she could feel the hardest substance on earth within her, growing, a million facets reflecting all the complexities of life. It was too much to bear.

"I'm not feeling so good," she said, plunking herself down on the pew. "I miss my husband, even though he's cheating on me. I miss my house, even though the spare room's empty and white. I want to go home. I just want to go home and sleep this off."

It was Jessica's turn to talk. "What are you going to do about the woman, though, Annie Lee, the one who's missing one of her possessions?" Both of them seemed to be ignoring the Lucas-cheating-on-her part, maybe because they assumed it was possible and there was nothing friends could do but gloss over it. Val fetched a bottle of sparkling water from the refrigerator and cracked the twist-top open as if all the answers were inside.

Annie Lee turned to Jessica. "I'm going to ignore the whole thing until tomorrow morning," she said. "Then I'll call her, tell her I swallowed it by mistake, and had a hard time tracking her down. Then I'll see what she says. That's the current plan."

Val was looking at her disapprovingly, and in her state she could not tell whether it was because she was drunk, a thief, a husband-deserter, or someone who flirted with men in bars. She shrugged at him. "I'm only human, Val," she told him, reaching for her shoes. "Just like my husband. And I'm going home. Home is where the heart is, you know, however ravaged the heart might be. It's where my bed is, too. And Libby Wolverton doesn't know who I am or where I live. She'll just have to have one wickedly bad night as penance for being rude to me. Then I'll figure out how to get the damned thing out of my system. Literally and figuratively."

Jessica, concerned for Annie Lee's feet, had retrieved some felt-lined snow boots and put them before her. "Lucas didn't say much at work tonight, Annie Lee. He seemed not to notice the world around him—which isn't really like him. I hope you guys work it out, whatever it is." Jessie's trusty compassion, especially for wounded things, endeared her to nearly everyone. Annie Lee smiled at her, thinking with satisfaction that at least Lucas seemed miserable. She hadn't noticed before, but Jessie had a couple pimples around her mouth that looked painful. Annie Lee couldn't help staring at them.

"My hormones are going nuts," Jessie apologized sheepishly under the scrutiny, and looked to Val. "He says bad skin on a pregnant woman is a sure sign of good skin on a baby!"

Annie Lee stared at her without immediate comprehension. "You guys are—"

Jessica turned a splotchy red, then faced her husband before addressing Annie Lee. "Oh, God, you didn't know?"

She shook her head. Lucas hadn't even told her, he'd kept it from her. No, kept her from *it*. Well, why wouldn't he keep it from her? Why would he want to see her face fall, watch her writhe in pain at someone else's good fortune, as if there were a limited amount of it and it was a race to get to it first. He was right, her vortex had sucked him dry, made him grip his little pieces of life to himself rather than release them into her atmosphere, a black hole sure to annihilate whatever it came across. How much of life had she missed in her all-consuming crusade to become impregnated? How much of Lucas had she missed? How much of him had she ruined?

She looked at the worry on Jessie's face, and on Val's, and thought it disgraceful that she should be the center of attention instead of Jessie, who deserved congratulations at the very least. She straightened herself up. "Well, you look great, Jess," she said, noticing for the first time the paunch in her dress, the excess oil on her face. "You look really great." Annie Lee flashed her widest, toothiest smile, and as it spread over her face, it heartened her.

Val rallied. "Lucas should have told you, man. He should have said something. That was not cool."

Annie Lee was shaking her head as she headed toward the door. "Lucas has had a lot to contend with at home. I've been sort of a spoiled brat, lately." She looked at them. "My husband was driven to being someone he's not, so don't blame him." Staring at Jessica, she wondered what you got when you crossed a black-haired Mexican with a blue-eyed blonde. A coffee-colored baby with light hair? Or one of those dark-haired, freckled types? "What's the baby's last name going to be?"

"Mars-Valdevino," Jessica said, looking at Val as if prompting him to explain.

"You can't exactly name a baby Vinegar," he said. "When the baby's born, we're all legally changing our name to Mars-Valdevino. People never stopped calling me Val, anyway. And I proved I could stop drinking, that was the biggest thing for me. I can reclaim my name, now that I'm not afraid of it anymore. Plus add Jessie's name to make it something completely new. An American name!"

Annie Lee stumbled down the front steps, waving good-bye as the two of them stood and watched her. It was a curious thing to play the drunken and screwed-up friend, the one she normally sent home from her own porch, waving, as she stood there with her own husband.

Sometimes you're the bat, she thought, sometimes you're the ball. And sometimes, like right now, it was hard to tell just which. By all accounts, she should have felt hollow with infertility, especially in the glowing light of Jessica Mars; but she did not. She should have felt the cleaving pain of having been cheated on; but she did not. And she should have been just a tad worried about grand theft jewelry; but she was not.

What she felt, besides tired and spent, was defenseless, like a cat without claws. She did not know what she would say to Lucas when she got home. Maybe the diamond, lying there in the pit of her stomach, would spin out some brilliance from within. She had that, if only for a few more hours.

Fourteen

When she opened the door of her house, the wind hustled in behind her as if cold and tired itself. Only one light was on, not in the kitchen but in the living room. Maybe, she let herself hope, Lucas felt like talking.

"Annie Lee?" The timid little voice calling her name was not Lucas's but Megan Doyle's. Now Annie Lee was confused.

"Megan?" She found the girl on the couch, sitting up straight, pale as paper, Klink beside her, one full cushion away, like a sentry at his post.

"What's up? Where's Lucas?"

Megan motioned toward a note on the dining room table. "The note says he's at the sisters' house for the night. That—well, you'd better read it yourself. I thought this was someplace I could come to get away from domestic strife . . ." Annie Lee raised one eyebrow. "I thought things were fairly secure around here."

Lucas never left notes. He would leave messages on the machine for her, or she would simply find him not at home. She picked up the piece of paper and stared at the pencil marks, unwilling to feel the growing panic that lay in her chest like a chick ready to hatch and flap its wings helter-skelter. "I am next door for the night. I'm trying to sort things out and need privacy."

No signature. No pencil nearby. Just the old pictures of the house the sisters had mentioned, lying beneath the note, two of them, which she glanced at now, since, by sheer proximity, they had all of a sudden become relevant. One had Orna Vitale out front, hands on her hips, with all the windows and doors open on the house behind her. The other one was a picture of all the townsfolk gathered there for a big party of some kind.

Annie Lee looked back at Megan while thinking to herself that Lucas had actually done what she'd considered doing earlier: gone for refuge next door. And Megan had done it, too, the Fleck house being her refuge. Everyone was seeking comfort tonight, wherever they could get it.

"So," she produced a smile and shrugged casually, as if capable of dealing with great undulations in the cosmic fabric. "People are entitled to privacy, aren't they? It isn't the end of the world or anything, and I'm glad you felt you could come here. Now tell me exactly why you are here, Miss Doyle. Do your parents know?"

"My parents aren't home. Mom's been out all night, and Dad finally went to look for her. I left them a note saying I wasn't comfortable with the situation and that I'd be here." She had on flannel pajamas and a down jacket and had an old leather satchel by her feet.

"Harold knows I left and knows to tell everybody if they wake up that I spent the night at a friend's house."

Annie Lee loved this responsibility the children felt for each other, as if they knew to take over when their parents became idiots. She motioned for Megan to go with her into the kitchen so she could make tea and take some aspirin. As she swallowed the two tablets, she recalled the diamond and its itinerary and decided on two full glasses of water rather than tea. "Have you heard any sirens or anything lately?" she asked her young ward.

"No, why?" Megan was taking off her coat.

"Nothing to do with your parents—whom I saw at the Hole in the Wall, by the way—but with an altercation that took place there. I left before it was over."

"My parents were at that gross bar? That place is for drug addicts and losers . . ."

"Whoa, girl! Who told you that?" "Loser" was a word Annie Lee considered better left unspoken, even unthought.

"My parents!"

"Well, there you go, then." Case in point. "I guess it's also for regular nonlosers with problems. What is the problem, anyway?" She remembered Jim's attempts at getting his wife's attention, the way he'd left the bar. Then maybe gone on to some other bar, who knew?

Megan, whose skin was so white Annie Lee had to fight an impulse to get her a hot washcloth to bring life back into her face, started to cry.

"What?" Annie Lee went to her and enveloped her in her arms. "What's going on?"

"Mom's pregnant again!" she blurted it out, as if confessing to one of history's most heinous acts. Annie Lee said nothing, head throbbing at being forced into thinking mode again. "You're mother's pregnant with number six . . ." the words came out slowly.

"Yes. They were only supposed to have four, Annie Lee. I've heard them talking, you know, listening in. I knew Jimmy was kind of a mistake, that they didn't plan on five. Of course it's obvious that we were meant to have Jimmy in the family now that we know him. But now this? Dad's angry because he says he can't support another kid in Pike. He says we'll have to move back to Chicago where he can get his old job back, where things are more straightforward. Mom feels like it's her fault, even though she was wearing a diaphragm and everything."

"Boy, you really were listening in." Annie Lee was impressed.

"Well, Harold and I put our information together and have a pretty complete picture. Mom's mad at Dad for blaming her; even though he says he doesn't, she thinks he does. Dad's worried because he's never seen Mom like this. She's spending all her time with Mrs. Bupke—"

"Yeah, what's with that?" Annie Lee thought the combination logical on a casual level but not on a best-friends, talk-three-times-a-day level.

"Mrs. Bupke is like my mom's oldest friend in Pike and she feels like she can tell her anything—I heard her say that to Dad. Dad got all huffy and said Sheila Bupke was a tart. What's a tart—a slut?"

"Slut is a little harsh. You should watch labeling people losers and sluts, Meg. A tart: someone dangerously addicted to getting attention and whose lipstick is too bright. She certainly does suck down the cocktails. They were at Mathilde earlier on. Your mom looked really sad, though—I guess about being *pregnant*—"

"I don't want to go back to Chicago—I have a life here. Friends. Quilting class. A huge crush on Olivia Davis-Hamblin's brother, Quinn. I don't see why my dad can't just deal with it." She lowered her voice. "My dad's being kind of a jerk, Annie Lee. He seems to *want* to go back to Chicago!"

"Why's that?"

"I don't know. So we have less money here. So what? I don't need much. I do need to see Quinn Davis-Hamblin on a regular basis. Even if he does just smile at me and say hey. If I don't see him I think I'll just vanish into nothing. Die or something."

Annie Lee couldn't think that straight, but something wasn't adding up. What was one more in the big picture when you already had five? Was it really a money thing? Or some sinuous, small-town plot lapping over itself, once hidden in the alley shadows and now about to burst forth onto Main Street?

"Your mom must have some reproductive system," she said, thinking of open tubes and chubby ovaries and happy sperm doing the butterfly. Everything going just as it was supposed to go in the primordial womb.

"The other thing . . ." Megan started in tentatively.

"Yeah?"

"Is that in a fit of rage, my mother put the cradle out on the sidewalk for put-out-your-garbage day tomorrow." Four times a year people were allowed to put unwanted items on the sidewalk for others to take. In March, the people of Pike did it to convince themselves that spring was just around the corner, that they could stroll about in March just as other people did, people at sea level, that is. Sometimes they were wrong. Tomorrow there would be snow on top of people's giveaways.

"So, since I thought she might regret it later, I hauled it to your house. Only while I was doing that, the sisters came out and pried the whole story out of me. They told me to take the cradle up to your spare bedroom. That that's where it was meant to be. And you know it's hard to argue with the two of them, Annie Lee. They're like—well, like Stephen King characters or something. Anyway, once I took it apart and got it up there and put it back together, they washed it off and stuff and found a spot in the spare bedroom to put it. Then right when I was thinking I'd done the wrong thing and that they were going to put me in a cage and fatten me up, one of them went home and brought back cinnamon buns and tea for me, and some squares for a tiny quilt. Said she'd been keeping them for me."

Her lip started to swell and twitch, and she picked up the squares to show Annie Lee. "See?" She started to cry again while fingering the multicolored and carefully cut pieces of material.

"Oh, Megan," Annie Lee put her arms around her. "I'm sorry, honey." She couldn't think of anything else to say. "Your mom and dad are too smart not to figure it all out in the best way." That's what she'd always thought about Judy and Jim, anyway.

"I don't want to figure it out in Chicago, though. I want to stay here! I hate Chicago. I hate my parents for not being better at birth control. I mean, how stupid can you get? It's like they're teenagers or something!"

Annie Lee laughed so loud and so spontaneously she sent Klink scooting off to a more distant perch. She was about to share whatever wisdom she could drum up with the baffled Megan when the phone rang, unexpectedly, and sent Annie Lee surging to grab it.

Eddie was calling from his house, an endangered-list tarpaper shack he shared with three other males, a dog, two cats, and the occasional month-long girlfriend. His room was the only spotless area in the whole house, CD's organized alphabetically, tee shirts folded, the whole nine yards. It said a lot about wisecracking, big-talking Eddie.

"I thought you should know," he sounded stressed beyond belief, "that that woman had four cops come to the scene of the crime, as she called it."

"Yeah?"

"Annie Lee, enough is enough. You have to give the diamond back. This isn't funny anymore. This is grand theft. Larceny. Robbery. A felony, even."

"It was never funny, Eddie, not for me. It was serious. Very serious. The thing is, I accidentally swallowed the diamond—and now, somehow, as serious as it's gotten for you, it's gotten pretty amusing for me." She heard him gasp. Eddie the con artist, all bark, no bite. Toothless in the face of a real situation.

"And so," she continued, "it's temporarily untraceable except by X ray. Did she suspect anyone?" Megan was staring at her.

"No, she was too wasted, I think. She said it vanished into thin air and waved her hand around and around like a drunken conductor without a baton. Almost waved herself right off the bar stool. They hauled her back to the Hotel while she threatened to sue everyone in the whole town. Said her husband was a famous Park Avenue shrink who knew people. She said he *knew* people, Annie Lee!"

"Wow." Annie Lee's tone was mordant. "Imagine that."

Eddie got peevish, "Just forget it, Annie Lee. I wasn't there. I don't know a thing." He hung up.

She looked at Megan, whose color had started to come back. "It's true. I have a very big diamond in my stomach." The phone rang again. It was the Magpie, calling from a bar from the sound of it.

"I heard what happened," she said, at which point Annie Lee's mouth dropped open.

"How is that possible, I just now told Eddie I swallowed it."

"You swallowed the diamond?" She actually shrieked with glee. "I heard from Claire that you'd vacuumed it up and had it snatched from your hand. Then I heard from Stevie T. that he saw you at the Hole—we bumped into him a while ago here—at the Miners' Union—and that the woman had had her diamond stolen at the bar. I didn't know what happened after that. I heard it was huge."

"How'd you hear that?"

"Stevie T. said she told the cops it was a four-carat diamond! Oh, Annie Lee, four carats! In your possession! How did you swallow it?"

"Can I ask you a question? Why do you think you can call here at almost 1:30 in the morning? What if my husband were asleep? What if we were doing something private?" Anything was possible.

"Stevie T. said he saw Lucas down by the river and said something to him but didn't get a response, so he figured you were having a fight or something, or that something was up. That wasn't that long ago, so I figured either he hadn't gotten home yet or he'd just walked through the door—and I just had to know!"

Annie Lee wanted to go out and grab Stevie T. by the scruff of the neck and hurl him against a yellow snowbank. "Does Stevie T. have any opinions about anything else you'd like to share with me?"

"What do you need to know?" Kathryn was a person whose most petty inclinations took over after a few beers.

"I need to know if he's seen Jim Doyle on his night patrol—I mean, since he seems to know everything." She heard voices through the palm of Kathryn's pudgy hand over the speaker.

"He wants to know what you need to know besides the fact he's boinking—" It wasn't a regular word for Kathryn, and she started hiccuping with laughter. "Boinking Sheila Bupke." She stopped again to listen. Annie Lee, not unused to such news, mentally tried to corroborate the connections. Stevie T. would know this because Jim was a Realtor and Stevie T.'s girlfriend, Amanda Roebuck's karate teacher, Chili Hicks, also happened to be the receptionist at Jim's office.

"And from the looks of his wife," Kathryn continued on with Stevie T.'s information, "who's still friends with Sheila Bupke, she doesn't know." Annie Lee was silent.

"What?" Megan wanted to know.

"Tell Stevie T. he should keep his big boinking mouth shut, because it'll all come back his way—"

"What?" said Megan again, as Annie Lee heard Kathryn start to repeat her message to Stevie T. and then stop.

"You wanted the information, Annie Lee," Kathryn said accusingly.

"Yeah, but I can still wish he didn't have it." She hung up on Kathryn and unplugged the phone.

"What's going on?" Megan was pleading with her.

"Everything," she said. "I guess everything is always going on. Sometimes you're just lucky enough to be ignorant of it."

"I wish you had cable," said Megan, who had sensed bad news. "Then I could watch infomercials or something, fall asleep on the couch." She made it sound like it happened to her often enough, sweet little Megan, needing an antidote to her life. That home wasn't as orderly as that mess kit Jim was so good at packing.

"Well, let me set you up on the couch anyway. We have some movies you could watch." Annie Lee hustled here and there, gathering blankets, a pillow, rummaging through a box of videotapes. She settled on a romantic comedy from the forties, the kind of movie that made you feel that the present state of the world was directly related to the fact that women didn't wear suits anymore and men didn't wear hats. It fit her mood to a tee.

"My dad's having an affair with Mrs. Bupke, isn't he, Annie Lee?" Megan asked as she allowed herself to be nested. Annie Lee felt her face burn with embarrassment at the way adults behaved and kept tucking the blankets in so tight that Megan looked like a mummy.

"It looks that way," she said, unwilling to lie to someone who could sense what was in front of her anyway. "But it happens to couples a lot; it's something lots of couples have to deal with at some point in their lives. It doesn't necessarily mean the end of everything, especially for a family like yours. I don't know the details—don't want to know them. But probably the best thing you could do is not jump to conclusions too quickly. Be nice to your mom."

"Maybe Dad will go to Chicago by himself for a while. Leave us here. Then come back when he's figured it out." Megan sounded sad. "I just can't figure out why he'd do this to my mom." Annie Lee didn't know how to answer. Megan was already making practical plans. "Well, if everything goes crazy and stuff—can I stay with you for a while? I mean if it's okay with Lucas, and you two work your own problems out?"

Annie Lee stopped fussing. "What do you know about our problems?"

"Well, nothing. I mean I heard Mom tell Mrs. Bupke that you were *barren* . . ."

Annie Lee felt the word in her face like a desert sandstorm. "How would *she* know *that*?"

"That's what Mrs. Bupke wanted to know. Mom said Dad told her he saw you looking at pregnancy stuff at the pharmacy a couple of times, and one time you bought something—I can't remember what he called it. That was a while ago, so he figured you'd been trying to have kids all this time. Mom told him he'd been nosy, and what was he doing spying on people? But then there *she* was, telling Mrs. Bupke. I didn't think it took a long time to get pregnant."

"Or that anybody really cared. But what do we know?" Annie Lee had tried to be as discreet as possible. When she'd bought the ovulation testing kit at the pharmacy, she'd scanned the cash register area to make sure no one was watching. She had asked herself at the time who the pharmacist might tell—which friends they might have in common. It had seemed safe enough. Jim Doyle must have been lurking in combs and brushes next to the convex mirror. She sighed.

"Anyway, everybody has problems," she said. "And everything is relative. I mean, just when you think you've got one big problem, a bigger one comes along."

"Is that supposed to make me feel better? Geez, Annie Lee, I'm just a kid . . ." Megan shook her head. "So could I stay with you if I needed to?"

Annie Lee looked at the girl, whose heart-shaped face and

bitten-down fingernails reminded her so much of herself at that age. At thirteen, Annie Lee had been infatuated with a strawberry-blond boy with freckles all over his face. Kenny Flakstrom. She had started painting with oils in her mother's studio, desperately needing to do something, anything, with her hands while she thought of him twenty-four hours a day.

And though she believed her life would end when Kenny went off to boarding school in seventh grade, it hadn't. She had continued painting Kenny's world. An old plaid shirt he'd given her. His red five-speed bike, still leaning up against the side of his house. After working him out of her system, canvas after canvas, she had kept right on painting, everything she could, things in front of her, things from pictures, things floating in her mind.

Her mother said nothing but supplied as much paint as her daughter needed and as much canvas or board. Although Annie Lee chose not to study painting in high school or college because it had seemed ill-fated to take such a private activity into a classroom, she continued to paint in spare moments and back at home on breaks.

During her early years in Pike, inspired by her job in the deli section of the grocery store, she had started painting from slides of construction workers eating sandwiches and chips and drinking Cokes. She was getting somewhere, doing work that felt honest and interesting. Then her mother announced the divorce, out of the blue. The suddenness of it, the breath-snatching surprise, knocked the wind out of Annie Lee and stilled her hands.

How can I paint the blond guy on a girder eating roast beef, she thought, while my father, a member of the same race of roast-beef eaters, cheated on my mother? In fact, she was incapable of painting at all from that moment on. She found herself completely uninspired, even after she'd met Lucas and felt her idle hands itching as they had with Kenny Flakstrom. By then not painting had become a habit. It would have taken too much to pick up an artist's brush and a tube of red, and then try to figure out where she was in relationship to everything in her life—how the loss of a father truly affected her in spite of the acquisition of a mate. What would her subjects be? She had no idea.

Lucas had always known she'd painted through ten years of her life, had been given most of the details by his mother-in-law, who considered it unhealthy for her daughter to have abandoned her gift in this manner. Annie Lee secretly knew Lucas had told Isabelle that he didn't think his wife should be pushed to do anything, that in time she would come back to it. And in the meantime he put her in charge of painting walls.

"It's a brush," she'd actually overheard him tell his mother-in-law, not long after Annie Lee had started painting rooms. "And it's pigment. Believe me, it's a start."

That's what trauma could do to a life. It could suspend one's best instincts, shove them down deep and bury them, for who knew how long. Annie Lee hoped Megan wouldn't give up her quilting because of all of this. She would do what she could to offer support.

"Yes," she kissed her young friend on the cheek. "You are welcome to stay with us if you need to."

Megan closed her eyes at last, and as Annie Lee trudged up the stairs to her own bed, she thought about Lucas next door. Would he make the sisters breakfast? And what about pajamas, had he brought them? Somehow this question seemed of utmost importance now. At home, he never wore pajamas, he was strictly a nothing-at-all man. If he'd opted to bring pajamas, that would mean he considered his night away from home a sleepover, nothing more. He'd return to nothing at all when he got to his real home. If, on the other hand, he didn't take the time to grab his pajamas, that would mean he'd started treating other places like home, that he was ready, at a moment's notice, to sleep elsewhere. To be himself and not just a visitor someplace else.

With trepidation, Annie Lee pulled open the drawer that held Lucas's tee shirts and his only pair of pajamas. There they were, yellow pajamas with little light blue diamonds. Just the sight of them gripped her so fiercely, she crawled into bed clutching herself.

Fifteen

The next morning it was snowing wet flakes the size of quarters. Four inches had accumulated by the time Annie Lee raised her aching head. Cigarette smells rose from her pile of clothes on the floor. And while a hangover sneaked up on her from one direction, from the other came a great longing for bacon and eggs and strong coffee so hot it burned to drink it.

Rummaging for one of Lucas's sweatshirts, she finally snatched a hooded one of heather gray he'd had since high school, and then made her way to the bathroom, where her initial impulse was to lean over the toilet, something she hadn't done since that infamous green-card party. Staring at the cracks in the porcelain as her head neared the rim, she thought of angles and facets and with that she yanked her head up with a jerk.

"Ohh," she said aloud, half clutching at her throat as if to keep all contents down. What was to say a big regurgitated diamond wouldn't go the way of lost earring posts and pinkie rings, mysteriously rolling down the drain never to be seen again? Klink appeared and sat down, staring at Annie Lee.

"He's next door," she said to the cat, who, by the look of his flaccid tail, appeared to be depressed. "Oh, he'll be back," she added. "His set of kitchen knives is here. His Cuisinart, his mixer, and his cookbooks. Would he leave those? Never. Whatever else happens, he'll be back for his kitchen things."

During the last fifteen hours, and under a mantle of conclusions already made during her week alone, Annie Lee had decided that it was her fault that Lucas had cheated on her. That there was no question but that he had, and that she had been the one driving him to do things he might otherwise not have done. She had, in creating her own vortex, as he'd called it, alienated him, been unfaithful in her own way. On top of everything, she had emasculated him by withdrawing from sex. The combination of her self-indulgent vortex, aloofness, and frigidity had sent him—surprise! as Con would say—headlong over the edge.

She wondered, now, if deep down she had not meant to put him to the test, and even worse, had not set him up to fail it. Desperate for coffee, she tiptoed down toward the kitchen, passing Megan in the living room before being stopped in her tracks by the sound of the phone biting into the silence like a fire alarm. She ran back up the stairs to grab it in the den and was greeted by her mother. Again.

"Mom!? What are you doing calling me this early?" Her breathing was labored, her heart sent crazy beats into every part of her. "What—is—going—on?"

"It's not that early, " said her mother. "Besides, I thought it was your day to make breakfast for your friends. Sunday. So you'd all be up anyway."

"We did that yesterday. Or I should say Lucas did it. Crumpets for the sisters. Is this a state of emergency or something?"

"It's important enough," Isabelle said, then paused. "Doesn't

Lucas usually answer the phone?" Worry in her voice translated for Annie Lee into an irritating strain of nosiness.

"It's not a rule we live by, Mom. Sometimes we deviate just a teeny bit from the usual patterns. Believe it or not." She looked at her watch: 8:30. It really wasn't that early, especially back East. Her mother wasn't prone to early phone calls since she worked late these days, disappeared right around dinner time to work in her studio—an old garden shed that Annie Lee's father had converted, added skylights to, and furnished with flea-market furniture, water closet, and a hot plate for the tea kettle. In the studio, Isabelle had dabbled as a spoiled young wife, done sketches and studies as an art student and mother of three, and become quite accomplished as a divorcée.

Now, Isabelle's soul, as well as her body, lived in that studio. In recent years success had required that she spend many daily hours there, working at her odd and singular art form—a combination of collage and paint, and family history gleaned from whatever sources she could fathom and then turned over like black dirt, rich with life and with surprises. Stories, letters, photos, genealogy, history, imagination. Her ancestral portraits, as she called them, were not so much standard portraits as interpretations of the time, the family, the person. Quirky individuals, some collectors even, paid Isabelle Lemarr large sums to see their past come alive through her eyes. What had begun as a sideline ended up a lucrative métier.

Consequently, Isabelle, once a traditional mother and now an eccentric, postmarriage artist, left a trail of confused daughters in her substantial wake. Both of Annie Lee's sisters were divorced. It was by virtue of Annie Lee's own faithful husband, her charming home, and her relatively stable lifestyle that she became a sort of default moral showpiece, the last of a dying breed. Ironically, Isabelle's misguided way of maintaining her belief in the integrity of her daughter's marriage was to take Lucas's side in every argument—as if fearful that the natural course of anything having to do with two people was, *enfin*, a state of disaccord.

Though Annie Lee could understand the behavior, she didn't necessarily relish the idea of her mother's involvement, especially at this juncture.

"What's going on that you have to call me at work—which you've never done in all these years, by the way—then at the crack of dawn?"

"I called you at work to tell you about that color. Which, of anyone on earth, I thought you could comprehend. I called you this morning to find out what's going on in your life. With your husband."

"My husband," she said, unable to withstand the temptation of turning Isabelle's image of the hero-husband into something more realistic, "is following the designated pattern. He's attached to his mother by his umbilical cord—"

"Meaning?"

Her mother's snorting rather than speaking the word caused Annie Lee's shoulders to tense. "Meaning I didn't go to Seattle this year, and Lucas did, and he spent time with his mother by himself."

"You didn't go . . ."

"I didn't go. We needed time apart—or so we thought. Evidently, the last thing on earth *I* needed was to be out of his sight and out of his mind." She may have driven him to his deeds, but Isabelle didn't need to know that. And besides, he was still a traitor.

Isabelle began banging dishes around, removing them from the dishwasher from the sound of it. Making noise. "You've never needed time alone before," she said.

Annie Lee did not like the way her mother was pegging her. Isabelle took liberties with dead people—changed a nose here, a hair part there—reinterpreting them to make them into art. Maybe she took liberties with the living as well—maybe she gave them qualities they didn't necessarily have or even deserve to have. Qualities she felt they needed in order to measure up in the personality area.

"Well, we needed time alone this time, Mom. The infertility thing has been making me nuts—I haven't been able to get it out of my head. It was getting to the point that I didn't want to have sex anymore because it set me up for failure. There was a lot of tension." She sighed, hoping that using the word "sex" to Isabelle the artist—a person she could actually say the word "sex" to—would cause her mother to sympathize with her daughter's selfishness, or at least see the logic in the situation. Not so. It was not the artist but her mother who answered.

"What have you gone and done, Annie Lee?" Her tone was somewhere between shrill and supplicating. "Have you alienated him completely? To the point of driving him away?"

Annie Lee finally had her hands on the coffee beans now. "As a matter of fact, I probably did. As much as I hate the way you made that assumption without getting to the root of the matter. But the thing is, it appears he had an affair in his time away." It felt good to say this to her mother, to tip the scales with a *whomp* in the other direction. She put her nose inside the coffee canister, hoping for a good whiff of the oily beans.

"How do you know that?" her mother sounded defeated now, as if regardless of her coddling of Lucas, and her belief in her daughter's marriage if not her own, the inevitable would, inevitably, happen.

"A woman knows," is what Annie Lee recalled her mother saying to her when she had made up her mind to divorce her father. Her lips were pressed together in a thin line, her pride refusing to be wounded as she stood there in a paint shirt, looking at the half-eaten apple she'd just finished painting. "A woman just knows." What had Isabelle's Polaroid picture been? Catching Annie Lee's father in a lie? Lipstick on his collar? A comment made about the faded-hyacinth color of a dress?

"How do I *know?*" Annie Lee's tone was slightly patronizing. "Margaret took a Polaroid of this woman, Cindy Sherman, and Lucas together. They'd been high school sweethearts; well, he'd lost his virginity to her, at least. Margaret, believe it or not, recognized her in the supermarket and invited her over for dinner—evidently in a tribute to the olden days, when Dr. Fleck was alive and everything was different."

"So," Isabelle interjected, "they got their picture taken. Maybe—" she interrupted herself. "Maybe Margaret wanted to make you jealous—she wanted you to be grateful to have Lucas at all."

"No, that's way too convoluted. You might do that, but not Margaret. I'm sure she didn't really care that I wasn't there. Her most personal comment about the two of us was that we should reconsider in vitro if we were serious about children. But in essence I think she may view us as a failing couple, a weak link in the chain of life. Survival is for the fittest. Why not usher the matter along, given such an inferior example of coupling as ourselves?"

"You cannot be serious. You're making her sound like a monster!" Though Isabelle's tone was chiding, Annie Lee could tell she wanted more. The two mothers had never actually met, so Isabelle's knowledge of Margaret was solely based on what she'd eked out of her son-in-law weighed against the heavy-handed commentaries of her daughter.

"You're right," Annie Lee said, thinking of Margaret Fleck in a white lab coat, live wires in her hands. "In a way, I think I see Margaret as a representative of the force of entropy. Allowing things to erode, disintegrate, to hustle them on to their final destination . . ."

At that point, just as Annie Lee was about to push down on the button of the coffee grinder, there was a knock on the door so loud it sounded like the sisters with their jar of jam again. Megan jerked up from the couch with a little scream;

and Annie Lee marched toward the door, phone in hand, only to find two local deputies standing on the porch.

"Ma, I got the police at my door, I gotta go."

"Police? What's going on? Isn't Lucas there?"

"Lucas didn't come home last night—another bad sign. He spent the night at the sisters'. As for the police, well, this is the part of the story I hadn't gotten around to. You see, I swallowed a diamond that belonged to this customer at the restaurant. Now it's in my stomach. I gotta go—I'll call you." She disconnected her mother.

Through the door's window, she waved to the duo outside, whose uniforms were consummated by air-force blue baseball caps emblazoned with the town logo. Then she saw Lucas standing behind them, staring at her with so many questions she could feel them pelting her like corks from a popgun.

"Good morning," she said, opening the door and letting all three of them in as if it were the most natural thing in the world. When she saw the sisters bringing up the rear on the steps, however, it seemed to her that every plot line in her life was intersecting at this time, at this house—not squarely in the middle or orderly up top like a tepee, but like a pile of pick-up sticks, each one, when pressed in a certain spot, affecting the lay of them all.

Sixteen

They all filed in, the sisters coming through the doorway last, with muffins and a Thermos pitcher of coffee. "Lucas made the muffins," Bea said, not without her customary reverence. "He used vanilla bean—actually went to the store to get one!"

A good sign, Annie Lee thought, he was trying to impress someone. And it worked: they smelled heavenly—somewhere between butter and warm sun and custard. Annie Lee took the basket and motioned for the local law enforcement to sit around the table. She put on water for more coffee. Megan had made herself upright and was rubbing her eyes as if unable to believe them. Annie Lee fully expected the Doyle parents to show up any minute.

"You saw the crib?" Eudora said squarely to Annie Lee, ignoring the police. "And the pictures?"

"Uh-huh." Annie Lee, who was used to the sisters' interrogations, didn't necessarily have to see the point in order to answer obediently. But she did hope Lucas hadn't somehow pitted Eudora, whom she considered her regular ally, against her.

"Megan told me about the crib, I glanced at the pictures. Not that I understand anything."

She couldn't look at Lucas. Officers Hurley and Gerecke were quiet, probably in deference to the sisters.

"I'm not sure what the point is about the pictures." She looked at Lucas briefly.

"It's about the house, Annie Lee," he replied, his tone verging on enthusiasm. "It has—physical powers."

"Uh-huh," she said again, as each of the cops nearly lunged for a muffin. Annie Lee still needed bacon and suggested to the group they have bacon and eggs as well. Lucas looked at her as if she'd said she wanted fried alligator and then inquired if she were hungover, since that was practically the only time she showed any interest in crispy slabs of pork fat first thing in the morning.

And what did his astonishment mean? First, that he hadn't realized she'd been out last night until he'd gotten home, hadn't seen her at the Hole. Second, that the idea of a hangover was problematic to him, that he might be wondering what she'd done while drunk off her derrière. Very good.

"Real bacon?" Fen Hurley stood about six feet four and had the look of someone who took in calories every ten minutes. The collar on his blue deputy's shirt was too tight—so tight Annie Lee wanted to wedge her fingers inside and release him.

"I could eat something," Nadine Gerecke chipped in. "We've been up since the incident, you know." She was staring at Annie Lee's tattered sweatshirt and violet-flowered pajama bottoms. "Geez, Annie Lee. I haven't stayed in my pajamas in front of company since I was seven years old. Should we give you a few minutes to make yourself presentable?"

Annie Lee looked at the cop, all buttons, belts, and brass and raised one eyebrow. "You walked in on *my* morning Nadine," she said. "And *my* morning looked like this."

"What incident would that be?" Lucas's tone was casual, but

his animated organization of breakfast materials belied it. Meanwhile, the sisters settled themselves—permanently, from the looks of it—at the table where Annie Lee had placed mugs and cream and sugar. Megan had shyly joined them at the table and had indicated to Lucas that hot chocolate would be better than she could have hoped for.

"The incident whereby one Elizabeth Wolverton of New York City reported the loss of a four-carat diamond that she claims was stolen from her person at the Hole in the Wall bar at approximately 12:45 this A.M." Nadine had flipped open a long, skinny pad that had the words "Reporter's Notebook" on the cover.

Lucas held an egg in suspended animation before cracking it into a bowl. "What does that have to do with Annie Lee?"

Annie Lee deferred to the authorities, and Fen continued. "The woman reportedly had just recovered her diamond from Restaurant Mathilde, where an employee, Annie Lee Fleck, allegedly found it after vacuuming it up."

Lucas was looking at Annie Lee, who stared at his bowl of eggs before speaking. "The woman was probably at Giancarlo, too, earlier in the week," she said by way of an explanation. "A real piece of work, believe me."

"So," Lucas said, cracking two eggs at a time. "Annie Lee vacuumed it up. Then what?"

"Well, that's where it gets fuzzy." The bacon in the pan had started to sizzle, and Fen Hurley began talking as if word count would pay for his breakfast. "We have reports that Annie Lee was seen near the woman in the bar at approximately the time of the incident. When the diamond disappeared from the bottom of a martini glass—"

"A martini glass? What was it doing there?" Eudora's tone was so full of fierce mockery, the implication being that only an idiot would do such a thing.

"The alleged victim has stated it was there for safekeeping." Nadine Gerecke was all business.

"In a glass in a crowded bar full of drunken people?" Bea wasn't buying it, either.

"And," Officer Gerecke added, "she said she felt the vodka would clean it better than soap and water."

Eudora, who had started repositioning everything on the table so that nothing was askew in any way, stopped short. "Ridiculous," she said. "And asinine."

"It has been noted by one Steven Titus," Fen Hurley continued, looking down at Nadine's notes, "that Annie Lee was allegedly seen drinking from an analogous glass right around the time the incident took place."

Annie Lee didn't think anyone had been paying attention to her. "So I was drinking from a martini glass, big deal." She thought of Gabriel Salt, remembering his advice that the diamond would have to go back to its owner but perhaps not before she had gotten some use out of it. "Hey, maybe we should fetch her, the woman, get to the bottom of things right now. And Stevie T., too, that worthless piece of shit—excuse me Bea and Eudora."

Breakfast was served, and Annie Lee noted with satisfaction that Lucas heaped enough scrambled eggs onto Fen Hurley's plate to get even his attention. Four pieces of bacon, too.

Nadine Gerecke ate with blue-collar manners. "You wouldn't want Stevie T. here, be honest," she said, blowing on her coffee, something Annie Lee could only remember having seen on *Bonanza*. "He's a dope." Nadine slurped. "A source of dope, in addition, but a dope himself. Off the record, of course." She grinned at her wordplay. "And mean, too. Ms. Wolverton, though, we for sure could get her in here. She's basically on call. Will do whatever it takes to recover the goods."

"Especially if she found out I have the goods," Annie Lee

interjected, freeze-framing the group in different stages of food ingestion.

"You have it?" Lucas could not contain his surprise.

This pleased Annie Lee. "In my possession," she said and then felt her face twist ever so slightly as she considered a more truthful phrasing. "In my *person*."

Officer Gerecke took the squad car, slowly pulling out of the driveway with both siren and flashers going.

"Well," Fen Hurley said, only after finishing his last bite of toast, heaped with as much jam as an entire slice of bread might otherwise have, "where is it?"

"We'll talk when she gets here," Annie Lee declared, and in preparation for the arrival of a complete stranger, excused herself and headed upstairs to make herself presentable. Nadine was right, after all: She ought to dress the part. She came back down in old black jeans, Redwing boots and a very tight and tubelike tee shirt of margarine yellow. The carefully selected garb made her appear several inches taller, ten pounds lighter, and ready for anything. She felt like a bumblebee; and with confidence and courage up, she was able to ask Lucas, in a private moment, if he'd even seen the east wall of the bedroom.

"I saw it," he said quietly. He seemed on the verge of saying more but was interrupted by sounds at the front door, first a knocking, followed immediately by the door's opening.

When Nadine Gerecke entered the premises with the victim, everyone stopped and pretended, somewhat futilely, not to stare. The woman was dressed in white stretch pants, furry white boots, and a white cowboy hat. Annie Lee then noted Jim and Judy had come up the steps, too, and waved them in with a gesture that said, "You might as well come in, everyone else is here."

Judy looked a little better and Jim a little worse for wear. Annie Lee couldn't help feeling sorry for the man, given the sheer silliness of Sheila Bupke, even as she told herself that the worst thing to feel at this point in time was pity for an adulterer. Megan gave her a pleading look then, a look that said, "Don't say anything," to which Annie Lee shook her head "I won't" in agreement.

Fen Hurley began by taking Libby Wolverton's hat and introducing her to everyone as if he were recapping a game of Clue. Jim Doyle, Realtor, next-door neighbor, father to Megan, found in the bar with the bimbo. Had Fen actually uttered that last? Surely it was Annie Lee's imagination. But when she glanced at the sisters, they were, in fact, giving Jim the beady-eyed glare. Oh-oh. How could they possibly know?

"Ms. Wolverton is from New York," Fen Hurley continued. "She claims to be in the middle of a divorce and in need of time away from her husband, a prominent Park Avenue psychiatrist."

"Elias Wolverton," the woman said with a measure of sarcasm. It was obvious her irritation was extensive. "Of the Long Island Wolvertons. The man who thinks he owns the diamond in question."

Fen continued on. "She claims to have had an upsetting phone conversation with aforesaid husband just prior to the incident—"

"One of many," the woman inserted crossly. "It's not like this was an isolated phone call or anything. But it was just as irritating as the rest of them. You might even say things were escalating."

Eudora, who had finally stopped scrutinizing the woman's attire, was focusing on her face now, something nipped, tucked, and plucked, and then outlined in I-Go-to-Auctions-in-My-Spare-Time Brown—not generally considered a morning color in Pike. "What was upsetting you?" Eudora gave her that piercing, pea-eyed look that required an answer. "What's this all about?"

Libby Wolverton wavered for a moment before answering.

"About assets, Mrs. Winkleman. Possessions. What it all boils down to in the end."

"Ms.," Eudora corrected her. "Go on."

"Well, it all boils down to dividing things up, doesn't it, as thousands of couples do every day. You know, he gets the apartment on East End Avenue, I get the house in the Hamptons. That sort of thing." She paused and quickly glanced around. No one said anything. They all waited.

"The spoils of war, I suppose," she continued. "Of course Elias gets the new green Jaguar. I get the old black one. He gets the Louis XVI salon furniture, I get the pre-Columbian doodads. He gets the time-share on St. Thomas, I get Hilton Head. I hate St. Thomas anyway. I think he really wanted Hilton Head. Nabberly wore him down on that one."

"Any children?" Bea and Eudora asked simultaneously.

"Two by his first marriage: he gets those. I get the Afghan hounds, which he said he'd always found outdated, like shag carpet. Nabberly told him to keep the personal comments to a minimum." She straightened up a bit and then, through the haze of her own private peevishness, added, "Nabberly's my lawyer." Then, "Is that bacon I smell?" Lucas pointed to the leftover slices on the table in a gesture of offering, and she reached for one, using her long, white-tipped fingernails like pincers. She took a bite.

"That's a personal comment?" Eudora asked the question for everyone.

"For a psychiatrist, believe me, yes!" She took another bite and looked around, scanning briefly for the first time, and then refocused on herself. "He implied I was outdated to begin with. That the whole relationship, because of me, was archaic. Oh, Elias knew full well Nabberly was right,"

"What's *his* lawyer like?" Even Nadine Gerecke was getting sucked in. Though the Doyles were silent, they too were engrossed.

"A woman. Thin, well dressed, and cunning. An ex-patient, of course. Julia Fraye-Cryer." She looked at the group and found them all attentive. "Who seems to think Elias has a legal right to all the art—get this—in both houses." She looked down at her fingernails and then, hardly aware of her audience, continued on. "Even the pieces that I'd collected during my first marriage! My Calder sketch. My Lichtenstein, which Elias always hated in the stairwell. My precious Francis Bacon charcoal." A small sigh escaped her lips.

"And what about the personal pieces I bought from artists I knew would pan out, people he'd never even heard of. My Sierra Woo? My Chuck Rainier? My beloved Isabelle Lemarr? Why should he even care about those?"

Annie Lee, sipping her coffee, began to choke when she heard the name of her mother. It was Lucas who spoke for her as she tried to recover, eyes watering, napkin over her nose. "Did you say Isabelle Lemarr? The portraitist?"

"Yes," Libby Wolverton had taken off her waist-length ski coat, revealing a white cashmere sweater and a necklace watch studded with enough diamonds to make it hard to tell time. "Isabelle Lemarr, one of her earlier ones. Of my mother surrounded by her six Siamese cats. Now, is that not pathetic of Elias? To try and swindle me out of something so personal, so—" her voice cracked. "Well, so precious to me!" She reached around to the back of her head to readjust her small ponytail, something she'd cleverly managed to make of all that big hair.

"What's the portrait worth now?" Eudora asked, visibly stimulated by the turn of the conversation. Of course, she knew Isabelle Lemarr was Annie Lee's mother.

Libby Wolverton paused. "Not that much compared to the other pieces. Probably about thirty. Maybe more."

"Thirty thousand?" Annie Lee gasped. Her mother never talked money.

"Possibly more, it is a collector's item at this point. Although, again, I have to ask you, who would want a portrait of my mother besides me? Elias, that's who—and just to show me who's who. Who pulls the strings of power. Who dominates over his mother-in-law." She looked at Annie Lee, and then at the sisters. "Why are you so interested in the portrait?"

"Because," Annie Lee interjected, unable to restrain herself any longer, "Isabelle Lemarr is my mother!"

"Isabelle Lemarr—" What was left of Libby's brows went up, archly. "Is your mother?"

"Yes," Annie Lee maintained, nodding, "my mother. Isabelle Lemarr. You know, 'Just because they're dead doesn't mean they're gone. Specializing in the resurrection of detail.'" She looked to the cops and the Doyles. "That's what her business card says. I spoke to her just this morning as a matter of fact." She looked back at Libby. "Obviously you've met."

Libby said she'd gone to the studio in Piermont—that Isabelle required that her clients seek her out. "Absolutely stunning studio. All that light, and color, and all those vines! Like a dream cottage. I could sell that in an afternoon."

Annie Lee thought of the morning glories climbing up the Dutch door of the studio, and the image saddened her. She hadn't been home in five years, wanted no reminders of happier family times or of painting. When they went back East, they stayed with Uncle Louis, her mother's brother, in his apartment in the city. "Were there paintings everywhere?" She tried not to sound morose.

"There were paintings on stretched canvases lined up along the walls; and there were canvases rolled up in long cubbies; and there were paintings hung on the walls. Not hers, she said, her daughter's . . ." She looked at Annie Lee slowly as if the connection were too improbable to be made. "Yours . . ."

Annie Lee frowned. "Mine," she said.

In the momentary silence, Fen picked up the announcer's role. "This is extremely coincidental, people, even for Pike."

Bea glared at him. "Of course it's not coincidental. There is no such thing as coincidence, young man. None at all. It is a gross falsification of life to see it in such terms. Is there order in nature? Order in time? Why should circumstances be any different—completely chaotic, haphazard, nonsensical, why?

"Mysterious forces draw people and their stories together so that, like quilts with holes," she looked at Megan and smiled, "they can be sewn up into something that makes sense. Crazy sense, sometimes; painful, other times." Annie Lee had to wonder why the sisters were staring unequivocally at her with such intensity. She looked at them and shrugged, trying to think of something smart.

Eudora took center stage. "Perhaps we should try to explain, just as we tried to explain to Lucas earlier, *about this house*. Ms. Wolverton, bear with us, please. We'll be briefer than we might otherwise." She crossed her hands on the table. "This house is a magnet house. By virtue of the original owner's obsession with magnetism, it is insulated to the two-foot level with lodestone, or magnetite. Lodestone is a naturally occurring magnetic ore that the man had shipped in," she turned to Annie Lee, "from all over the place, Lord knows how—"

"He firmly believed," Bea continued on, "that magnetism held untold powers. Over the years, we've witnessed certain things, irrefutable things having to do not only with the physical but the metaphysical. Why do you think we are all sitting here today, weaving these stories together as we are?"

The group said nothing, not even Libby Wolverton, who'd somehow managed to find a muffin and a cup of coffee for herself and, much to the surprise of everyone, had undone the top snap of her ski pants. She appeared to be thinking.

"Or, if you prefer," suggested Eudora, "look at the houseplants in this room. Ever seen anything like it? Ask Lucas and Annie Lee when the last time was they were sick, either of 'em. Ask 'em why they had to move the VCR around so many times before it worked! Ask Megan why she likes it so much here. Why the cat's so big." She laughed. "Lord, we thought they'd have figured it out by now!" She sniffed. "And if you need to see to believe," she concluded, rising slowly as if tired of dealing with idiots and nonbelievers all day long, "watch this."

She reached for a cast-iron pan from the hanging rack and walked over to the closest wall. Holding it against the wall right below knee level, she released it. And there it stuck. To the wall. She smiled and then crimped the smile into something crooked and very fetching. "I haven't done that in years," she said staring at the pan. "It still feels good."

Annie Lee sucked in her breath. Megan laughed, as did Judy Doyle.

Lucas smiled, then dropped his head. "Look at this picture again." He spoke in an undertone to Annie Lee while reaching for the photo of Orna, standing all alone outside the house. "Check out the tools."

Annie Lee took the small, square black-and-white photo from him and scanned it. She had not noticed it before, but dozens of yard tools and utilitarian implements were stuck to the house. Without hooks or nails, just—stuck. She stared at the picture and then went over to the pan stuck on her wall. It took a good deal of strength to pry it off, but finally she did so, staring at the bottom of the pan as if someone had sprayed it with glue.

Libby Wolverton picked up a fork and placed it gently on the wall, where it stuck, just like the pan.

"Why didn't we see this before?" Annie Lee said, as she began to collect metal objects and place them around the periphery of the first floor.

Nadine Gerecke was either unimpressed or tired or both. She took the floor. "Let's move on to the diamond, now, if y'all don't mind, before we lose sight of the matter. Annie Lee here has indicated that she is indeed in possession. Isn't that correct?"

Annie Lee, still preoccupied with metal objects, said, "Well, yes. That is correct. This is really unbelievable—" She had fetched her box of pins and, emptying them into her hand, tossed them all at the wall. Only one hit the floor. "I can't believe we didn't *notice things* . . ."

Bea was about to slap an answer on Annie Lee, but Nadine got to her first, and, taking her by the shoulders, was redirecting her. "Can you please show Ms. Wolverton her rock—I mean gemstone—so as to ease her mind, and mine, about the matter? We'll talk magnets later."

"I can't do that," Annie Lee said, feeling at that moment that it might be her time of the morning to use the bathroom and wondering how she should put it, what she should say. The entire group, highly expectant of resolution, especially in the face of the new magnet-theory of plots and subplots, looked at her.

"Why not, Annie Lee?" Lucas asked. "Do you have it, or not?"

"Because," she said, heading toward the powder room, "I swallowed it last night." In response to the gasps she heard at the table she added, "By accident."

Seventeen

Libby Wolverton stared at the wake of air left by Annie Lee. "Elias," she finally uttered, "is going to have a nervous breakdown." Thinking about her words and the image they'd conjured, her lips spread into a wide grin while they all watched and waited.

Finally, Eudora blurted out, "For the love of Pete, don't flush, child!"

Megan started giggling then, and crossed the room to her pile of quilting pieces to try to disguise the fact that her chortling was about to become uncontrollable. Libby Wolverton was looking to the cops now for appropriate action, but they obviously didn't have a clue.

Annie Lee was tucking in her tee shirt as she reappeared. "I stuck the Glade to the wall, down low," she said to the group as they stared at her. "What??"

"Well, Annie Lee . . ." Fen Hurley lowered his voice to point out the obvious. "What if—well what if her diamond went down the proverbial drain?"

"Oh." Annie Lee shook her head. "It's unlikely that something I swallowed last night would reemerge this morning." Having captured the complete attention of everyone in the room at last, including Libby Wolverton, Annie Lee turned to her. "I need to be straight with you now, Ms. Wolverton. I saw that diamond in the glass and went crazy inside. I switched glasses, put the diamond in my mouth, and replaced the glass—and then a friend came up from behind—Val," she said to Lucas, "—surprising me, and I felt myself start to choke. And swallowed. Believe me, I, too, was too drunk for my own good. I didn't even mean to be drunk, either—it was just the end of a really long, strange night, and I was mad, among other things, about the way you snatched the diamond out of my hand at the restaurant. You snatched so much more than just a dumb rock."

She felt her voice crack and cleared her throat. "I was in the middle of a revelation . . . and you . . . well, you know you were a bit of a bitch at dinner, not to mince any words here. I mean we're all—*all of us*—going through something in life, believe it or not. You can't just go around being *nasty*." She reached deep inside for a breath and exhaled. "Why are you getting divorced anyway?" She must have picked up the Winkleman cross-examination tactic—rapid-fire blunt questions—and it worked.

Libby Wolverton began fiddling with a bracelet of gold and silver links, and then stood up. "My husband has always cheated on me," she said flatly. "He was the kind of man you knew would cheat on you even as you married him."

"Well, why *did* you marry him, then?" Bea's sweatshirt today, the kind of avocado color only a matched appliance could love, had a cream-colored turtle standing on a box in which were placed the words "Slow and steady wins the race." Annie Lee, noting a theme for the week, felt a pang of worry that Bea was starting to feel her age more sharply.

"Oh." Libby Wolverton looked off into the distance. "He

could be very witty. Charming. He has exquisite taste right down to the label on his pajamas. He pursued me, called my company relentlessly—I own a real estate business—and had me show him apartments here and there, and he'd talk about what he'd do with them. Clever psychiatrist, he knew just what would get me. It was in showing him one of my listings, a beautiful brownstone on East End Avenue—that same one we're fighting over—that he proposed. I found it impossible to say no. Isn't that how love is? People become irresistible, and then you really can't resist."

"So what happened?" Fen Hurley had found the sage chicken from the fridge and some chopsticks and had Klink on his wide lap. Lucas was studying the man's dexterity with utensils.

"In the same way he seduced, he began tearing things apart." She cocked her head now. "Why on earth am I telling you this?"

"A psycho," Eudora uttered, as if having had quite enough of them herself already, thank you. "Because you're in the magnet house, dear. Go on."

"A shrink," Libby Wolverton corrected. "And utterly charmed by the deviancies of the human personality, including his own." She paused. "I used to vacation alone. Loved it, the freedom of it. But this trip has been nothing if not excruciating. I told him I wanted a divorce the day before I left, and he's been calling me up every day at 6:30 New York time, right before he leaves the office, to hash out the minutiae. I've spent half my time on the phone. The rest of the time I've spent eating and drinking, which is why my pants feel so *tight*." Again, she worked the positively miniscule waistline of her ski pants.

"Well," Fen assured her, "you look great—eating and drinking agree with you. And believe me, I'm an expert on that particular subject."

In spite of herself, she smiled—and when she did, her whole demeanor changed. Annie Lee couldn't help wanting to feed her, fatten her cheeks. Give her a flannel shirt and some cotton sweats and get her started on the healing process.

"So. Ms. W. . . . Can we, excuse me, get back to who gets the diamond?" Nadine Gerecke was needling again.

"We hadn't come to that yet in our *dialogue*. It was part of my engagement ring. Which I've never really taken off, or cleaned, or been careful with. It's a minor miracle that diamond stayed seated as long as it did. Anyway, by use I suppose it's mine."

"And technically," she continued, holding her hands at arms' length and staring at their nakedness, "it was a gift to me, which should also render it mine; but Elias won't see it that way. The whole idea of his having given it to me will drive him nuts, as if part of him will have escaped with me. He's too watchful and retentive for that to sit well. Plus he'll need it for his next victim: There's a consistency factor there."

She looked around at her audience, focusing briefly on Fen (who had the look of a man smitten) before facing the sisters. "What do you two think I should do?" she inquired.

Eudora was still hung up on the stone in the glass: Why had she put it there? Libby replied that Elias had driven her to drink and that her judgment, especially given the altitude, had suffered considerably.

Annie Lee then felt she ought to recap her version of the night, just for balance. She mentioned Sissy Spacek and Mia Farrow and all those shots of ten-per tequila.

Nonsense, the sisters interrupted, couldn't people see past the cheekbones? Lucas acknowledged people sometimes did liken her to the two celebrities, a very noncommittal statement, Annie Lee thought, made for the purpose of sounding noncommittal. She continued on with brief character sketches of the Brazilians and the four orthopedists, the vacuuming, the rock snatching, and the arrival at the bar. "The Hole was the obvious choice," she said, looking at her husband as she watched him become less aloof before her eyes. "And, in fact, I ended up learning a thing or two about men there. Like last time." She wasn't about to protect his feelings at that point and was not beyond making insinuations.

It came as no surprise that the Doyles were itching now to go home. They sensed the story soon might be taking a turn too R-rated for their tastes. Except for Megan's. She had to be cajoled up, her chair physically shuffled, to get her out of it, but the way Jim and Judy did it, with affection and understanding, truly comforted Annie Lee.

"Hey," she heard herself call out as they walked toward the front door. "What about the crib?" As soon as she said it, she regretted it, for as soon as she said it, Judy stopped in her tracks and turned around, two round, red blush dots highlighting her porcelain skin as she looked at Jim and then at the sisters and then finally at Annie Lee. "You should keep the crib, Annie Lee. I wish I could give you some of my luck conceiving to go along with it." She flashed a brief smile at her hostess and then visibly slumped.

"You might as well all know," Judy continued, influenced no doubt by the confessional nature of the proceedings. She turned to her husband. "It's twins this time . . . so it's all going to be different anyway." She put a hand on her just-bulging middle. "Might as well start fresh with everything." She gave another quick glance at Jim. Accumulated heavy snow fell off the roof and landed with a dull thud on the ground, shaking the foundationless floor beneath everyone's feet.

"Twins . . ." said Bea, straightening up her shoulders. "That *is* news."

Megan had already begun jumping up and down, eyes sparkling, every ounce of her a joyful sibling-to-be. "We're having twins! We're having twins!" Everyone else was staring at Jim, waiting for his reaction. Judy had done a kindly thing in mentioning a fresh start, but poor Jim didn't know what to do with the news. He had an unmistakable look of swallowed panic on his face.

While Judy waited for a response from her husband, Nadine provided interim excitement by grabbing Jim's hand and shaking it almost maniacally. "Seven!" she belted out. "Get out! You'll be the only family in Pike with that many kids! That beats a diamond any day of the year. I for one am happy for you." Nadine was looking around for support.

"I am too . . ." Bea spoke so softly she got everyone's attention. "But they're going to need all the help they can get. You let us know if we can be of assistance, Jim. Eudora and I have always fought over taking care of babies—with twins it'd be even-Steven. We'll sure love that." Judy's eyes filled up, and she fought hard not to blink but held out too long. Two big tears rolled quickly down her cheeks and onto a crisp white blouse.

Eudora went over to Jim and looked him in the eye. "And that goes for me, too," she said. "Now. You take that wife of yours on home, James. You fix her a cup of tea with milk and honey and you tell her what's in your heart and you don't come out of the house till y'do. And you'd better thank the Lord for your wife's forgiving nature." *They knew,* Annie Lee thought. Then she looked over at Lucas, who seemed confused. *He must be the only one without a clue.*

Judy glanced over her shoulder with a face and forehead that seemed smoother now, her eyes more relaxed and hopeful. To his credit, Jim put his arm around his wife's shoulders, carefully, without laying claim to her. Possession, he must have gathered, would have to be earned anew.

Libby Wolverton jumped right in once they'd gone. "Well, I'm not sure what that was all about. Anyway," she turned to Annie Lee, "can we get back down to brass tacks? Where were we?"

Lucas was still staring at the front door. "Was Jim Doyle

cheating on *Judy?*" he whispered, as if Judy, of all women, would be impossible to cheat on. Well, it was impossible to find any woman who was impossible to cheat on, *that* seemed to be the going formula. She had until recently considered herself impossible to cheat on. Bea was whispering into Lucas's ear until Eudora told them to stop.

"Everybody knows about Jim and Sheila Bupke," said Nadine, just to clear the air. "Can we get on with this? I mean, my shift is going on nineteen hours—" She stopped, cupped her hand to her ear. "Your phone's ringing upstairs, Annie Lee."

Sure enough, it was. Annie Lee had unplugged it downstairs after the Magpie's late-night call. Lucas, the closest one to the telephone table, picked up the receiver after quickly plugging in the line. Annie Lee had begun to feel at this point in time that the phone was playing an integral, almost autonomous role in her life.

"Yes," Lucas was saying, "this is the Fleck residence . . . Annie Lee is my wife . . . Poison Control?" He looked at Annie Lee and furrowed his brow and then flicked on the speakerphone without further ado.

". . . Gabriel Salt," they all heard. "I spoke to your wife last night. You must be the chef."

The look Lucas gave Annie Lee was worth a thousand stammers. He shrugged. "Yeah," he admitted. "I guess that would be me."

"Well, your wife called here about having ingested a diamond," he began. The group stared at Annie Lee, who whispered quickly that she had become paranoid and needed some oral instruction.

"I feel remiss," he said in his quiet way. "I neglected to mention, and perhaps you could tell her—she's probably exhausted from her ordeal—how many people in history have swallowed things of value in order to hide them. Jewels, of course. The family jewels, so to speak. All manner of silver and gold. And of course drugs, usually wrapped in plastic and then evacuated via purgatives." He paused. "Am I on speakerphone?"

"Hi, Gabriel," Annie Lee said. "Yes. As a matter of fact, we have the woman who owns the diamond here! And the cops who brought her here. And my next-door neighbors as well, the Winklemans."

"Oh my," he said, seemingly put out by the audience. "Well, I didn't want to cause you undue worry, what with the mention of X rays and such. I should let you get back to your people, didn't mean to barge in . . ."

"Oh, no," Annie Lee assured him. "You're not barging. You actually belong here: I mean you were the one who told me I had to give Libby her diamond back."

"He did?" Libby had gotten up to stretch her legs and resnap her ski pants. Fen rose as well, pitting his height against hers. Libby seemed impressed.

"I told her," Gabriel said, "that it would be *bad karma*, so to speak, to keep something acquired in said manner."

"Well," Libby was looking at her fingers now, free of jewelry of any kind. "What if I was *meant* to lose it? What if my own karma sent the stone to the bowels of a vacuum cleaner then on to the bowels of a human? I mean, I have to say I feel sort of unfettered without it. It was an engagement stone, you know, Gilbert."

"Gabriel," Annie Lee corrected her. "What do you mean by what you just said?"

"Well, I don't want Elias to have it. And I don't really want to have it myself, since then it remains a point of negotiation between us. I want neither of us to have it. In fact, I'm beginning to appreciate the fact that the diamond is gone. That I lost it in a bar after recovering it after having lost it at dinner."

"I'm not sure I should be hearing this," Fen said, turning his ham-sized shoulder away.

"No, you knew Annie Lee here had it, which is why you're here," Nadine piped up. "Then Annie Lee went to the bathroom to evacuate her bowels, at which point the trace ended. Deputy Marshal Nadine Gerecke attempted a quick search of the porcelain toilet, an antique, water-wasting model, and turned up nothing. Nada. Zilch. She had her suspicions that the diamond was inadvertently flushed down the drain from the very moment she heard the torrent of water go down."

"So the intestinal evacuation part is true, then," Gabriel practically whispered the words. "And so is the part about the owner not really wanting it—"

"I said I don't really want anyone to have it," Libby reasserted. "I'd like to get on the phone right now and call Nabberly and tell him. But it would sound so—well, flimsy. The thing is it's a perfect solution to my problems. It's a little power play. Little in the great scheme, but still worth, well, $28,000 or so. True, the size would indicate greater value—but it's got plenty of imperfections, certainly to the trained eye. Now, if Elias were to have gone on the two-months'-salary rule—we'd be talking gemstone with a capital G . . .

"Anyway, I didn't really research diamond values until this whole divorce thing, at which point Elias gleefully told me he'd sacrificed quality for size. And at which point, I said, 'Kind of like your lovemaking.' The man was blessed with an organ of considerable magnitude."

Eudora burst out laughing, and managed to explain through her guffaws that she wasn't and never had been a prude, old maid or not. "But," she started laughing even harder, "your way with words tops 'em all, I declare!"

"As I said," Libby continued, pleased to have gotten a laugh, "it's not that big a deal in the assets lists. But it would drive Elias nuts to be told he couldn't have it back. I almost wish you *had* flushed it down that toilet."

"Well," said Annie Lee, "I suppose nothing is impossible. It could certainly have settled, by weight, and taken a speedier course than anyone would have imagined. Or, we could simply say that for the purposes of investigation, the diamond is as good as gone, since no one has any intention of searching for it."

"Okay," said Libby. "I could accept that. Now what do we do?" Annie Lee was only a little surprised by her use of the word "we."

It was Eudora who suggested that Fen be the one to call Elias with the news that the diamond was lost and not likely to be retrieved. Annie Lee said that made her a thief, didn't it, but Libby protested that, no, they could say it had been an accident, free and clear. The glass mix-up, and so forth.

"You can't call him now, though," Annie Lee interjected. "Because with that medical background he'd claim nothing was certain until everything in my intestines had been thoroughly evacuated. How long does that really take, the passage of yesterday's food?"

"Two or three days, I would say," Gabriel said from inside the phone. The rest of them glanced briefly in his general direction, having forgotten he was there.

"So Ms. Wolverton can't go home yet," Fen said, trying to hide his satisfaction. "How do you feel about staying a few extra days?"

She stared, thinking, at Fen's badge, which hit her at about eye level, then spoke. "We could call Elias right now—on speakerphone—and I could tell him something . . . I don't know, *something*. I twisted my ankle and didn't want to fly with the swelling. Or . . . no, I needed a few extra days—to learn snowboarding!

"Yes! He'll have a hard time believing that; and either it will drive him batty that I'd want to do something so out of character, or he'll wonder why I'm lying . . ."

"So, I'll take my leave then," Gabriel's voice seemed to be

getting softer and softer. Annie Lee felt sorry for him; for so big a behind-the-scenes player, he was getting short shrift.

"I'll call you tomorrow, Gabe," she said. "I want to talk to you some more about your cookbook idea." She turned to the group. "He has this great idea, isn't that right?"

"Well . . . yes," his voice brightened. "A cross between the Meyers-Briggs personality test and cooking yourself a meal. But perhaps now's not the time . . ."

Gabriel Salt had barely signed off before Libby was at the phone, punching in a multitude of numbers. "Elias?" she barked out before the man at the other end had a chance even to say hello.

"Elizabeth, you know Sunday morning is my time to read professional literature." Elias cleared his throat with the sound of papers rustling in the background. Annie Lee pictured him in his wing chair with racing forms or the *New York Post*. "It's a matter of import, I take it? Should we conference with Julia?"

"Great import, Elias." Libby rolled her eyes while keeping her voice steady. "I'll be coming home a few days late. I've had such a good time here—in spite of everything—that I've decided to stay and learn to snowboard."

Elias said nothing. "Am I on speakerphone?" he finally asked. "You sound very hollow." Libby hushed the group with a wave of her hand.

"No, nothing like that. I'm at the hotel. It's the sticks, Elias. The phone systems out here are not what we're used to."

"Movie stars and such live there—it can't be that bad. Arthur Tweedel's ex has a place there, a deluxe time-share. That guy from ABC news—what's his name?—has the one next door. Anyway. Snowboarding? Isn't that for kids, Elizabeth?" He sniggered.

"Not according to my instructor, who is in his forties. Said it was more fun than *sex*"—she whispered the word—"once you got the hang of it. Of course I'm in the never-ever group."

"Never-ever group . . . this doesn't sound like you, Libby. Yesterday you were peevish, contrarian, nearly as whiny as that middle-class attorney of yours. Yesterday, I knew you, Lib. Today—"

"Today I'm a shredder, Elias, a knuckle-dragger. What can I say? I doubt you've ever gotten inside the mind of a snowboarder. And I bet that drives you cr-r-razy."

Elias's voice went up a quarter of a notch. "Are you sleeping with the instructor, Libby, because if you are I must say—"

"I have to go Elias," she interrupted him. "I have to be on the hill at 12:30. I'll be home in five days. I've called my office, so there won't be any calls at home for me. Good-bye." When she'd hung up, she actually got a round of applause from the group.

"I'd like to throttle *that* man," Eudora said. "No offense intended, Ms. Wolverton, but is that what your marriage is built on?"

"Well," Libby was rubbing what remained of her brown lipstick off with the napkin. "It does take two to *tangle*, you know." She sighed. "I suppose every woman is vulnerable to a man who listens to her. Deduces. Surmises. Studies her character. Yes, Dr. Freud, I secretly did love my father and all that—now that you know my deepest secrets, can I marry you?" She laughed.

But Annie Lee silently agreed with her statements. Usually men didn't try to figure out women. Not really. Not like the hours women spent trying to figure men out, or at least trying to figure out why it was men didn't understand women. So when it did happen—a man actually trying to comprehend what made a woman tick for more than the singular purpose of getting her into bed—yes, it was intoxicating.

"Yeah, but what if he only *thinks* he knows you?" She looked at Libby, Libby looked at her.

"Exactly," Libby said, pushing up her sleeves. Finally, she

turned all her attention to Annie Lee. "Look," she said, "I'm sorry about last night. The way I barged in, barged out. In those heels that hurt, and which consequently broke on the way to the bar—I bet you didn't know that, that I was operating without a heel. Anyway, the whole trip has been extremely stressful . . .

"However. It turns out you're Isabelle Lemarr's daughter! It's incredible, isn't it? That here I am, trying to hold on to a piece that means a lot to me, and I meet part of the artist's family. And in such a manner . . ." She pointed right at Annie Lee's nose. "I see Mia Farrow more than Sissy Spacek, by the way. But really neither of them. Cleaned up, you'd be a stunner, you know that? Anyway. I'm curious. Say you find the diamond. Recover it. After I've collected the insurance money—"

"Whoa there," Nadine cut in. "I'm an officer of the law. Eating breakfast, or not." She stuck her chest forward, badge first.

"Say I give the insurance money back, Nadine, and say just for the purposes of argumentation I let Annie Lee here keep the diamond. All big ifs granted." She paused as though listening to her own crazy words. "What do you two . . ." she looked hard at Lucas for the first time, but Annie Lee had no doubts she'd sized him up throughout the course of breakfast, ". . . do?"

Lucas and Annie Lee stared at each other before answering, both of them wondering if his dreams still knew hers and vice versa. Let him say it, she thought, I refuse to utter the words.

"Start a restaurant, I suppose," he finally said, with a certain breeziness, even though it was a subject they had broached many times, many times indeed.

Libby was already rolling her eyes, on the verge of dismissing the idea completely. "In Pike?" She threw up her hands.

"With these leases, where? In a back alley two miles down the road?"

"Here, in our house," Lucas said matter-of-factly. "Which is zoned for mixed uses—one of the reasons I bought it all those years ago. I loved it, of course, but when I found out it was rezoned two years after the ski area opened, I realized it had everything. The new gondola's three blocks away."

Libby, the New York real-estate agent, thought about this, calculating. "So you'd spend the money on . . ."

"The obvious," Lucas said. "A regulation kitchen—we could use some of what we have here, actually—and some necessary remodeling for the dining room. We'd live upstairs, like people did in the old days. It's the only possible way we could ever afford to open a place in Pike. And I'm not about to move. Sell the house or anything," he looked at Annie Lee. "Especially now."

"And what kind of food?" Libby's registers were still cachinging.

Annie Lee looked at Lucas and he looked at her. "Breakfast," he said. Annie Lee nodded, despite her will to remain neutral. "All this training in this and that," he continued, "and it turns out I like people who eat breakfast and I like the people who cook it. Maybe the magnets have, over the years, been bringing me back to my most basic self."

"I'd be the hostess," Annie Lee broke in. "And the cashier—it would have to be an antique cash register. Magnet-proof. Boy," she added, "I bet we'd see some stories come together here, everybody all magnetized and stuff." She had a thought. "We could call it the Lodestone Café . . ."

Libby was eyeing the two of them. "Most people dream of a trip around the world," she said. "You two dream of opening a coffee shop? You must be some cr-r-razy masochists."

Bea was pacing in the dining room as the conversation took place, and she stopped in front of Libby. She looked worried.

"Why on earth would you torture these two, whom you hardly know, I might add, with pipe dreams of a big chunk of money? People like you don't give away things, Ms. Wolverton—why even insinuate that you might?"

Libby smiled. "Fair enough," she said. "But I just realized something, and that is how much of my marriage has been about ownership, about tit-for-tat. I got my first taste of leveraging power—and I'm very grateful for the revelation! I mean, what Elias said about my being pissed off and contrarian and whatever else—that was me! But not today. Today, I'm a little less tense. Possibly even ready to go through with a snowboarding lesson. All thanks to someone," she indicated Annie Lee, "who inadvertently took the diamond out of my life. Set things in motion." As if wanting everyone to join her in revelation and problem solving, she faced Annie Lee and gave her a thorough stare. "Are you two trying to have kids, is that what that crib thing was all about?" She looked at Lucas and Annie Lee, who were not offering her any response.

Libby did not wait for an answer. "A few years ago, I checked out all the options. Behind Elias's back, of course. I thought I wanted kids. Which I simply wanted because he didn't, that sort of thing. Frozen eggs, frozen sperm, IVF, ICSA. Assisted reproduction is big biz, believe me; I have friends with big-time gyno husbands. Well, I became a behind-the-scenes expert!"

She looked at Lucas and then ran her fingertips over her eyebrows to groom them. "You know, twenty-five percent of the time it's the man's problem. Elias never told me he'd been snipped—never. So when I went off the pill, secretly, you know, and nothing happened, well, I started blaming myself and had to do a little investi—"

"Ms. Wolverton," this time Eudora interrupted, crossing her arms. "Enough! I have to ask you to hold your tongue. Even if you feel your own marriage has benefited from public comment, why, some things are private, at least for these two.

"We know your intentions are good," Eudora continued, "but I suggest you let Lucas and Annie Lee work out at least some of their own problems themselves. Let the Pike police take you back to the hotel at this point. Relax. Get outside. We'll tell you when the diamond reemerges, and then you can decide what to do. In the meantime, why don't you all, Fen and Nadine included, come to our house tomorrow for elk stew—we found meat in the deep-freeze last night . . ."

Libby Wolverton seemed surprised but then genuinely pleased by the invitation. She admitted she'd never had elk stew before, and added it had been too long since she'd had a home-cooked meal. Fen busied himself collecting her various articles that were stuck on the wall, then handed them to her with a big grin. Then he turned and bent himself toward the sisters, "I would love to be here tomorrow night for some elk meat. Throw in some scalloped potatoes and I'll dig out all the dandelions in your lawn this summer . . ."

Eudora said nothing but solemnly nodded in agreement. She said they'd have lemon meringue pie, too, with three full inches of meringue on top, even at the edges.

Eighteen

Then it was just Bea and Eudora and Lucas and Annie Lee left around the table, and Klink on top of it, perched where he knew he was not supposed to be. The sun had chosen that moment to break through and cast its light onto the storm-blue walls almost as rapturously as it would throw a rainbow onto the mist. A flaring sunbeam struck Klink right at the bone of one shoulder blade, and he closed his eyes blissfully. No one had the heart to tell him to get down.

The Winkleman sisters, a well-oiled and wordless team, scooted their chairs out and gathered dishes together, tidying up the kitchen. They ignored protests from Lucas regarding fussing with housework on a gloriously sunny put-out-your-garbage day, the day they traditionally scoured the neighborhoods, arm in arm, doling out advice like helpings of that lemon pie. Tart but awfully sweet at the center.

The snow could be seen and heard melting everywhere at once now, off the steep metal roofs, branches of fir trees, and newly steaming streets. In great rows of drips and then rivulets, it coalesced into gutters, then into creeks, and finally into the river, where at this very moment chunks of ice were breaking off and traveling downstream as if winter itself were migrating at last. Outside, the world looked newly born, precious, and purified by water.

Lucas was cleaning the stove, enjoying some final moments of refuge with the sisters. Annie Lee knew that he was thinking about the conversation they would have to have when they found themselves alone at last, speculations on magnets and diamonds notwithstanding. For her part, she was not quite ready for that *tête-à-tête*, either.

"I still can't believe," she said, grabbing the broom, "that we didn't notice this *force* all around us. I mean, we never questioned why cable TV didn't work, we just figured we weren't meant to have it. We got lucky or something with the stereo alignment." She ran the broom up against the wall. "And I always thought I had the greenest thumb in Pike! I mean, for that matter, why didn't some other old-timer in town tell everyone? Why didn't we hear it through the grapevine, like everything else in this town?"

"Well, they're good questions." Bea was smiling. "But think about it: It's compelling now because of the revival of interest in magnets, but it really wasn't that interesting back then. People thought Speranzo Vitale was a little off—another oddball. There were a lot of those types in the old days, believe me: inventors, gamblers, people out to make money any way they could. Orna never made a big deal about it because she didn't really want the notoriety, and I'm not sure she knew what her father was getting at anyway, maybe nobody did. But I'll tell you the woman was never sick a day in her life. Not one day. And the plants she grew indoors, Lord'a'mercy . . . just like yours, Annie Lee."

"Clearly, the man was ahead of his time," Eudora stated unequivocally. "He was a genius. And that's how geniuses get treated—they're ignored or ridiculed. In time, people simply forgot about him. Why *you*-all never figured it out on your own is simple enough: Why on earth would you ever suspect you had magnets in your walls? Unless by sheer coincidence, some loosely held nails or a tool in Lucas's hand got close enough to the wall for him to feel them pulling toward it. Now, the question of the garden tools is quite another matter . . ."

"Yes." Bea stopped fluffing her hair with the cake-cutter she'd retrieved from her purse. "Every spring we'd sit tight, with bated breath, waiting for that discovery to be made: for one of those garden tools of yours to stick itself to the side of the house! But it never happened. We just got so we couldn't tell you—until last night, that is, when Lucas came knocking on our door and it seemed like the time had finally come."

Annie Lee considered this. "Well, why didn't Orna inform Lucas when he bought the house? Seems like it might have been her responsibility."

Lucas was struggling with it as well. "Maybe I didn't pick up on Orna's trying to tell me something. I do remember her showing me some pictures. She was very clear on the house not being remodeled, said I should live in it for a while before even considering changing things. And if I didn't like the house after all, to let her know and she'd buy it back."

"You never told me that," Annie Lee said, feeling the time had come to look him in the eye. Just how many things were out there, floating about, that he'd never told her?

"It just didn't seem that important." He held her gaze briefly. "Like I said, I figured she was an eccentric. I would have told you if it had seemed relevant." It appeared he was telling the truth.

In the silence that followed the sisters saw fit to excuse themselves. The promise of put-out-your-garbage day loomed before them. "I'm hoping to find a good read," Eudora said, relishing the prospect. "And I know just where to go. You know those people on North First with the house they painted up in about a dozen colors of a garish nature? Well, she buys every new hardcover on the bestseller list and then reads 'em and then throws 'em all away! Can you imagine? She always writes her name on that first page, and I just cut it right out. I want me a thriller!"

"You'd do well to remember," Bea said, slipping on some gloves and ignoring her sister, "that your lives may be charmed by this peculiar magnetic configuration here. You want proof? Well, that's difficult. The subtler effects of such a force are mysterious indeed. They seem to be the more interesting forces, in my mind, but hardly calculable or quantifiable. And certainly not predictable."

"Not," Eudora said, "that there's anything wrong with keeping the body healthy and the plants thriving. You know, the Chinese have been using magnetism for thousands of years—"

"No, of course there's nothing wrong with that," Bea concurred. "I could certainly use a couple of years of not getting that dadblasted January cold . . ." She yanked an old pom-pom hat on her head, one that matched her gloves. It was a pale shade of dioxazine purple, the color of a turnip's stripe just before it meets the white. A good old-fashioned acrylic-yarn color from the seventies, and it suited her perfectly.

When the front door finally closed behind their last guests, Annie Lee was thinking how foolish it had been to believe that the timing of a fortune from a cookie could have any direct relation to her life. Or a tea-bag quote, or bubble-gum wrapper, or the random reading from some book cracked open blindly. In the face of such a force as magnetism right in her own house, it seemed almost preposterous. It would be like saying a two-foot wave had seen your dinghy to shore when it had actually been the current from some tsunami-sized rogue a mile out.

On the other hand, what about "Seize the day" and the sagacious little mouse and "You will soon inherit money and jewelry?" Maybe magnetism made everything relevant, sucked everything of pertinence right to you like dust to a balloon. She made a mental note to buy a piece of Bazooka later to see what the wrapper said and whether it was stupid or true.

"Annie Lee, we have to talk now," Lucas said to her as she walked back into the living room. "Before any more time passes. I—I need to tell you . . . We need to talk."

She slumped herself hard into the couch, still made up as Megan's bed. "I know we have to talk." Balling up the sheets, she looked at them and tossed them in a pile onto the wood floor. "You have to confess, I have to forgive, and somehow we have to get on with our lives." Annie Lee, not generally so short and blunt in her summations, looked and felt sad.

Lucas, palpably on the verge of relevant speech, continued to grind his gears. At his wife's tragic tone, he stalled and stared obliquely out the window toward a house half a block away that had been lifted from its base and put up on stilts in order for a new foundation to be laid beneath it. House moving had become very popular in Pike. You raised them up, you excavated another thousand square feet of living space beneath them, you put them back down, and figured out how to turn what was once an old house, a yard, and a rickety outbuilding into a massive, multiwing showpiece. Most of the interior walls of this particular big old box had already been demolished, making it possible to see right through the windows clear to the other side and through those windows as well.

"When did they pick that one up?" Lucas asked, then added he hadn't even known it had sold.

"Of course you knew it sold. The Piellis got sick of Realtors beating their door down." The news had made Annie Lee want to cry and throw a tantrum. The old place sat on two lots and boasted a dozen mature trees, including a miraculously fruit-producing apricot. The creek cut through one corner. "They bought a little house in Grand Junction not far from one set of grandkids. The new people haven't shown their faces yet, though. I hear they're from Atlanta, he's a cracker heir or something. Course I suppose it makes a bit of a difference whether it's Carr's Table Water Crackers or Cheez-Its . . . Anyway, lifestyles change. Before you know it he'll be running for town council and I'll be waiting on him."

Annie Lee positioned herself next to Lucas and stared at the Pielli house, already hardly a shadow of its former self. A broken window flashed in the sun. "You slept with her, Lucas," she said, with more control than she thought possible. "We can't talk about anything else until we talk about that."

He continued to stare at the exposed structure, while Annie Lee wondered if lives could be temporarily suspended, like the house, and then laid gently back down on a new foundation. Was it possible?

At last, he spoke. "I had sex with her. I did do that." He glanced at his wife, whose look of surprise and hurt registered fully.

"I know you did." Though her tone was weakly flippant, her armpits were wet. "By the time you came back I'd already decided that my bad behavior was enough to ruin our relationship. I was going to apologize, move forward, stop being so selfish. I had a reunion scene all sketched out in my head—and I kept wondering how I could pull it off without seeming too pushy or manipulative. It's truly a miracle any marriage lasts, you know? What with the timing of things, the separate personalities. Then you throw in hormones, addictions, temptations, and unforeseeable circumstances . . . and different rates of personal development. My God, lasting marriages are miracles!" It was a good preamble, she thought, and it gave her strength to go on.

"Anyway," she continued. "When that picture fell out of the magazine, it was as if I just knew. Just *knew*. After the initial shock—and panic and rage and jealousy—everything shifted. I started to feel crazy and to think I understood just how people had affairs, something I've never understood before, even in the abstract. I told myself I couldn't really blame you, you had your reasons, and I was probably most of them; then I started to wonder if *I* could do it, just to get even, just to feel attractive." Right now, she felt just like that house across the way, with its punched-out windows and hollow insides.

Lucas was shifting from one foot to another. "I felt trapped and abused by you, Annie Lee. I felt impotent." He sat down, uneasily, on the arm of the couch.

"Which brings us to the next subject . . ." she said quickly. "Not that I don't want to know how truly disgusting sex with that trashy Cindy Sherman really was."

"It wasn't anything like it is between you and me. It was—"

"Maybe you should quit while you're only in the third ring of hell. Sometimes people don't really want to hear what they ask you to tell them."

'Look," he said, standing up again and coming toward her for the first time in what seemed a glacial crevasse of an interval. She didn't move backward but held her ground. "I did it because I was angry at you and felt helpless." He swallowed. "I went through with it, then felt like a real lowlife the second after ejaculating."

"I see," Annie Lee said. The use of the physiological term shocked her—not unpleasantly—and then made her think of sperm, their big heads, their little bodies. Like windup toys, they couldn't help blindly moving forward. Men were a lot like sperm. "What about birth control?"

"She said she'd had her tubes tied after her second child."

Ahh. Cindy had become *she*. Maybe they would never have to speak her name again. "What about sexually transmitted diseases, did you ever think of that?"

"*She* thought of that," the incipient scorn in his voice did not seem insincere. "And whipped out a condom."

Annie Lee feigned admiration, nodding as she spoke. "Covering all her bases."

"Evidently."

"So I'm just supposed to forgive you, the victim, for cheating on me Lucas, because (a) she seduced you and (b) I was to blame for the transgression in the first place because I made you feel impotent? Maybe I deserved that kind of behavior, but still, forgiving seems worlds away to me." She paused and for a moment thought of herself on a milky white moon, looking across black space—the chasm of the relationship—to earth. "Well, it's not something you can summon. I realize there are magnets involved and everything, but there's a distance factor now." She shook her head, slumped a little, and then lost any interest she might have had in long, complicated sentences.

"Why did you have to go sleep with her, Luke? Do you realize how hard that is on a person's imagination? What it does to that part of you that has finally trusted another human being completely?" *Don't cry*, she told herself. *Don't listen too hard to what you just said.*

She could see Lucas swallow hard. "Yeah, Annie Lee. Yeah, I do. Just the idea of you rubbing up against someone at a place like the Hole in the Wall—makes me feel—"

"Like shit?"

He nodded and shrugged at the same time. Annie Lee looked at him sadly. She could think of nothing else to say as they stood there, as close as they were far apart. Finally, she turned toward the kitchen.

"By the way," she said, "the undisclosed wall colors, FYI, are Canary in Your House for the foyer, Grandma's Lilac Apron, attic, and Dark-and-Stormy-Night Blue for the living room. I recently got reprimanded by Marty at the paint store for keeping the color names from you. They're just colors, for God's sake, not matters of national security. I'm sick of harboring that information. And I hate that word, 'harboring.'"

She could hear the smile on Lucas's lips. After a brief pause, he asked her if she knew about her paintings being up all over the walls of her mother's studio. He was happy, no doubt, to have been given a new conversational trajectory. No, she told him, but tried nevertheless to recall which paintings those might actually be.

"Did you know from the very first time she met me she's always tried to get me to ease you back into canvases?"

Annie Lee didn't like his chummy manner. "I know she tells you things and you tell her things." She endeavored to make her own tone as icy as possible. "Meanwhile, I've benefited from painting walls all these years. There's nothing wrong with painting walls."

"No, especially not these walls." He paused. "Do you suppose that by virtue of them, we have become magnetized—and that mysterious force makes us more attractive to each other than we might be otherwise?"

"I don't know," she gave him the wary eye but some latitude to continue. What was he saying, that without the magnets they didn't stand a chance?

"On the other hand, we've never had a problem with sex away from the force field of the house, even at the very beginning of our relationship. Remember the old Highline Mine ruins that day? Remember that?"

"Don't try to get me off course here." She felt Klink's back arch against her calves, as if he'd become a part of the team of lawyers pleading this case. She was thinking of those ruins, though, the second after the words came out of his mouth. They had made long and luscious love in the hundred-year-old stone foundation ruins of a miner's cabin. Lucas had packed a picnic of salami and cold potatoes and ripe peaches. The air at tree line had been cool on their naked bodies even on one of the hottest days of the year. How wonderfully everything had smelled of dry sap and rock and the last of the snow wafting down from the icy couloirs.

"Well," she said, reining herself in, "I'd have to agree we had a good thing going even without magnets. From the word go."

Lucas was nodding. "So," he was playing with a leaf on one of the philodendrons. "Did anything happen at the Hole? Anything, you know, at all?"

Annie Lee looked him smack in his gray-green—Olive Branch?—eyes and thought hard about lying but couldn't quite manage it. "I contemplated it." She crossed her arms. "I had lustful thoughts it might have been interesting to pursue. The man was attractive and seductive and dark, and he was coming on to me without any ambiguity . . . But then he did something that irritated the hell out of me."

"What's that?"

"He started presuming too much. Treating me like Anywoman in Anybar."

"Uh-huh." Lucas masked his relief by pretending to get a male's grasp of the situation. "Of course." His whole body had visibly relaxed. "He didn't want a real relationship, he wanted the game. That's the difference between a one-night stand and a love affair. Did you dance with him?"

"No." She lost the will to keep up appearances and sighed deeply. "I got sidetracked. Eddie dragged me over to Libby and we gawked at her and then, well, you know. The diamond. Val. Going to their place where Jessica, *his pregnant wife*, was eating a sandwich . . ." she smiled. "Val was going to deck this guy Carlos!"

"I would have decked him . . ." Lucas reached toward Annie Lee's face and pulled a stray strand of hair out of the corner of her mouth and then very slowly retracted his hand from under her jawline.

"Annie Lee," he mumbled as she clenched her teeth, trying not to feel aroused.

"Hmmm," she could smell him, the bleached smell of his clean shirt. Why would she want to rub up against this man who had betrayed her, dragged her and their marriage into the polluted waters of infidelity? But there it was. That smell, the feel of his hand on her jaw. Two months of abstinence had made an enemy—well, a dissident—of her body. She had to struggle for control. Was this how men felt all the time, perpetually struggling for control?

"I want you to know," she took one step back. "The body is willing even as the deep part of me knows you're not to be trusted. I mean, I've loved you more than anyone I've ever known . . ." She paused to pull all other wispy hairs away from her face. "But we screwed up, even with that amount of love between us. I mean what does that *mean?*" She wanted to smack him in the nose for making her feel as if cynicism fit her now, whereas it never had before. What color was cynicism? The color of tear gas? Of smog? Was it a cloud around you that had to be burned off by the heat of direct sun?

He shook his head. "I don't know," he said. "I thought about it last night at the river but couldn't come up with anything. Even the river seemed disillusioned with me. I made a mistake, Annie Lee . . . I can't take it back. But on the other hand, now that you've told me all this other stuff, well, it's almost as if some of it *had* to happen. If you *had* come with me to Seattle, you wouldn't have had a run-in with Libby, learned about the magnets, or had a diamond in your possession. Imagine a restaurant."

They thought about this.

The diamond and related reveries seemed to stop all other thoughts cold, even the preeminent one about the solo trip to Seattle being precisely that which had occasioned his lapse into abominable behavior.

"Wouldn't that be something?" It took an eighth of a second for Annie Lee to see herself delivering food in her own coffee shop. Charitably forgiving the slack waiters. Giving them Christmas bonuses.

"Yeah," said Lucas. He seemed to be waiting for Annie Lee to give him some signal that it was okay for him to hug her or kiss her, something to seal this image of a dream shared.

She couldn't do it. "I'm going skiing and then I'm going straight to work," she said at last, the words "tit-for-tat" echoing somewhere deep in her psyche. "I'll swap with someone for tomorrow so I can go to the sisters'. Think you can?"

"I already swapped a bunch of shifts for the time I took off. But it's getting slower. Maybe Lina will let me off—if I tell her it's a matter of saving my marriage." Alina Lacomaggio, who ran her kitchen like military basic training, managed at the same time to secure both love and loyalty from every one of her employees. Annie Lee's theory was that it had to do with the regular and frequent hugs she gave to everyone, as well as occasional slaps on the butt.

"Which would not be lying," Annie Lee said, then excused herself to gather her gear and head out. Today, she would leave Lucas alone to contemplate the forces at work in his life. And to make him wonder about it all alone in his wonderful house, which had, as yet, not been gutted, grafted, or lifted off the ground.

Nineteen

Eddie spent the entire night at work begging Annie Lee to tell him what had finally happened with Libby Wolverton. All he really wanted to know was whether or not he was in trouble, if he was implicated. Aiding and abetting was one thing, but could he be in trouble for having come up with the idea in the first place?

Virtually everyone, against all restaurant odds, had been in good spirits that night. Con's orthopedist, Elliot, had come to visit him and invited him out again. Flushed with the attentions of a suitor, Constantine Premus had even forgotten to be snide and sarcastic, which was lovely, just for a change.

It was Sunday—the chef's night off as well as Marc's—and with the imminent closing of the ski area, it had been slower than usual, just as Lucas had predicted. They hadn't really needed all the floor personnel, but no one was complaining of a skimpier tipping pool or of not having enough to do.

There had been no large tables, very few young children, and not even the trace of a bottleneck at the 7:30 peak. Not one customer had whined about allergies to the onion family or to caffeine or anything with cream in it. There had not been a single request for either a vegetarian plate or grilled vegetables, and nothing had been sent back to the kitchen for any reason whatsoever.

Yes, Sunday night had been a waiter's dream come true.

In their spare time, all through the shift, they'd played at one of their favorite staff pastimes—Customer Capers—where they would come up with schemes and gizmo ideas to throw the clientele off balance. Waiters wearing headsets and pretending to talk to the kitchen. Waiters using *Star Trek* language like "affirmative" and "engage" and "make it so." Waiters all wearing Buddy Holly glasses. Mumbling waiters who will not repeat anything louder no matter what. Waiters who mimic their customers' accents. Waiters who blink too much. Waiters who add frozen peas to the plates of complainers. Waiters who pretend to write down every word at a table, like reporters: *"I'm not a big cauliflower fan," she said, taking off her reading glasses and looking up from the menu.*

Tonight Eddie's mind was on one thing and one thing alone. "What if we all wore big, huge diamonds on our fingers? You know, paste, costume jewelry. All the guys could wear those pinkie rings encrusted with diamond bits. The girls could wear fake nails and solitaires the size of gum balls—" He wanted the rest of Annie Lee's story, but she only smiled and said she was saving it for dinner.

When the sous-chef brought in hamburgers made with ground-up tenderloin for staff dinner, the waiters practically raised him up on their shoulders. The perfect end to a perfect night. With dinner and a half glass of wine before her, Annie Lee was able to recap the highlights of her implausible big-gem story, careful to leave out the parts about Lucas cheating on her and about magnets in her walls. She concluded by saying, directly to Kathryn, "Libby was so grateful to have gotten a grip on herself—and out of the grip of divorce fever—that she's not all that anxious to have the diamond back."

Kathryn had a mouthful of meat and some mustard seeping from between her lips. She started having trouble swallowing; everyone could see it. At the sound of Annie Lee's words, she attempted to eat too quickly, to swallow the huge bite of super-lean meat before its time. Clearly, she was too eager to speak her piece.

Con, proud of his vigilance in a world of potential choking victims, was behind her chair in a flash with his fists clenched together right below her sternum.

"I'm okay." She forced the words out quickly after finally managing to gulp. "Too dry," she said, pointing at the meat. After drinking half a glass of water and wiping her eyes, Kathryn focused again on Annie Lee. "You're lying about keeping the diamond. You almost killed me with that lie."

"I'm not lying. Of course for all I know, it may no longer be inside me . . ."

Jay, who was eating his bun-less burger with a fork and knife, stopped for a moment. "This doesn't sound like the same woman we witnessed last night. The one with the fur coat. And all those sticks in her hair."

"Sure as hell does *not*." Eddie had procured a few tomatoes from the walk-in and had managed to unearth an ancient bottle of ketchup, too, from a secret place that no one had known about. Which one of the cooks was sneaking condiments in spite of the chef's specific instructions to the contrary? He'd sworn if he couldn't find a pickle or some regular old lettuce, he'd call Elmo's for some, but those necessary garnishes also materialized from deep in the bowels of the kitchen.

"People change," Annie Lee replied simply, thinking, however, that Eddie might be one of the very last to do so. He would always find his pickle, his mayonnaise, and his ketchup;

he would always be able to turn ground filet into something recognizable, perpetuate the established order. Keep things right.

"People do not change," Jay countered. "They merely adapt to changing circumstances."

"Well, what's the difference? We're talking semantics here." Annie Lee was making a special pink sauce of mayonnaise and ketchup. She herself believed fully in the world of condiments. One day, she hoped to start her own line, based on that phoenix of the refrigerator door, mayonnaise. She wanted to do a south of France line. Basil mayonnaise called Basinnaise. A black olive spread called Tapennaise. And a roasted red pepper one called Peppannaise.

Jay was wiping his mouth and shaking his head. "I'd be careful, Annie Lee. This woman sounds—"

"Too good to be true?" Con finished the sentence, and Jay shrugged a reluctant affirmative. "That's what I thought about Dr. Elliot Neehigh. Bright, attractive, wealthy, unattached." Was he talking about the virtual surgeon? The cross between the nutty professor and Mick Jagger? She smiled at Con, who had blossomed like a buttercup.

"Maybe it was a fake." Kathryn was still drinking water in numerous tiny sips as if practicing her swallowing skills. "You know—sometimes people wear their paste and keep the good stuff in the vault at home. In which case, no big deal. She lost her zircon and is not enthusiastic about its current location. Can you blame her?" She sneered.

Annie Lee remained calm. "It was the engagement diamond given to her by the man she currently loathes and is leaving, a prominent Park Avenue shrink. Fen Hurley, on the other hand, seems to be interested in making her feel attractive again."

"The goofy giant cop?" Eddie Stahl was noticeably relaxing with every bite of his burger as his involvement in the matter continued to evanesce. "What would she ever see in him?"

Annie Lee shrugged. "He sort of had her number, or played like he did. It means a lot to a woman."

There was leftover ice cream—caramelized hazelnut—for dessert, which Annie Lee did not even have to fight for. Con was already vacuuming since he was about to be in the throes of something too good to be true. Kathryn had her lips pressed together in a tight seal as she gathered her dishes.

"Well," she summarized, "I'll believe this when I see it." A few minutes later, she could be heard thrashing around in the bar, slamming things around pettily like a spoiled brat. Then it was just Jay and Annie Lee, and they were sharing the ice cream, taking turns with the plastic container.

"Please be careful, Annie Lee," he said. "This situation sounds . . . fishy."

"You don't know the whole story—"

"No one ever does."

She laughed at him then. "I'm auxiliary tomorrow night. Think I could have the night off to stand watch over my intestines and sort out these details? Among other things, I'm having dinner with Libby and Nadine Gerecke, Fen, Lucas, and our next-door neighbors."

Jay considered it. "The Winklemans or the Doyles?"

"The Winks."

"I knew that, actually," he admitted. "The taller one grabbed a book right out of my hands this morning. Up at the big, ugly house, you know, on North First?"

"Was it a thriller?"

He nodded. "Then she put it back into my hands without letting it go—as if we were having a tug-of-war over it—and said 'You can have this book if you see to it that Annie Lee has the night off tomorrow. It's a matter of great import . . .' I didn't even know she knew who I was. Of course I agreed. So I got the new Robert Ludlum, and I'm giving you the night off." He paused. "What're they cooking over there anyway?"

"Elk and lemon pie."

"Elk and lemon has never been one of my favorite combinations," he said, scraping the last driblets of ice cream out of the box and then looking up to see whether he'd gotten a smile out of her. He had. He got serious. "Somehow you get the feeling those two are pulling strings."

"Uh-huh," Annie Lee said, wanting to tell him about the magnets but opting for a quick departure and keeping her mouth shut. That was twice in one night she'd been able to bite her tongue, and this she considered a great accomplishment indeed.

When she got home, inspired by the idea of restraining oneself for the higher good, she asked Lucas about his night, gave him a quick peck on the cheek, and then went about gathering enough blankets for a pallet on the couch. He watched her, slow to realize what she was doing.

"Look," she said to him, fluffing this and patting that. "Maybe we should take our time sorting this one out. I'm not sure we should be bumping up against each other in the night. Having sex and then pretending the next morning that we did it in our sleep—all this while I'm deeply angry and we're unresolved. It's true we've always had chemistry on our side . . ." Swallowing the lump creeping up her throat, she continued. "But for the time being, I am not ready. I'm still mad at you, you piece of shit, I don't care what the percentage is of men who cheat on their wives. You need to sleep somewhere else." More arranging and tucking in.

"Someday, when we have sex again, it will be with not one remnant of that awful woman on your skin, under your skin, under your nails, anywhere. I mean," she added, "sleep on the floor if you want, or in the truck. I just thought the couch would be easiest."

Annie Lee felt Lucas watching her as she prepared his bed. "What is the alternative?" She kept the patter going. "We can't share our bed right now. And I don't think it would make sense to give you the bed. I mean, why should I sleep on the couch?"

Lucas said the couch was fine. He didn't play the martyr at all and said he'd make his own bed from now on, she didn't need to be doing that. Right before she headed upstairs he called to her, and when she turned around, he said, "I know there's a lot going on, Annie Lee. But I want to tell you something. A small, happy part of me exists because of you. Because you see it and have faith in it. I thought about this a lot in Seattle, why your misery made me so miserable, made me feel so helpless. And part of it was really selfish: I was mad about not getting the regular, upbeat attention from you, the reaffirmation of the part of myself I like. And what I said about the vortex? Well, everybody has a vortex, we all do. Relationships are in some ways just headlong meetings between people's personal tornadoes. So it really wasn't your fault at all. People are entitled to have crises in their lives."

There was no reason not to believe something so frankly spoken, and it made her feel just a fraction better.

"Okay," she said to him, before heading off to bed.

Twenty

Though the couch—velvet, moss-colored, overstuffed—was beautiful and even welcoming to readers and guests, and was probably even adequate for the occasional teenager needing a getaway, it was hardly meant to be slept upon night after night by a full-sized man.

Lucas stretched inconspicuously all that next morning, trying to get the kinks out. He walked to the bakery early for croissants and found Annie Lee brewing coffee when he got home. No mention was made of the dialogue of the night before, and much of the day was spent cleaning and conversing politely, crossing paths nimbly as people used to each other's company are able to do. Lucas went cross-country skiing around noon, and Annie Lee had tea with Megan a little later. Megan was working on a quilt comprising pieces of snowboarding logos all interlocked together in kaleidoscopic geometric patterns.

"Is Quinn a snowboarder, by chance?" Annie Lee asked, to which Megan answered, shrugging lightly, that the quilt was for the twins. Little babies liked to look at bright, bold things, she said, not pastels: pastels were just for the people making them.

And snowboarding logos, she said, reflected Pike's visual vernacular. They had learned about such things in art class.

Dinner at the Winklemans had been set for seven o'clock, and in spite of Pike's lackadaisical stance on promptness, everyone showed up precisely on the hour. The sisters accepted little gifts from everyone who walked through their door, not surprised but pleased by the offerings. A Venus flytrap from Nadine Gerecke. A bottle of crème de menthe from Fen Hurley. Annie Lee and Lucas brought a pound of Seattle coffee as well as two bottles of wine. Even Libby Wolverton, fresh from a shopping spree, thought to bring six bars of beautifully wrapped lavender soap from the most expensive of the lingerie shops. She herself was wearing a new fleece pullover and had managed to get her jeans to go over the tops of her fur boots.

"Well," she told the group, after they'd all settled in the living room with their glasses of wine, "my office keeps calling to make sure I'm all right . . . Meanwhile, I let the hotel voice mail get Elias's daily call today. Guess what the message said? 'We need to talk, Lib.'" She was addressing her remarks to the sisters, but Nadine Gerecke was the first to comment.

"You know," she said, "men constantly need to be challenged: They need to be chasing, chasing, chasing." She looked at Fen and Lucas and then at the sisters. "Women need to remember how to dangle the carrot, that's all. And they need to remember that on a certain level it's all just a game." The off-duty Nadine had dressed in brown work pants and one of those low-cut V-neck thermal shirts with the first two eyelets undone, in plain, ordinary orange. She had a knockout off-duty figure, evidently the one that went with her off-duty personality.

"It's a game until you start losing," Annie Lee noted, hoping not to sound too much like an expert. "Then it becomes life again."

Eudora wanted to know how Nadine knew so much about

dangling carrots. Had she been reading books lately or had she actually dangled some?

"Dangled," was all Nadine said, obviously smart enough to know that in a town like Pike, if you cherished a private moment or private encounter, you kept it to yourself. Now Annie Lee found herself desperate to know whom Nadine had set her sights on.

Lucas, who, to his credit, could be quite good at regulating conversational flow, was inquiring politely of Libby how she'd spent the day, to which she replied half of it had been spent on the mountain and the other half looking at real estate. "That house down the road, for instance, the one up on stilts? Sold for over four hundred thousand dollars," she said. "And it requires a complete renovation. A top-to-bottom overhaul. Four hundred—"

"Unfortunate it's being overhauled at all," Bea cut in. She motioned for everyone to sit down, that dinner was served. "Tell us about snowboarding. Was it hard? They say it is at first . . ."

Annie Lee could see Lucas trying to pick out more pearl onions than his share and then sort of scatter them on the plate to make them look scanty. Fen was having a slice of buttered bread as he waited for the serving spoon to come his way.

Libby had worked up an appetite on the mountain, evidently, for her portions surprised even Fen. "Well, funny you should ask," she said. "I had a grand time snowboarding—although *falling* is closer to what I would call it. And I had another revelation. They seem to be coming fast and furious in Pike."

"Tell us," commanded Eudora, who had reached over with her fork and stabbed one of the pearl onions right off of Lucas's plate.

"Well," Libby said, after taking a sip of wine and remarking how good it tasted, "I learned to be a beginner again. To feel stupid, and awkward, and fall and get up and fall and get up again. I learned it makes all the difference in the world if you can smile just a little bit at yourself. Of course it helped that the instructor was so young and such a darling . . ."

Bea was clucking at her guest. "And how will this information serve you, if you don't mind my asking?"

"Are you really interested?" Libby seemed surprised when everyone said, yes, they were.

"Well, I realized how much our marriage—Elias's and mine—needed a shot of being beginners again. I'd love to see that man flat on his ass on the slopes. And I bet you he'd love to see me flat on mine!" She laughed out loud. "Oh, well." She dropped back down from the land of ifs. Eudora noted dryly that it sounded as though she still had feelings for the man, at which point Libby changed the subject about as subtly as a rock might be thrown through a window.

"So. About Pike's *demographics*." She was busy-working the sauce with a small piece of bread. "Looking around town, it would appear everyone is under the age of thirty-five."

"Not everybody." Eudora pinched her face into a punctuation mark of some kind. "But the old people are disappearing. They move away. Or their families come and haul them away . . . It's not an easy town to live in when you're up in your years. If you fall on the ice, you break your hip, you know."

"But you're here," Libby countered. "You've survived." There was not a single driblet, crumb, or morsel of food left in front of her. The immaculate state of her plate seemed to endear her to the sisters.

"We're here because we don't have any children bossing us around!" Eudora proclaimed. "Telling us to move into those retirement centers or what have you. Selling our house from under us." She looked to her sister to continue, as if it were getting too personal for her own tastes.

"The closest we've ever come to having children," Bea obliged, reaching up to fix her bangs, "is Lucas and Annie Lee."

It was the first time they had ever said such a thing, and Annie Lee, noting pressure in her tear ducts, stared down at her plate. The sisters just didn't get sentimental all that often, they were of no-nonsense extraction—practical, stubborn, and plain. They were the venerated rough-hewn sentences in a world of purple prose.

"Yessir," Eudora agreed, now that the words had actually been uttered. "We've enjoyed our adopted children. Of course," she added, "most children are not married to each other. But then, most parents are not two old biddy sisters, either." She shook her head. "It's quite a family." She started laughing at the idea then, and the laughter, loud and raucous and contagious, took hold of the group, and they all laughed until their faces were flushed. It was true, though: Families were flung together only initially by genetics. Later on in life, surrogate families coalesced more like mercury blobs, pooled together by geography or fate or any number of factors arguably still far thicker than water.

A pleasant lull followed just as the clock struck eight. Annie Lee took the opportunity to begin clearing away plates, which raised an immediate objection from Libby. "I don't think you should be clearing, Annie Lee." She scooted out as well. "You don't need to wait on us. Why don't I clear the plates while you help the sisters get the dessert ready?" It was a sweet gesture, but no one wanted to see Libby struggle with the plates, so they all helped her, everyone except Annie Lee, who refrained, not without difficulty, from clearing anything at all.

The magnificent pie, wheeled in on an endangered-list TV cart, lived up to its reputation. Sweet; tart; not too rich; and a pillow of puffy meringue cushioning the roof of the mouth with every bite. When Lucas inquired how much extra lemon zest they actually put in their pie, however, the Winklemans' faces fell to the floor.

"It's what we *do* to the rind that makes the difference," Bea finally proclaimed, "not how much extra." She and Eudora had both clamped their faces shut, laying a silence on the table that hurt.

Lucas was swift with the remedy. "Well, anyway, what do you think about making that jam for the coffee shop we might someday actually open? We could hire someone to pick the berries, and you could make it. We would under no circumstances give the secret away . . ."

As fast as they'd shut down, the two of them came back to life, eyes twinkling as they chatted gaily about labels, the name of their company, how much fun it would be to become entrepreneurs at their advanced age.

With coffee came talk of Pike in the old days. The sisters had a story for nearly every house in town, and photos of them, too, and in a matter of minutes had blithely put the guests under their spell. Lucas, familiar with all the photo albums and scrapbooks, became the errand boy and took to finding this photo or clipping, passing around that. It was during Bea's digression on the prostitutes of Pike (a liberal view to say the least, and one that surprised no one) that Annie Lee felt an unanticipated need to use the bathroom. It must have been the coffee, which she rarely drank after noon. Tonight it had smelled so good, she'd indulged with everyone else, and now her body was behaving as if it were morning.

The back powder room was chilly and smelled of rose water and hoary plaster. Annie Lee picked up an open copy of an old *Farmer's Almanac* from a basket near the toilet and began to read about using Ex-Lax to get rid of skunks and cedar chips to get rid of spiders. But, the final remark read, why would anyone want to get rid of spiders?

It was almost anticlimactically, in a state of mild bafflement as to why the question of spiders struck her as so poignant, that Annie Lee experienced—swiftly and obviously—the reemergence of the four-carat stone from its alimentary journey. With a bottled soap smelling of pine that she found under the sink, she vigorously took to scrubbing the diamond and her hands up to the elbows, and then returned to the group, gem safely stowed in the tiny, heretofore obsolete, watch pocket of her Levi's. Now was neither the time nor the place to share her repossession of the article. She needed to show it to Lucas first, keep it to herself until that happened.

The group, captivated still by the Winklemans' histrionics, barely noticed Annie Lee's return. Even Libby seemed to have capitulated, smitten more now by the old Pike than the new. Certainly, none of the guests seemed to recall or even care about the issues that had brought them together in the first place. Cheating spouses, for instance. Or stolen diamonds. The diamond, in fact, was never once mentioned, even though Annie Lee herself could think of little else once she'd recovered it.

On the way home, after good-nights and thank-yous, and after Lucas hugged the hostesses and apologized for picking apart the pie, and even after he'd told Annie Lee he'd actually held back what he'd figured out about the meringue, Annie Lee said, as offhandedly as she could, "By the way. I have the diamond in my pocket. It came out." She opened the door to their house and strode in.

Lucas had to struggle to keep up. "What—just now?!"

"Well, ten minutes ago. The coffee was what did it, I guess." In the front hall she switched on a small lamp and reached into the little pocket of her jeans. She couldn't feel the gem at first and panicked for a moment as she wriggled her finger deep into the pocket before touching it, crooking it out.

Lucas's eyes focused hard when he saw it. "Whoa," he said. "I guess I've never really seen a diamond until now." She dropped it into his palm, and together they stared at the thing, which twinkled away, heedless of who, if anyone, was looking at it.

Annie Lee had to tear herself from what might have been

construed as a shared moment. She plucked the diamond from Lucas's hand and then stowed it in one of the eggcups before going to brush her teeth. She loitered in the living room just long enough to watch him make up his bed. Only before heading up the stairs did she waver for a moment, teeter on the brink of a false move, nearly compromise her new and powerful language of holding back. Overall, restraint seemed to have the effect of making Annie Lee feel consummately virtuous. Nevertheless, at this moment, she could not curb the desire to fluff Lucas's pillow, which she did with great vigor—like a good scratch of the scalp—before saying good night.

The next morning they had buttermilk pancakes and stared at the diamond, still in the eggcup, while eating. Annie Lee revealed that she didn't necessarily feel ready to call Libby just yet, that they needed some time alone with the object. Lucas enthusiastically said he agreed, it seemed important to have it there, in their house, to gaze upon. Perhaps, he said, it would become magnetized, which would be like doing Libby a service, however intangible the results of that service might be.

By Thursday afternoon, though, Annie Lee felt so guilty about secretly hoarding the gem that she walked to the Hotel hoping to find Libby had already returned from her day on the slopes. She had. She was scheduled for a manicure but begged Annie Lee to come with her. "I can't spend one more second talking to the hotel staff as if they were my closest friends!"

"Libby," Annie Lee said to her in the elevator, which, aside from the two of them, was empty. "I have to tell you something . . ."

Libby matched Annie Lee's pause with one of her own. "The diamond just resurfaced, no doubt," she finally said, as if she were tired of having to think about it. The elevator door was about to open, but Libby pushed a button that caused it—magically, it seemed—to keep right on going.

"Well, yes," Annie Lee admitted in the security of their private elevator. "It finally did. It took a while." It felt terrible to lie, but she didn't want Libby to think of her as someone who hadn't come clean right away, someone covetous of what was not hers. Even if, in fact, she was lying.

"Well," Libby said, "I've been thinking about that thing quite a lot. I know I don't want Elias to have it; and I don't want it in my possession, either. I mean, think of what it's been through. I'd almost rather get the insurance money." The door opened and, together, they exited, met by wafts of pool-room chlorine as they continued on past four hot tubs teeming with people, some of whom Annie Lee would undoubtedly soon have the pleasure of waiting on. Libby led them through a gift shop (where she purchased some of those Life Savers that made sparks) and then on into one of the salon areas.

Finally, Annie Lee said, lowering her voice, "Well, it's perfectly clean, Libby. I mean it's been washed and bleached. If you want we could have it professionally laundered."

Libby wasn't listening. "But then that's problematic, too: You see, I called the insurance company, and guess what? Elias, in his frugality, underinsured that stone, just to save a few bucks. So the insurance money is not an option. I mean why be stupid and take a loss?" She smiled at the attendant and indicated that Annie Lee would be sitting next to her during the manicure. An extra chair was brought in.

"You could *sell* it," Annie Lee said. "Cash it in. Get the money."

"Uh-uh. I don't like that plan, either. Then Elias and I would have money to fight over, which is even uglier than cars, jewels, and art combined. No, there seems to be only one way to end this thing. *You* cash it in, Annie Lee. You and that darling husband of yours. Elias will have a fit of course, but that will be part of the beauty of it. It was mine, I gave it away—before we could settle on it. He'll be furious! It will mark the day I took control." The manicurist was approaching with that all-too-familiar long-lost-friend look service-industry people gave customers who tipped them. Her smock had the hotel emblem on the pocket. Small rectangular glasses hung on a chain around her neck.

Annie Lee was thinking she certainly didn't want to be responsible for any of Libby's revelations, she wanted Libby to have them all on her own. But before she could utter one syllable, Libby continued:

"You cash in the diamond, dear, yes you. And use it for that restaurant—only God knows it won't go far in terms of remodeling. But it's a start, I suppose . . ." She smiled at the manicurist, who was assembling her tools, much like a dental hygienist.

Annie Lee couldn't think of anything to say, especially in front of the nail-tender whose ears, she knew, were wide open. She thought of keeping the diamond, but then flashed on Elias, hot on her trail, hunting her down like a common swindler. With dart guns or psychological torture—something out of a Joseph Conrad novel. He would work Libby over until he'd gotten Annie Lee's name out of her. Then he'd come after her, nail her. Probably accuse her of brainwashing his wife with simple-minded hogwash from the sticks. A place where people read the likes of Venus Philabaum—and worse.

"I'll tell you what," Libby continued, "as a tribute to me, put blini on your breakfast menu—like my great-aunt Babi used to make. Now *there* was a cook—the world lost an artist when she died. She had some secret ingredient in her buckwheat blini that no one ever did discover—of course they didn't have Lucas working for them. Babi's blini. God they were good."

Annie Lee faltered. "I—I really don't know what to say." She glanced at Miss Lab Coat, whose head was down. "I mean, I don't think I ever seriously thought about keeping the diamond—even if I toyed with the idea. And Lucas's comment about the Winks making jam for our coffee shop—it had nothing whatsoever to do with his assuming we'd be keeping it. It just got us *thinking* about the possibility of a breakfast place again."

"I realize that," Libby said, laughing.

Annie Lee decided at this point to bare her soul, manicurist be damned. "And what if Elias comes after me, Libby? Comes after me and snatches it out of my hand, just like you did the first time around?" One upward glance, over the tops of her glasses, from Miss Lab Coat. So she could identify Annie Lee, if she had to, to her friends when she told them what she'd overheard at work that day.

"Oh, don't you worry about him, dear. I can handle the man. I know his little secrets—and I'm getting a better handle on him every day. But take my advice and sell the thing pronto. I mean, why tempt fate? You might lose it yourself, or swallow it again or something!"

Annie Lee said, "Are you sure?" four or five more times before following up with a chorus of "I-don't-know-what-to-says."

"Say okay!" said Libby. The manicurist was finally ready to get down to business. Libby looked at her hands, then at the woman before her. "I want you to cut them short . . ." she said, scheming, as if speaking of military tactics. "And put clear polish on them." Though Annie Lee had not ever seen a nervous nail technician, she was sure this was what one looked like. The woman hardly knew which scissors to begin with.

Annie Lee was exiting the salon. "Sometimes," she heard Libby say to the woman, "we must pare things down to their most basic nature."

Annie Lee ran all the way home and told Lucas, panting, of the conversation, and there the two of them stood, stock-still and speechless, as the diamond glinted, glistened, even winked at them in its new spot: the only crystal bowl they owned, one that had always held olives or small pickles but that might someday soon hold a bit of caviar, the way things were going.

A question flashed before Annie Lee: Would she trade the diamond in for her old life—the one she was living before her husband had cheated on her? Surprisingly, she couldn't answer the question. In its full-spectrum presence, she felt the same sense of opportunity that she'd felt before, only this time Lucas was there, standing right alongside her at the brink of something new. The diamond, like a three-dimensional dot at the bottom of a prodigiously vital exclamation point, might very well be the thing that would reestablish the bond between them.

Four days after that conversation, the words "You cash in the diamond!" still ringing in her ears, Annie Lee FedExed it to her uncle Louis in New York, the only person she could think of who could help her get the stone appraised. Louis knew people in every walk of life, from parking-lot barons to backgammon players to Swiss bankers. Annie Lee still didn't know exactly how he made his living, only that he spent half his time eating out and the rest of it on the phone.

"Should I ask where you got this?" He'd called her upon receiving the parcel.

"It's legit, Louie. It was a gift from a customer . . ."

"Wha'd you do? Save her life?"

"No, I interrupted her life. It needed interrupting." Given Louis's penchant for a good story, Annie Lee gave him the long version, complete with names, faces, occasional reenactments.

"Well, you couldn't have made that up, *chérie* . . . You could probably sell the story to *People* magazine, for that matter. Anyway. The diamond. It's a flawed specimen. I mean it's obvious it got chewed up—you know diamonds aren't nearly as impervious as people say."

"They're not?" She'd considered it very sparkly indeed for such a mangled rock.

"Certainly not. This one is big, but it has internal flaws, the color is off, and it got banged up. I'd say it's worth no more than twenty thou." Louis talked about any number of subjects in this manner, with the appropriate insider vocabulary. "You want me to try to sell it for you?"

Annie Lee heard herself replying, "Yes, that would be nice. Please do." The conversation, like a lava lamp, had surreal yet inevitable qualities; a question burbled up, and she released it. "Louie," she said, "do you think there are good reasons men cheat on women?"

He was silent a moment. "The reasons seem good at the time, no doubt. Of whom are we speaking here? Of your father?"

"Well," she tried to sound detached, "only partly. And of a situation closer to home." If Lucas had known of her capabilities of running off at the mouth, blabbing to her family, he might never have married her. Although at this point there was only her mother and Louis to go blabbing to.

"I see." Louis could not conceal his voice's shifting to a minor key. "So what we're saying here is that Annie Lee is now in her mother's shoes and is confused about which road to walk down."

"Correct." Louis's use of the third person soothed Annie Lee; she was sure it was some sort of meditation exercise in other parts of the world. "I mean, my husband may have had a good reason for dipping into the tawdry. Maybe Dad had a good reason, too. No one ever said he didn't."

"Nevertheless. My sister wasn't—isn't—the type of woman to do that to."

"I realize that, Louie!" Annie Lee had raised her voice. "I mean, of all people to say that to! I haven't spoken to the man for a third of my life! Most people would consider that insanity. Sometimes *I* do. But Mom deserved loyalty from *someone*." She caught herself and readjusted her voice to a whisper, which might have been more effective in the first place. "Am *I* the kind of person a man does this to?"

"What I meant, darling child," his voice was raspy, "was that your father probably did have a reason. But Izzy wasn't supposed to find out. He loved her more than he could possibly have loved anyone else, that much was obvious. Now, don't tell me that you're going to make the same mistake Izzy made." As her brother, he was the only one who could get away with the nickname or with calling what she'd irreversibly done "a mistake."

"No. Not that my ego isn't at worm's-eye level, or that Lucas doesn't deserve public flogging. Physical punishment, supervised by me, would fit this crime. But—and don't ever tell him this—the kind of loneliness I would feel without him seems like it might be worse than going through what I'm going through now."

"I see. Smart girl. Not that what he did was excusable." He paused. "But both you and your mother have the capacity to drown out others with those personalities of yours—given certain circumstances. A drowning man, you know, is not a happy man." He cleared his throat. "Enough said. I will sell the *item*," he summarized. "And I will send you the *cash*. What are your plans? Not mutual funds, I hope, or *anything* to do with the stock market, or boring IRAs. I have more lucrative suggestions if you need some . . ."

"We want to start a restaurant, Louie, here in Pike. Lucas and I."

Another pause, then a groan of disbelief. "A restaurant? With a mere twenty thou . . . Are you nuts? They break your back! I have a friend who started a little bistro on the West Side, very trendy—authentic—whatever. And you know what? He *lives* there, Annie Lee, and sleeps there—a few hours a day at best. He's there all the time." He sighed as if he'd been the one working all those hours. "Well, what kind of food are you gonna do?"

"Breakfast." She said the word like a secret weapon.

"Breakfast?" he barked back, then considered the concept. "Breakfast could be a different story. An American breakfast might work. Your grill items have got to be—"

"We know. Breakfast is good if it's perfect. It has to be perfect."

"Right. You can't have bad coffee; you can't have over-poached eggs. Your bacon has got to be fully crisped, not burned. You thinking of doing popovers? Your mother used to make the best popovers. To this day I still beg her to make them. They were like velvet."

After she got off the phone with Louis, Annie Lee retrieved an old photo album from the study and stared at pictures of her mother and father from fifteen years earlier. She tried to see just what a drowning-out personality looked like. She scrutinized her father's expressions to see if it looked as if he were suffocating. Then she looked at photos of herself and Lucas, scanning for clues of her tendency to drown *him* out. She couldn't see it. Couldn't see it in her mother, either. Maybe people put on airs for photographers. Maybe Lucas hadn't felt as happy as he'd looked in that photo of him and that woman.

Twenty-one

By the time the end of the ski season rolled around, Lucas had been sleeping on the couch for two weeks. After work every night, the knots in his neck had tightened so badly from leaning over food at the restaurant that he had to force down a glass of scotch before laying his head on the pillow. He didn't complain, though, and didn't move himself to the floor, probably concerned that he wouldn't be seen as doing the proper kind of penance there.

Finally, unable to take the pain any longer, even with the end of the work season just days away, he made an appointment to see his chiropractor, a sorceress of a bone popper by the name of Eloise Daniella. She called Annie Lee later in the day to inform her that it felt to her as if Lucas had received a severe blow at C5.

"When pressed, he admitted he's been sleeping on the *couch*, Annie Lee." She mumbled something about his jaw being out of whack, too, and then said, "I'll tell you what I told him. I can realign his body, but I can't realign his life. Sweetheart, the man needs to get back into a proper bed. Soon. Or stop doing what he does for a living. He's stubborn about things, so I'm asking you to help me out on this. Subtly, of course; use your womanly wiles."

"Of course," Annie Lee said, embarrassed to have to be asked to help her own husband. "My womanly wiles will be summoned." Unsure of how to proceed, she tried to imagine what someone else would do with wiles summoned—a Katharine Hepburn, even a Libby W. But all she could come up with that night, and the following, was a genuine offer to massage her husband's neck before bed.

He was all knotted up, there was no doubt about it. She had to use all her strength to knead and stroke and rub and apply pressure. Just when she thought she was getting somewhere, though, after maybe ten minutes, he would send her off to bed, swearing she'd made all the difference, swearing he felt good enough to sleep. It was almost as if he didn't want her to feel too guilty about leaving him down there on the couch.

Finally, the end of the season came. At last.

Every restaurant in town closed the night before the final day of skiing because management everywhere knew not a single employee would be in proper shape to work after the blowout finale on the mountain. Giancarlo and Mathilde would remain closed for the full seven weeks, until early June when the summer season began. Lina, who knew Lucas and Annie Lee's plans for opening their own place, gave Lucas a little going-away party, plenty of advice, her lucky white apron, and two more German knives for his collection as going-away gifts. She also gave him a kiss right on the mouth, something she'd never done before. "My condolences," she said. "You won't get any sleep or make any money the first year at least. I hope you know that. And I'm gonna be checking up on you. I'm gonna miss you Luca . . ."

At Mathilde, the end of the season meant comparing off-season notes. Con said he had no real inclination to do anything, but everybody knew he'd be hightailing it to Chicago to visit Dr. Elliot Neehigh, man of mystery, charm, and pocket pencil holders. Kathryn said she and her husband were thinking of having kids (stared right at Annie Lee as she said it) and wanted to conceive their first child on a beach somewhere. Annie Lee smiled at Kathryn's lies and wondered, staring at the mole right above her lip, how a tiny brown spot could say so much about someone.

Claire was going to Martha's Vineyard for a month to mooch off her sister's fiancé's parents. Shep was heading to California for more skiing. The chef, Michel Gaufrette, would make his annual trek back to France for a month, to eat good cheese, drink good wine, and visit his mother, in that order. Marc Broyard, aka Lover Boy, whose entire off-season itinerary was to hit Las Vegas for four days, blanched with homesickness at the mention of his native country.

Donna, that night's busser, couldn't leave town since she'd gotten on the framing crew of the first $5 million home to be built in Pike. Mikey was going surfing in Mexico, he said, and might not be back for opening, but would they please not give his job to anyone else? Jay was taking his family to Lake Powell for a couple of weeks. Annie Lee told the group she and Lucas would probably take a road trip to Wyoming for some big sky, some wide-open spaces, and no vanity plates. Though Lucas had quit his job, Annie Lee would remain on at Mathilde for one more season.

Eddie, who had restrained himself from making his usual running commentary, finally revealed that he would be returning to school for his MBA. "I mean, I love this town, but what am I going to do? Work in a restaurant for the rest of my life?"

"Gosh, no, Eddie." Con narrowed his eyes into black lasers. "Why would you want to waste one minute more of your distinguished life? Time to get a move on, youngster! Get the degree, get the wardrobe, get the babe. Get happy! And while you're at it, don't forget to step on all the little people on your way up!" It was not a nice way to say good-bye to Eddie, but Eddie had not chosen a nice way to say good-bye to the restaurant.

Things might have gotten really ugly had it not been for Lover Boy (who missed the exchange) and his entrance with the going-away cake Jay had instructed him to make for Eddie Stahl. Cake does not begin to describe the three-tiered espresso-chocolate structure festooned with nut baubles hanging from spun sugar. Fireworks, it looked like—or a fountain. Evidently, his talents *had* been stifled at Mathilde—he had never really shown his stuff. His stuff was outrageous! Openmouthed, the staff gawked and then clapped like children at what was before them. With Marc smiling proudly, the end of the last night was spent eating cake and forgiving—or at least forgetting—Eddie's crass behavior.

Annie Lee brought a large piece of the cake home for Lucas, who said it was the best mocha cake he had ever tasted and set about figuring out how Marc had gotten all those slivery layers of hazelnut praline inside of it.

The chocolate/coffee combination, however impeccable it was, kept them both up. Lucas closed his eyes around 2:00 A.M. Annie Lee studied his face briefly before heading upstairs where she lay awake for another hour and a half before nodding off. They woke up late and ate Irish oats for breakfast. Lucas made a huge pot of black tea instead of the usual coffee. The tea was quenching and fortified them to head out for that one last day of skiing. On their way out the door, he handed her a megavitamin, with everything in it but the kitchen sink, and a glass of Gatorade, the orange kind. She took the supplement obediently and willed herself to be strong, despite the lack of sleep, for the day ahead.

Traditionally, everyone went out on that last day of the season. It was a day when Pike turned into a version of its former self, a town where everyone knew everyone else and said hello with the ease of those having fun and enjoying life. Like Brigadoon, it reawakened for one day only—though once a year in Pike instead of every hundred. This year, the second Sunday in April was so unseasonably warm the snow base seemed to be thawing an inch at a time beneath the friction of the hordes of skis and snowboards. Annie Lee and Lucas, who had not skied together at all in recent months, had forgotten how pleasant such a day could be. Carving turns through slushy snow, peeling off layers of clothing after every run, and then relaxing at the midmountain lodge, surrounded by smells of barbecue and coconut sunscreen.

When they finally returned home, bronzed and blessedly fatigued, they put their feet up and had a few beers. Annie Lee could not remember the last time she'd felt so content. But why? Her husband had still cheated on her. She was still incapable of conceiving. The only differences in her life were contained in the facets of a diamond and the forces of magnetism. Realistically, they could have borrowed all the money needed for their breakfast joint before all this had come to pass—but somehow it hadn't happened, didn't seem feasible. Now, it seemed inevitable. Lucas felt the same way. "Maybe the magnets have cumulative effects," he ventured, handing a bowl to Annie Lee.

"Beer nuts," she said, looking at him. "You hate beer nuts." She took the bowl and stared down into it, then reached in for a handful.

"I bought them for you," he said. "To try and bribe my way back into your good graces."

"Kind of a cheap bribe," she said, trying to look unmoved by the gesture. The look on Lucas's face made her wish she hadn't tried quite so hard.

Exhausted, not so much from skiing as the bad sleep of the night before, Lucas fell asleep on the unmade couch at 8:30

that night. Annie Lee draped a heavy blanket over him. She could not stop herself from staring at his face again before heading up to bed. Isn't it remarkable, she thought, as she noted a single, newly sprouted freckle on his lip, that you can agree to make a life with someone without really having any idea at all what you'll be in for. What makes us do such things, have such faith? Simple desire? Is it all just a matter of chemistry?

It was the middle of the night—awakened by wind and branches breaking, a gale whipping through the trees with such force the double-hung windows began rattling—when Annie Lee sat up in her bed, instantly attentive, as if someone had called her name loudly and come to fetch her. The wind continued to whip and howl and thrash until Annie Lee, as if in harmony with the elements, let the cobwebs in her heart come down one by one, ousted by the great gusts around her. With no forewarning, she started to feel free again and light. Unencumbered. It was hard to tell, but it had the feel of forgiveness, a kind of weighted weightlessness. Certainly it seemed ridiculous now to think of Lucas sleeping downstairs. Ridiculous.

She slipped out of bed and went to the rattling window, which she felt she must yank open. Wind rushed in and fluttered things on the walls. Annie Lee stuck the upper half of her body out and breathed in the air, the moisture, the wind. Everything was alive.

Then she turned around and tiptoed downstairs, through the shadows, and over the boards she knew would squeak, and right over to the couch. Lucas was lying on his back, one hand hanging down and brushing the floor. He was snoring and appeared not to have moved at all since he'd fallen asleep. Colonel Klink lay on one arm of the couch with his portly body spilling over the sides. Another enormous crack of a tree branch caused the cat's eyes to open but not Lucas's.

Annie Lee approached the couch, her heart thumping like

a teenager's. Bending down, she laid restraint to rest and put her lips to his and remained there until he stirred; and then she kissed him. Really kissed him, the kind of kiss that builds up inside and brings every live wire of longing to the delicate forefront of two lips.

He did not jerk up but opened his eyes dreamily as if waiting for that very thing to happen. "Annie Lee . . ." he stroked her hair gently and pulled her down toward him and found her mouth, her neck, slipped his hand under the tee shirt she'd worn to bed. She felt herself tingle, his warm fingers on her cool skin. "M-m-m-m," she murmured as her juices began to flow.

Oh, yes, she thought: This is what gets people together.

Lucas carried her to their bed upstairs and then loved every inch of her that stormy night as if he had been waiting a lifetime to do it. Outside, the wind raged on. Inside, microdrafts rippled the gauze of the mosquito netting. Annie Lee let herself be rubbed raw, then caressed delicately, and felt herself return to the eager lovemaking of their past.

They fell asleep as dawn broke and were awakened midday by the sounds of rain and snow, an apt beginning for the six-week season of weather mixed with mud. Annie Lee looked contentedly outside, feeling snug in her house, even more snug in her bed. At one o'clock, after a leisurely breakfast of roast beef hash, they grabbed their jackets and went to walk the emptying streets together.

"Isn't spring wonderful?" Lucas said, cold raindrops falling on his head and face. "For a few brief weeks we get to live in a ghost town. Nobody wants to come here. Even people who live here go away. There's no fine dining, no espresso, no *New York Times*, no nothing. Just a few people, dwarfed by these mountains and numbed by eight months of winter. I love it. Let's walk to the river."

"Okay, the river," she said. "Then let's go back and do that again. If you think you're up to it."

By the second day of off-season, every employee of every resort-oriented business in Pike—which meant everyone but construction workers and government employees—had disappeared. The children were given two weeks off from school, and most families tried to get out of town, at least for part of that time. The Doyles were no exception.

Annie Lee was giving the blow-by-blow to Lucas as she watched Jim from the living-room window. He was loading up the Suburban for their drive to Chicago, which was not, after all, a move but merely a visit. With his mouse-brown polo shirt neatly tucked into his khakis, sleeves rolled up, he wrestled earnestly with the great task before him. Wedging this bag, inserting that one. He lay certain suitcases flat, some upright, twisting and turning the bulky puzzle like a Rubik's cube until finally he had nothing left but the family-sized red cooler and a hole of accurately matched dimensions. He paused as if reflecting on his worthiness and then hoisted the cooler up and slid it in slowly, gently. Annie Lee did not see gloating today, what she saw was relief. Jim could still pack a vehicle.

He hitched up his pants, slammed the back doors of the car, and then looked toward the house in a fleeting moment of panic—as if gripped by a fear that his *Wonderful Life* family had never been anything more than a figment of his imagination. But in the next split second, the flesh-and-blood brood emerged—Judy, Harold, Megan, Oliver, Helena, and Jimmy came tumbling out of the front door. Jimmy ran to his father, who scooped him up and cartwheeled him in the air, and the rest of the children dutifully found their assigned seats, placing their backpacks at their feet like well-trained passengers.

Judy wasn't smiling. She wasn't frowning, but she wasn't smiling, either. As they pulled out of the driveway, Annie Lee speculated on how they would possibly fit two more babies into a vehicle. Would they have to start over, as Judy had said, with new cribs, high chairs, strollers, even cars? She wondered if it had been hard for Judy to part with the lovely old carved crib, which Klink had lately adopted as his nap spot.

As the Doyle family turned the corner onto Crabapple, Annie Lee was overcome with a yearning to paint and headed to the spare bedroom to evaluate her supplies. Though her hand seemed at this moment to be the rightful place for a brush, or even a roller, it was not clear to her what she would cover with color until she entered the room, its whiteness screaming mutely against the rich wood of the room's only piece of furniture, the newly acquired crib. The room, naked and cold, was begging for color now.

With no doubt in her mind that none of the colors on hand would do, Annie Lee put on a coat and told Lucas she was going to the post office to check her mailbox.

There were no other customers in the paint store. After briefly studying the ready-made swatch cards in their tidy rows, she grabbed the one with four colors verging on celadon and then pointed at the third one down. "Marty, could you give me two gallons of this color here—#427, in eggshell. Artichoke Leaf. I have one white room left and I'm going to paint it!" Marty stared at her lips—they must have been red and swollen from the kissing—but said nothing. He mixed the paint. He smiled as he put little handles on the paint cans for her.

When she got home, Lucas had his own surprise. He was staring at something they'd received by Federal Express. It was a personal check from Louis.

"We'll still have to get a loan, Annie Lee," he said to her. "A pretty big one. But it's seed money. We'll start as small as possible. Val said he'd come and work for me—" He saw the paint cans.

"I'm painting the—spare bedroom. A nice artichoke-leaf

color. It's been white long enough." She tapped the lid of the can with her finger. "I figure if we want a child that badly, we can go the in-vitro route like your mother said." She took the check from him and stared at it. She tried to contain herself. "What will $22,496 buy in the real world?"

Lucas already had an answer worked out. "A grill. A dishwasher. A big refrigerator. Some more sinks. In vitro. That's probably about it. But it's somewhere to start."

"Libby wants us to do blini."

"Buckwheat blini?" Lucas smiled and scratched his neck.

"And Louis says we should definitely do popovers like my mom used to make in her early days as a homemaker."

"Popovers," he nodded solemnly.

Annie Lee stared at him. "Aren't you going to get bored with breakfast?" she asked. "Dream of more complicated meals, experimentation, virtuosity? You're not going to get sick of flipping eggs and cakes and slices of ham and having people beg you to do Belgian waffles and eggs Benedict? 'Can you do a half Benedict? Can you do real poached eggs?' Aren't you meant to be cooking up creations instead of Number Twos with sausage?"

"Not right now," he said. "Right now I'm supposed to be doing breakfast."

Klink was waiting in the nursery when Annie Lee arrived with her painting clothes on. He was perched precariously on a pile of cans with his tail hanging down like the letter *J*. She couldn't resist flecking the appendage with just a dab of the new color to make him not quite so gray through and through, (from footpads to nose to actual splotches of gray on his tongue, which had always struck her as spookily deviant).

The paint went on darker than she figured, but she liked the shade right away. With each stripe of the roller, the room came verdantly alive. A few hours later, after scanning her progress, she only wondered about having painted the ceiling. Maybe, she thought, she should have painted it with some contrasting color. Darker? Lighter? Back to white? Unsure of how to proceed, she started opening the stacked cans of leftover paint, one by one, to see what she could come up with. Finally, she decided to try mixing a bit of Canary in the House with the Artichoke Leaf.

Klink meanwhile had discovered the irregularity in his tail and was biting at the fur, yanking at it and then spitting out the paint as if it were contaminating the pure tonal value of his very life. For Annie Lee, just the opposite was happening. It was in mixing the paint together in a clean bucket that something multilayered but simple clutched her—like coming up for air after a plunge into icy cold mountain lake water. This minor act of watching green paint stream into yellow and then disappear before resurfacing in blobs thrilled her. She mixed them together with a stick and watched the swirls, like ribbon candy, fold into each other, creating a new color, slowly converging. It filled her with yearning. She opened all the remaining cans of leftover paint before her and stared at them, overcome with the notion of color, of being able to spread color upon the world as if it were a blank canvas.

Lucas always left his wife alone while she painted a room, but when she still had not emerged at 1:00 A.M., he quietly stuck his head in the door. What he saw was not only a freshly painted room, but an immense shadow of the crib projected on the wall and painted a thick plum color. Annie Lee was sitting cross-legged on the floor when she heard the boards creak and turned to find him there, loitering, with a bowl of buttered egg noodles for her.

"Nice shadow," he said, testing a noodle before handing her the snack.

Annie Lee's smile took up the majority of her face. "Well," she said, "I was thinking about the colors of shadows, the way certain balloons actually cast colored ones. Have you ever noticed that? So I mixed Dark-and-Stormy-Night Blue with a mistake pink, and it gave me this wonderful—"

"Bitten Plum color," Lucas finished.

"Yes." She nodded, feeling understood, and then ate her food ravenously, like a starved animal, before heading to their bed where she fell into a dreamless sleep.

For the next week, Lucas researched restaurant equipment over the phone and tried to sketch out what had to be done to the kitchen. Annie Lee set up an easel in the spare bedroom and told herself she would just be playing around with paint, not to get nervous or be too critical of herself. For her first painting she'd used one of the Orna Vitale photos and "repainted" their old white house. "It's just another form of house painting," she said, trying to calm herself. But, still, it took her four or five attempts—with gesso between—before she felt she could leave it alone.

"Here I am," she summarized upon the completion of her first painting in over a decade, "finally realizing that a white house is not really white at all. Nothing in a painting is white. Hardly anything in life is white except the paint in the can before it's opened, but you can't see it *until* it's open, and by then it has shadows. Nothing is pure white."

The Flecks also spent countless hours speculating on their house and what Speranzo Vitale's true intentions had been with regard to his magnets. In all the histories of Pike, Lucas could find no mention of the magnet house except for a small notation in a paper dated 1912 regarding Orna's never missing a single day of school. Nothing more directly relevant than that. Annie Lee and Lucas felt there was something the sisters weren't telling them, but Eudora swore they'd revealed everything except the fact that Speranzo had died relatively early in life—

from a broken neck after a horse had thrown him—with his life's work probably unfinished and certainly unpublished.

"So I don't know," Eudora said, "what to tell you. So much of history is unrecorded, you know. Speranzo found a proportion of magnetic material that worked—that wasn't overwhelming or destructive—but that was before the age of appliances and electronics. You've been witness to a certain number of devices going haywire. Lucky for you the microwave works. I doubt cell phones will function inside the restaurant, though—"

"God bless that idea," Bea interjected. "The only thing worse than phones in restaurants is being at the movies and hearing that awful ringing from someone's pocket. What kind of ignorant barbarian does such things? Why, what was that we saw recently? The movie was practically ruined for me because of that very thing."

"She was headed down toward the front to find the man and confiscate his phone"—Eudora had to struggle to keep her tone serious—"but she bumped into someone in the aisle, and all the Whoppers from the box in her hand fell on the floor, rolling toward the front, causing more commotion than that man's phone."

"Yes, well," Bea said, "he got lucky that time. Whoever he was; I never found out."

With such neighbors and such stories around them, Lucas and Annie Lee only halfheartedly began packing for their off-season trip. It was tempting just to stay home and try to feel the force, figure it out. But an excursion to Denver's big restaurant suppliers was mandatory; and, given all the work required in opening a restaurant, they knew it would be a while before they would take another vacation. And so they made haste to leave town.

Twenty-two

They spent three days in Denver in a condo Lina persuaded her son Paolo to offer for the Flecks' use. While Lucas went from warehouse to warehouse, looking at ovens and pans and grills and becoming discouraged at the high cost of everything, Annie Lee waded through the other aisles, the ones filled with syrup pitchers and straw holders, plastic trays and coffeepots, a new world of morning essentials. Finally, Lucas got hooked up with a guy who sold used commercial equipment and was cheered up considerably. Then he and Annie Lee started conversing again, hashing out plans and ideas, especially during the midday and evening meals. Breakfast, however, was sacred.

Each morning they toured coffee shops, sampling and studying and staring at the cooks, the boss, the waitresses, the food, to see how things flowed. On Tuesday, at yet another place called "Coffee Shop," it was painfully obvious to Annie Lee after sitting at her table for five minutes that the waiflike waitress on duty was having problems taking orders and delivering food and everything in between. The boss was following her around, yelling at her like one of those little dogs whose mouths are bigger than their heads.

Meanwhile, all the customers needed coffee.

Annie Lee, perceiving the raw material of nightmares in front of her, slid out of her booth before she had a chance to think about what she was doing, and moved toward the coffeemaker, where she grabbed the two pots. She made a round, refilling cups at every table. As she returned the pots to their burners, she noticed a lone plate of eggs slowly turning to rubber under the heat lamp and felt she might be remiss in not delivering them to the only single guy in the place.

"Two eggs scrambled with ham," she said placing the plate before him. "Enjoy your meal." She then scanned the rest of the tables to see if any necks were craning for the waitress. Satisfied that things were temporarily under control, she returned to her seat.

By the time the owner caught up with Annie Lee to thank her and ask her if she wanted a job, she had grabbed the coffeepot again and was filling Lucas's cup. Their breakfasts had somehow miraculously appeared. Lucas looked up from his waffle at the man propositioning his wife and said to him, "You use extra baking soda in these, don't you?"

It was while in Denver, she supposed because of the geographic proximity of Poison Control, that Annie Lee had the notion to call Gabriel Salt. No emergency situations this time, no lies, no solicitations for advice. She just wanted to say hi, hear his voice again. She tried twice before being given Gabriel's shift hours, assuring the woman she was a friend and wanted to surprise him.

"Then why are you calling the Poison Control number, if you're his friend?" the woman wanted to know.

"That's part of the surprise," said Annie Lee. "Get it?"

Gabriel seemed truly glad to hear her voice.

"What are you doing when you're not on a call?" she asked, after giving him a brief synopsis of their trip so far.

"Right now I'm reading *Saveur* magazine, an article about making a Monte Cristo sandwich, which sounds divine. Of course my shift provisions include nothing of the sort." She heard the rustling of paper, probably waxed. "Banana sandwich," he enumerated. "Lay's potato chips. And carrot salad. I have a Thermos of tea."

"Well, pour yourself a cup, because I'd like to tell you how the diamond I swallowed finally materialized." She brought him up to date with a recap of the events of the past weeks, and by the time she'd finished, she could hear the smile on the other end of the phone.

"So you're putting the dirty diamond to good use!" he declared with satisfaction. "Well, breakfast is a great idea. Are you going to do those bran muffins like they have back East? You know, the kind they always sell right next to the corn muffins? I love those things!" Annie Lee had put him on speakerphone so that Lucas could hear the conversation, so he wouldn't think she was hogging Gabriel or anything. And it was Lucas who assured him their plan was to comfort people with a breakfast experience—"swaddle them in the pleasures of morning" were his words. "A coffee shop can, for some people," Lucas said, more pedagogically than Annie Lee thought fitting, "be more of a home than a home."

"It's the baseball of meals," Annie Lee tossed in.

"Well," Gabriel said, "there is much psychology involved in eating, of course. The different times and places people eat. The role of a restaurant in all of this. What people choose to fix for themselves and how they do it. For some, the nostalgia factor is key. Things must never change—ever!"

"That's right!" said Lucas, beaming at Annie Lee. "My wife fits that bill. She's got to have her sanctioned items, the things that never change—it's a personality thing." Annie Lee would have interrupted, but they sounded so happy talking to each other, she thought it better to leave them alone.

After several minutes, Lucas mentioned Gabriel's personality-test idea and suggested he write it up. "Breakfast is the one meal people actively seek out reading material for," he offered. "Why not write up part of the food/personality test on one page? Then we could put it in the menu holders. I mean, how much more captive could your audience be?"

Gabriel thought about it. He said it probably wouldn't make them a fortune, but that it did sound oddly charming. "It would have to be excellent," he mused. "Clever as well as deep. I could give it a try . . . Are you still there, Annie Lee? You with us?"

He was a sweetheart, wasn't he? "I'm with you, of course!" she said. "I love the idea . . . I just . . ." she looked at Lucas. "I don't want anyone pegging me as a food traditionalist. I mean, I am and I'm not. I try new things all the time—I live with an experimenter! Isn't it reasonable to constantly want standard breakfasts in the face of experimental lunches? It's a reaction! So somewhere in your test, you should include something about why we choose what we do . . . As pleasure? As antidote? As bodily need? As trend?"

"Good point," Gabriel said before Lucas had a chance to contradict his wife in any way. "And how that connects to other personality traits. Yes. And who we are is so much a reflection of whom we are with."

"That's what I meant," Annie Lee sighed. "Only I couldn't say it so succinctly."

Finally, a call came in. Gabriel quickly excused himself, told her he'd call her in Pike, and laughed when he said, "Have a good time in Wyoming."

Though the weather was patchy in Colorado, the second they crossed into Wyoming it was dry as a Milk-Bone. Meandering through the state with no predetermined itinerary, they car camped and even tent camped a few times. Occasionally, they would splurge on a motel to escape the bellowslike Wyoming winds, dry squalls that had a way of making craziness boil up inside until you had to stop, comb your hair, brush your teeth, and shower. Get the grit out.

Lucas liked stopping at gas stations in the godforsaken middle of nowhere where he would hope for a piece of authentic homemade pie or fresh peanut brittle or something basic that went with the territory. Though Wyoming restaurants were for the most part grim, according to Lucas's theory, you could usually find one decent thing on any truck-stop menu. He seemed to have a sixth sense about it and ordered different items confidently every time. Without fail, he fared better than Annie Lee, who had only bad luck to report at the roulette wheel of truck-stop dining.

In one such meal break, Annie Lee realized that she hadn't felt peevish for quite some time and that, by her calendar, she ought to. The notion of choosing between a bacon burger and yet another "chef salad" should have set her off, made her cranky at this time of the month. Instead, she simply ordered the chef salad—and didn't even flinch when it came out in retro shades of Iceberg, American Cheese, and Spam-pink. And at which point Lucas cracked a smile and said, "Oooh—maybe not such a great choice." He'd chosen correctly again: ham steak with the bone in.

No, not even the whisper of a peeve as she put a dollop of dressing as thick as mayonnaise (Miracle Whip?) on top of the iceberg wedge and picked up her steak knife and fork.

In Casper, Wyoming, however, at the tail end of their trip and only one long driving day away from home, Annie Lee woke up in her motel twin bed to the sound of the shower through the cardboard walls and felt nausea creep up on her from somewhere deep inside. She was quiet as they drove around looking for a breakfast spot. Finally they pulled in at Paulette's, on the far edge of town. A onetime trailer, its angular neon sign sputtered winsomely in turquoise. Neither of them, together or alone, would have ever driven past such a place without stopping.

Annie Lee was staring at her plate. White toast. White eggs. Hash whites. She popped a yolk and had dipped a corner of toast in it before gagging.

"More coffee?" said the waitress with practiced congeniality.

"I know this is a pain in the neck," said Annie Lee, trying not to look at her plate, "but do you think I could have some tea instead? Lipton or something?"

"No problem, hon." The woman finished her rounds with coffee before bringing Annie Lee an ample pot of near-boiling water, cream enough for four, and even honey. Like an oasis in the desert, the tea came just right.

"Want my eggs?" she said to Lucas while watching the waitress darting here and there in Uniform Maroon, the same color they used on lettermen's jackets. She had nine tables and no help, and could turn on a dime if she heard her name or the kitchen bell, or sensed anyone was in need of anything. It was beautiful to watch this person named Janelle.

Lucas shrugged and slid the runny eggs onto his plate, next to some grease-boat sausages. He hardly seemed to be noticing the food. "I want to remember," he said, finally taking a look at what was going into his mouth, "exactly what this place looks like. I like everything about it . . ." He stopped as if biting down on a particularly stubborn piece of gristle and then continued in a whisper, "Except the food." Annie Lee had to agree it had just the look they wanted in a coffee shop.

"Not hungry for a bad breakfast, huh?" Lucas finally asked, realizing he'd eaten not one but two listless plates of food.

She shook her head. "Even my fondness for grease was called into question," she said, the tea reviving her. "There was no correct answer on that particular multiple-choice menu." Lucas burped in agreement.

Back in the truck, she took notes, as she had been doing all along, on details not to be forgotten. "Never get honey in those little boxes with the peel-off lids, I hate those," she said. "You have to use a knife to get it into your tea. With the bags, you can dunk it right into the hot water, get it all liquid-y, and then it dissolves perfectly. See. Stuff like that is really important."

"I agree." Lucas was staring out the window at endless Wyoming with its blue umbrella of sky, the occasional solitary white cloud scuttling like a lost sheep to get back to its far-off fold. "Details are important. So is the actual food." Such was the nature of their conversation as they headed home that day. Through desertscapes dotted only by telephone poles. Through northern Colorado's rain and sleet and flickering sun. Through southwesterly fruit blossoms and full-on heat—and finally back up into the cool San Juan Mountains on the shoulder of the Four Corners.

Back in Pike, dandelions greeted the spring with their pompons of cheerleader's yellow. Aspen trees had started to unfurl their tender leaves. Irrigation ditches were running high, and kayakers had begun their love affair with the raging river. Lucas gloried in the return to familiar and well-loved surroundings. "Coming home from a vacation like that," he said to her as they drove down Main Street slowly, "is like being spun around and around with a blindfold on and then released, dizzy, into the light of day."

Annie Lee agreed with the sentiment and nodded with as much enthusiasm as she could muster. She was happy to be home and took exception only to the use of the word dizzy. Wasn't it more like queasy?

Klink met Lucas at the door with enough meowing, purring, and leg rubbing to suggest that separation had been unbearable this time, truly unbearable. Just as soon as he could put down his duffelbag, Lucas picked up the cat and draped it over his shoulders, uttering kind words of apology into its ear.

Annie Lee dropped her duffel at the bottom of the stairs and headed straight up to the bathroom to do what she had been thinking about ever since that last long stretch of road, while Lucas listened to famous essays about food. She'd caught a few paragraphs here and there, but found herself physically veering away from the discourse on buttery escargots and the essential wines of Burgundy. Lucas had not even replayed all the phone messages before she had found what she was looking for, taken the test, and gotten the positive results. In her state of astonishment, the nausea surged. She realized then, for the first time, that pregnancy was a physical condition, not just some highly elusive and desirable state unconnected to the realities of childbirth.

Her body had already begun to change.

Eudora, who had come over the instant she'd seen their red Ford pickup pull into the driveway to tell Lucas she had already hired the Doyle kids to pick berries this summer for the jam the sisters had been commissioned to make, said something looked different about Annie Lee; her expression seemed—different. When Annie Lee said that actually there was something very different, she was pregnant, Lucas swung around so fast he hit his head on the door of one of the kitchen cabinets, which he had opened to get a water glass. As he stood there, stunned by each of the blows and even dripping a little blood to prove it, Eudora ran home to tell Bea, and in the two minutes it took for them to return, Annie Lee assured Lucas this wasn't some mean trick, the test was positive, and she seemed to be having a mild but unrelenting form of all-day morning sickness.

"I don't even want *coffee*," she told him with the urgency of shaking someone to his senses.

* * *

They spent the next few days in a state of stupefaction as their brains spun, trying to figure out how this had happened. Had sex been different in motels and sleeping bags than it was back at home? Had their state of mind made a difference? Or had their physical lovemaking, after a two-and-a-half-month dry spell, gained such a potency as to render even the formerly infertile fertile again? After feeling like a deficient couple, dabbling with pregnancy in the way lackey masons dabbled with stones, both of them were jolted not only by the surprise of success but by a new respect for their bodies. But what had done it?

Several days later, it came to Lucas.

He had just awakened from a nap—with a stiff neck reminiscent of earlier couch episodes—when he called his wife over excitedly with a possible explanation for her unexpected condition. "I had to ask myself what we'd done differently, really differently, and the only thing I could come up with was my sleeping downstairs for two weeks—here on this couch—where I've never slept before."

She stared at him, not getting whatever he was getting at.

"Here on this couch, Annie Lee," he knuckled the walls. "Right next to the *insulation*. Remember Libby Wolverton's percentages about male factor infertility? Well, maybe it was me the whole time . . ." He continued on, postulating that while he slept, his slow-moving or otherwise deficient sperm were being magnetized, their motility and/or numbers increasing in the force field. Was it possible, they asked the sisters?

Of course, Eudora wanted to hear explicitly why he'd slept on the couch for two weeks before offering her opinion on the matter, smugly nodding her head to all he said. "Well, the Lord works in mysterious ways," she finally said, looking at Annie Lee. "And magnets seem to be the only explanation on the table. I suppose if a hot bath can slow spermatozoa down, magnets can speed them up!"

Annie Lee thought she should mention the Oram Advisory and the Klimps, just to play devil's advocate. Bea tossed off the idea as poppycock. "Imagine saying such a thing. Who wants to hear that they shouldn't try so hard at getting what they want? Oliver should stick to his bagpipes if he wants to blow wind! Lord have mercy on that man."

"He was good to me, Bea. And he was right." Annie Lee, in spite of her nausea, felt like being kind and generous to the whole world. "You miss things, wonderful things, if the focus is too all-consuming." She glanced at her husband.

"Well, his *be-here-now* didn't get you pregnant, though, did it?" Bea said, which, much to her delight, set Lucas laughing.

"And neither did his *Carpe diem*," confirmed Eudora, in a direct translation from Zen to Latin. "*Carpe lapem magnem* is more like it." She pursed her lips. "Seize the lodestone."

Bea was marching them up to the nursery, wanting to talk about babies. "Id like to see what old Ollie Oram would make of all this now. Spouting off as if he were some guru—the nerve!" She saw the freshly painted room and gasped. "Look at *that*," she said to Eudora, who seemed to be sneaking in a stroke (they claimed not to like pets) as Klink stole by them into the room. "They've painted the nursery! Even before they knew!"

Annie Lee was reluctant to reveal her pregnancy to anyone else until after the first trimester—until she looked at least slightly pregnant and felt less queasy. In the meantime, she met with Dr. Oram to confirm the matter. He would be her in-town obstetrician, while a doctor at the nearest hospital would deliver the baby. She waited (predisposed by Bea's comments) for Dr. Oram to gloat, to mark the occasion with an adage reconfirming his prior angle on things. But she waited in vain, her original opinion of the man confirmed. All he did, after verifying the pregnancy, was tell her how radiant she looked, prescribe some vitamins, set up her appointments with him, and advise her to take a nap every day before going to work.

"I knew it would work out for you two," he finally said in the last thirty seconds of the visit. Annie Lee tensed. Here we go, she thought, here comes the punch line. "All it needed was time," he said.

"Actually," she said, "it was more than that, Dr. Oram. It was a lot of things coming together at once. It was simple and yet complex. It was scientific, yet enigmatic. It was free will versus fate. It was . . ." She thought about how to get through to him. "It was the arrow, shooting itself, into the wind, through the fog, toward the target. *My* target. See?"

He laughed and shook his head. "The shortest distance between two points is a line connecting past events," he said.

"I'll see you in a month," she said to the man, searching hard for a return quip. "I'll come with my best footnote forward."

"I don't doubt it," he said, putting his arm around her shoulders. "Remember the nap, Annie Lee. Waiting tables is a lot of work for a pregnant woman."

And it was, even early on. She didn't tell her coworkers until mid-July by which time most of them had probably noticed even the miniscule augmentation in a bustline like hers. And like Jessica Mars, Annie Lee had pimples to show for a body that just seemed to be doing its own thing. One night, Con asked her if she'd ever heard of face powder for that kind of shine on her nose and then stared at her long and hard before hitting the nail on the head. Turning beet red, she nodded and was unable to keep from choking up as she revealed her January due date.

Con wiped her tears and kissed both her cheeks, and they all celebrated with slices of a flourless terrine of chocolate, which Annie Lee wished she could box up a dozen of to take home.

The next day she called her mother, a call which began with magnetism-the-concept and ended with magnetism-the-miracle-cure-for-sluggish-sperm. "I'm PG, Mom," she summed up. "Three months. And it seems magnetism is what caused it. Well, above and beyond Lucas, of course."

"Almost too unbelievable for words," Isabelle said once she'd recovered her voice and congratulated her daughter and said a few words about the rewards of having children. Annie Lee had a handful of saltines set before her in a crispy tower. Someone had told her they were good for morning sickness, but staring at the cheerful blue-and-yellow box seemed to help her even more than the actual crackers.

Isabelle asked about Margaret Fleck's reaction and Lucas's feelings on the matter and ended the conversation by saying she would have to try sleeping near the walls on her next visit, see where it got her. On her own, however, back in Piermont, she proceeded to launch the full-on magnetization of her own life. A rotated, north-facing bed. Magnetic insoles for all her shoes. A magnetic backrest for her favorite chair. Magnetic wristbands. Shortly thereafter, she reported a keener sense of smell and greatly improved appetite and digestion and also mentioned, with feigned dismay, that someone had asked her on a date.

"Wow," Annie Lee replied, riveted by the concept. "A date? Are you going to go? Who is it?"

"I might," Isabelle said. "Just a man. *Un homme*." The French word somehow clinched this idea of the essential nature of man, of woman, of coming together. Of complication. Annie Lee tried to remind herself that her mother might soon be the one uttering the word "sex" to her daughter, and that Annie Lee would have to be the one hearing it. And she could not stop that feeling of helplessness, the same feeling, in fact, that Megan had lately incited in her.

Megan Doyle was spending more and more time at the Fleck

home as fall approached. Interior walls were coming down. Lucas and Val had moved all the living room furniture upstairs so they could work on the coffee shop part, and Megan found it very exciting to be in the midst of such changes. Judy, as big as a blimp by now, was grateful that Megan had somewhere to go, and seemed to understand that at thirteen every child needed a place of refuge.

Sometimes Megan did her homework at the Flecks' and other times she brought her quilting over, attempting, without much success, to teach Annie Lee the stitches. Annie Lee was too distracted by the young girl's developing use of color and shape and theme, which she found exciting. One day, with a smile sweet enough, full enough of joy to radiate throughout her body, Megan informed Annie Lee that Quinn had almost kissed her in the school parking lot, but that his friends had shown up. She was holding a piece of work with stitches so fine it made Annie Lee want to cry.

A kiss, she wanted to tell the girl, is the first fracture, the tiniest hairline fissure in a heart that will be broken many times. A kiss, she wanted to say, is the beginning of inevitability. But she held her tongue. Instead, she hugged her little friend and felt, she was certain, the wings of a woman about to sprout from the bony shoulders of a girl.

Not long thereafter, Quinn did kiss Megan, and she took on the dazed yet unscrupulously focused look of girls of a certain age. Annie Lee asked Lucas what he knew about this Quinn. He stopped sweeping up plaster long enough to look surprised. "Is that who she's got a crush on? Our little Megan?" He shook his head. "Quinn's taller than me and his shoulders are broader. He plays soccer and basketball. He's verging on manhood."

"Oh, God." Annie Lee sighed, thinking that maybe she should send Megan over to the sisters for a little bit of a lecture on the shortcomings of men, some tea and cookies, and a blitzkrieg round of brainwashing, plus a few new quilting stitches, some sewing homework—stuff to keep her busy. But with that look in Megan's eye, it almost seemed like it might already be too late.

Before she'd decided on what to do, however, Eudora had called Annie Lee, her voice so panicky all other circumstances were temporarily put aside. "What is it?" Annie Lee's heart skipped a beat. "What's happened?"

Twenty-three

"Bea's gone and broken her foot, Annie Lee. Gone and broken her foot! I know she has, it's all swelled up."

Annie Lee hung up quickly to relay the emergency to Lucas, who swiftly nabbed Val, and together they carried the stiffly protesting Bea to the truck and got her to the medical center. Two hours later, Bea returned with a cast up to her knee, her face pale and worried. Eudora got her settled on the couch and handed her a lipstick and compact.

"This is not only uncomfortable and cumbersome," Bea said, impressively revived with the application of makeup, "it's downright embarrassing. And with all the swelling, I'll probably have to get another cast put on in a few days. So that doctor said, who looked about twelve. Dr. Twist."

"No one has to know you were doing television aerobics, Beatrice, that you needed to prove something or other." Eudora's tone, outwardly scolding, did not hide her inner agitation. "Landsakes. The whole town'll be happy to sign that monstrosity. You can tell 'em all it was a stress fracture, an old injury—that you finally had to do something about it since you'd decided to live another thirty or forty years."

"I feel old," Bea said, indulging herself for a moment while she allowed Lucas to prop up her leg. He followed Eudora's lead and brought Bea a comb and mirror from the powder room.

"Well, you're going to feel pampered soon enough," he said. "And then I'm going to set you to work handwriting the menus. We need an old cursive look." Bea's lip trembled as she smiled at him, and Annie Lee's heart ached.

Lucas made sure, in the weeks that followed, that Bea was kept busy doing small things for the restaurant. In addition, he managed the minor miracle of getting her to go see Dr. Daniella, who kindly refrained from lecturing the sisters on the importance of spinal adjustment for seniors. Bea admitted to feeling curiously better if light-headed, and Eudora had the propriety to note her sister's posture had clearly improved. Was she really doing aerobics? Dr. Daniella wanted to know, to which Eudora, answering for her sister, said it wasn't the aerobics per se but the cans of lentil soup she'd tried using as weights. She'd dropped one right on her left foot.

"This town has gotten to you both," Dr. Daniella answered, shaking her head. "Everyone in this sports-obsessed town is hell-bent on misaligning their bones. I'd heard you two were common sense incarnate, but frankly I'm not seeing it!" Lucas said the look on the Winks' faces was enough to make him smile for the rest of his life: they'd met their unlikely match in Eloise Daniella. Later, Eudora said to Lucas if Dr. Daniella ever came into the coffee shop, she was sure she'd be the type to complain if her poached eggs were even slightly off. And, she added through the side of her mouth, it took one to know one.

* * *

The restaurant did finally open. After six mind-and-body-numbing months of planning, remodeling, securing loans and a liquor license, getting equipment and supplies, and at long last watching that first truckload of food being unloaded from their own driveway.

Not that things hadn't gone wrong; plenty of things had.

But none of it had really bothered Annie Lee. Not that they were running three weeks late because of inspections and hadn't had time to get the hang of anything before opening their doors to the holiday hordes. Not that a new bakery had opened near the gondola, one that made cheap breakfast sandwiches and baked their own superior and crusty bread the likes of which Pike had never had before. Not that they hadn't had time to advertise in the *Winter Gazette*, the four-color guide to Pike that lay on every nightstand by every guest bed in town.

The only thing that really bothered her—unnerved her, rather—was that the house right across the street from theirs had a "For Sale" sign in front of it. It made her feel that just as she'd started wanting things to stay the same, they persisted in changing. That you could never really have that kind of frozen-in-time, on-the-outskirts-of-town Casper, Wyoming, coffee shop she and Lucas pined for; that their greatest challenge would be to keep things simple, out of time, slightly nostalgic. Was it possible in a place like Pike, where the forces of development and trend were so fierce?

She voiced her concerns to Lucas, who mentioned them to Val, adding that his wife saw the sign as *bad luck*. Val, sympathetic to such notions, stole out into the blackness the night before opening. Uprooting one leg of the sign, he rotated it ninety degrees and then sprayed in "Breakfast" above the "For Sale" and added an arrow pointing across the street. "It'll work for opening day, at least," he told Annie Lee the next morning, as she smiled, straining her eyes against the predawn dark to see what he'd done.

The only thing left to do was flip the sign on the door from "Closed" to "Open."

Annie Lee had stocked the old-timey cash register, briefed her wait staff—including Con Premus, who'd needed a change after a messy breakup with Dr. Kneejerk, as he took to calling him—and stood ready at the door as the hanging sign bearing the restaurant's name fluttered and banged in the fortuitously inclement weather outside. People wouldn't want to be outside battling the wind on skis, they would want to be inside a steamy room, suffocated sweetly by the smell of bacon and eggs and butter and fresh coffee. Eudora and Bea, who was finally cast-free but still limping after a full eight weeks, ate the first breakfasts at 6:32 A.M., giving the thumbs-up to their orders of over-easies and over-mediums.

On that busy opening day, friends, neighbors, and tourists entered in a steady stream all morning long. Annie Lee did not wait on customers but managed the nine tables and eight bar stools. She chatted, refilled coffees, cleared a few plates, and did anything else the kitchen told her to do. And despite unfamiliar procedures, a dysfunctional Frialator, a delivery mix-up, and a near-catastrophic problem with the grease trap, Lucas and Val and Annie Lee, along with one dishwasher, one evening prep guy, and two waiters, managed to make it through the weekend. Lucas only called Lina one time for emergency help; the other time he'd needed her she just happened to be there at the counter, eating an omelette. (Or *frittata*, as she dubbed it joyfully, after making Lucas put it under the salamander and serve it with balsamic vinegar.)

They were restaurant proprietors now, living in a blur of early mornings and full days, food-service headaches, employee management, and greater responsibility than either of them had ever known. Again, Annie Lee (who had still not mastered basic bookkeeping) was coping enviably well. Lucas, without the benefit of self-secreting chemicals, simply put his head down and worked as he had never worked before. He would reward himself with little touches he was very proud of: those blue New York City to-go coffee cups with the Greek motifs; a gumball machine near the cash register; curio salt and pepper shakers; and an oak display rack for the sisters' jam, which was sold as well as served. When he wasn't working, he was either sleeping, being molested by his perpetually "overheated" wife, or thinking of ways to streamline his business.

"The only thing I feel bad about," Lucas said, handing Annie Lee a tray of popovers about a week after opening—"put these over there—besides the fact that Bea is using a walker of all things, is Klink."

Since the restaurant had consumed the entire first floor of their house, the cat had been relegated to the upstairs. This was not received well at all. Lucas had gone so far as to build a shelf outside one of the windows so Klink could peer into the restaurant from outdoors. Thus, whoever happened to be sitting at table six usually got a big faceful of morose gray feline to go along with their eggs. Even on opening day, in a snowstorm, there sat Klink—perched stoically as the drifts swirled around him—blinking, as if to say, "What have I done to deserve this kind of treatment? What have I ever done, but be a loyal pet to you both?"

It became less disconcerting as people came to know Klink; Lucas thought also to include a little note about the cat at the bottom of the menu. Klink's blurb was right below several concise lines regarding the origin of the coffee shop's name.

These walls were originally—and still are—randomly insulated to the 27-inch level with lodestone, a naturally occurring magnetic material. Though we do not know the original owner's intent in surrounding himself with so many magnets—except that he may have believed in their special pow-

ers—we have spent many hours speculating. We urge customers to do the same.

Lucas had also posted a notice outside the door regarding pacemakers and handheld electronic devices, including portable phones. You just never knew.

Though Gabriel Salt's personality test did not make it to the menu rack on opening weekend, due to its being too lengthy for first-time customers, another one of his ideas did. In fact, the greatest surprise of all was that Gabriel showed up in person to deliver his "menu stuffers"—braved the six-hour drive in inclement weather to be there for opening.

He matched up to his voice completely, at least Annie Lee thought so, as he bent to give her a hug and pat her belly. Sharp nose, gunmetal gray eyes, and an overly sensitive look to his intelligent face. He had on jeans, a white tee shirt and a birch-gray sweater of good-quality wool, possibly cashmere. Having been kept up to date by his now regular phone calls to Annie Lee, he had chosen four additional sets of odd salt and pepper shakers as a restaurant-warming gift. Lucas was pleased.

For his first menu stuffer, he offered "Great Breakfasts of Literature," which was so well received that Lucas put Gabriel in charge of all reading material and started paying him to write it. He did "Breakfast Around the Little-Known World" one month; then a mini-cookbook on breakfast wraps. Annie Lee was most fond of a personal (and slightly hilarious) piece he did, called "Grandma Salt and the Oatmeal Conspiracy." Eventually, the personality test made it not only to the tables at the Lodestone but to National Public Radio's *Morning Edition*, during an interview with "Restaurant Reading Collaborator" Gabriel Salt.

Everyone said Gabriel had a radio-perfect voice—that he came off witty and shy and even mysteriously erudite, like some great undiscovered cult author. It was Annie Lee who suggested he try doing a two-minute Mr. Science–type show, highlighting a poison of the week and offering factual goodies on things ingested. Thus began Gabriel's radio career and *From Hand to Mouth with Gabriel Salt*. It was on his very own program that he did a piece called "Diamond in the Roughage" which earned him near-instant fame as well as an eventual offer of a book deal. Like great and oddly interdisciplinary minds before him, Gabriel became an essayist. He told stories with philosophical punch lines, morals, or admonitions. In due time, he quit his job in tel-emergency communications and turned to full-time writing. He purchased a lovely turn-of-the-century loft apartment in downtown Denver but visited Pike often, rubbing up against Annie Lee and Lucas as if he had found the rabbit feet of his life. This pleased Bea, who seemed to have developed a lively crush on him, enough to put the spark back in her eye, the spring back in her limp.

Libby Wolverton, who had not returned to Pike since her original trip but had also remained in touch, had arranged for six pots of white geraniums to be delivered to the Lodestone on opening day. Of course they were perfect. Libby never did divorce Elias, but had gone so far as to purchase a separate apartment, four blocks away, for her own sanity. "I realized, during that stay in Pike—when I actually started to get a feeling for the upper hand—that Elias loves it when people get the upper hand. Why, he eats right out of that upper hand now! He even walks Yin and Jung, the Afghans, when I bring them to visit. Can you believe it?"

Actually, it was very easy to believe.

In early November, Annie Lee had sent photos of the café to Libby to fully apprise her of just where the diamond had gotten them. Libby had called upon their receipt. "I got the pictures, Annie Lee, and I have to tell you first of all that you and that belly of yours positively radiate!" Annie Lee had, uncharacteristically, asked Lucas to take lots of pictures of her during her pregnancy, just so she could see what she really looked like. She did look happy. And, she didn't seem to have any sort of drowning-out look to her at all.

"In terms of the remo," Libby continued, "you've worked miracles! That wall color . . ." Annie Lee had painted the whole first floor a bombproof, glossy wax white with a tea-stain-colored glaze. "Wow, that is some change of *attitude*," she continued, touching then on the Formica-topped tables, the padded chairs. "I also wanted to ask you about that painting on the wall closest to the gum-ball machine. Your mother doing regular stuff now, stuff besides portraits?"

"That's my painting," Annie Lee said timidly. "Well, it was sort of an assignment. I gave myself parameters: house paints, a limited amount of time, and a saying. It's more of a poster than a painting."

"A poster, huh. Well, don't be so quick to make excuses, it's lovely! Even from what I can tell from the photo." It was a painting of a palm tree in a snowstorm, impressionistic, layered with shades of white paint. Underneath, in partially worn-off ornate script, were the words, *Carpe diem*. "Maybe you should think about doing a whole line of sayings . . . obviously it gets you going."

Annie Lee had thought of this, thought of it many times. She wondered during her entire pregnancy how she might incorporate her preoccupation with sayings into the restaurant. But it was not until that fateful conversation with Libby Wolverton that she got the brilliant idea—the best idea of her life, she thought—of hand-selected fortunes laced in with the gum balls. With every quarter spent on a sour apple, grape, watermelon, or orange gum ball, you got a fortune. They were about the same size as cookie fortunes, and Annie Lee printed them out in that same shade of magenta.

Thus did she spend countless rapturous hours looking things

up and thinking of sources of fortunes. She used phrases from that old Eight Ball game; from her favorite poets; from cookbook instructions; from etiquette manuals; from religious works of many denominations; from old postcards; from favorite song lyrics; from their own customers. Anything was fair game, from the ridiculous ("No more quazy whining. Get quackin' and get those ducks in a row.") to the sublime ("O body swayed to music, O brightening glance/How can we know the dancer from the dance?—Yeats").

The gum-ball machine became so popular Annie Lee had to replenish it weekly and found herself growing ever more adroit at the doling out of fortunes, warnings, pieces of advice, and restatements of the obvious. In the first year of operation at the Lodestone, they emptied $2,003 worth of quarters into a brand-new account. That represented over eight thousand fortunes. Some were used again and again, for obvious reasons. Eventually, she had to get a print shop to keep the fortunes on file and reprint them for her as she added a handful of new ones every week. She enlisted Eudora—who'd been dying for a crack at it—to help.

Though Annie Lee was not an epigrammatist, she had become an epigrammatist's best friend, thanks to an offhand comment made by Libby Wolverton about a painting, a whole line of sayings, and a gum-ball machine.

In mid-December, Nico Mars, after yet another last-minute last-name change, had been born to Jessica, whose labor had lasted—much to the horror of Annie Lee, whose turn would be next—thirty-three hours. Nico, named for the *Encyclopaedia Britan*nica, from which Val had learned most of American history, had dark skin and light hair excepting his eyelashes, which were long, black, and feathery and seemed to create a visor for his pale hazel eyes. Jessie let Annie Lee hold Nico a lot, but the baby felt strange, almost foreign. Jessie kept telling her, smiling indulgently, that after one full day with her own baby, everything would change. It was hard to grasp, though. Annie Lee had desperately wanted children, but she wasn't so sure she desperately wanted to have infants.

The Doyle twins, Bridget and Kelsey, had also arrived, three weeks prematurely, to join their five siblings. Though tipping the scales at barely five pounds each, they showed up with full heads of strident, stand-up, unripe-tomato red hair. Where had such locks come from? According to Megan, whose accounts of home life had now taken on the droll view of the freshly world-weary, this was the question that had sent her father deep into the annals of family genealogy. Megan pointed out that her father had recently started scowling at Rudy Colwick, the owner of the hardware store and the only one in town with hair the color of the twins'. Those twins seemed to be in the paper every week, too, which many said had to do with the fact that the sisters spent so much time taking care of them and couldn't be bothered to shoo away photographers anymore. What they didn't know was that the stroller had been custom-rigged for Bea, who was using it quite successfully as a surrogate walker. She swore her foot was on the mend because it was getting adequate usage outdoors.

Annie Lee went into labor on the tenth of January, at 9:14 P.M., during a feverish snowstorm that had blown in from the southwest without warning. Lucas, normally undaunted by the worst winter driving, reluctantly said he had a bad feeling about getting behind the wheel to drive the sixty miles to the hospital, that from his gut he didn't want to do it. Annie Lee was worried, but then she looked outside and figured it might be better to have the baby in Pike than at the top of some frigid mountain pass on the seat of a pickup truck.

So, in spite of their delivery obstetrician being at the hospital in another town, they stayed put and called Dr. Oram instead. His wife, quite put out, revealed that the doctor had gone to Grand Junction for an afternoon convention and had gotten stuck there in the same blizzard. There was nothing to do but notify the local on-call doctor at Pike's medical center and ask him to come help deliver a baby. Annie Lee told Lucas to call Judy Doyle and the sisters, all three of whom she needed nearby. With seven children, all born the regular way, Judy would know a thing or two about every phase of labor and delivery; and the sisters, who knew a lot about everything, just seemed to belong at her side for any ordeal whatsoever.

When Dr. Sidney Twist showed up, he found Annie Lee on a low bed—a foam mattress—they'd set up in the restaurant where table number four usually was, lined up right against the wall. He stared at her as if she'd chosen a stable in which to give birth.

"This will be my first baby," he said, rolling up his sleeves with a forced cheerfulness that slipped by no one. "Is there some significance to this spot?" he inquired politely.

"Yes," said Bea, somewhat stridently, "there is." She was probably happy to have a chance to confuse the "twelve-year-old" who'd put a cast on her. No one said "Magnetism is going to help push Annie Lee along," but it was obvious everyone was thinking it. Dr. Twist continued to stare at the low bed with its crisp white sheets. Eudora obliged him: "It's where the former tenant of this house came into the world. It's a birthing spot." Bea nodded in agreement, as if no more questions would be entertained.

Judy busied herself settling Annie Lee, whose contractions were coming closer and closer together. Lucas, the most nervous member of the group, finally went to kneel next to his wife and take one of her hands in his as much for his own comfort as hers.

"Don't worry," said Judy, putting her hand on his shoulder. "It's all going to be just fine, Lucas. You just sit there and let her squeeze your hand. You two are going to meet your child very soon!" Judy's words were like balm to Annie Lee. She looked at her neighbor, whose concern and goodwill were so evident in her face, and smiled at her until the next contraction came, and then the next. It was sheer, excruciating pain like nothing Annie Lee had ever experienced, sandwiched, in the respites, by the anticipation of more pain. Just when she thought she couldn't take it anymore, she felt an immense need to get the baby out and stared, panicked, around her, thinking that with the birth of her baby her body would burst like a balloon. That the baby's life would eventuate the end of hers. How could it possibly get out?

Dr. Twist himself panicked then. "What is it? What's wrong? She looks as if something's wrong!" He managed, as acting house doctor, to alarm the sisters as well as Lucas, who all jumped up, ready to do—they knew not what. Get the doctor? This was the doctor.

"Nothing is wrong!" Judy took control. "She's about to give birth: Now you men (she lumped the doctor and the husband together)—move back!" She lowered her voice. "It's okay, Annie Lee. It's time to push. Right when you feel you can't do anything but push, give it all you've got. Then rest and breathe, and I'll tell you when to push again. Don't hold back; scream that baby out of there!"

Dr. Twist, thanks to Judy, hardly had to do a thing to help that baby greet the day. Gemma Fleck came out as if she'd been greased—at 3:42 A.M. on January eleventh, after only eleven minutes of pushing and a total of just over six hours of real labor. Judy helped the doctor wrap the baby in a towel and showed him where to put her on Annie Lee's stomach, which he did with great beaming pride. It was almost as if he'd given birth himself. Eventually, they moved Annie Lee upstairs, where Judy helped little Gemma latch on to her mother's nipple.

"Look. At. That . . ." Bea said, both Winklemans standing together in their nightgowns and sweaters, holding each other's hands, while gazing at Annie Lee. "Landsakes, you two," Eudora was smiling through her tears. "What a miracle a birth is!" Neither of them had ever seen a child being born, as it turned out. This was their first. Lucas, who had nearly fainted as the baby's head crowned and then emerged, was shaking with relief to see his family intact.

Annie Lee's whole face was covered with tears. Gemma, named after the fateful diamond, had big eyes the color of the Atlantic during a hurricane. Her hair, what little there was of it, was a whitish blond, as were her brows and lashes. She had a seriousness to her upper lip that caused Annie Lee to reflect on how hard it must be to be catapulted into this cold and breezy world after the dark womb, and she vowed then and there to try to make her daughter's life as cozy—for lack of a better word—as possible. While she stared at her suckling baby, a tidal wave of questions overwhelmed her. What did I ever think I knew about anything before this? How much could I possibly know? How can I now pretend to show someone the way? What is the way?

"I'm really hungry," she said to her husband, both to signal her triumphant survival of childbirth and to give Lucas an opportunity to feel useful. "A chocolate shake and some salty home fries. Ketchup. Use the organic milk in the shake."

On his way downstairs, Lucas said his daughter's name aloud, "Gemma Louise Fleck." It had a certain steadfastness to it—and yet an undeniable grace. "Gemma Louise." He was cooking enough ham and eggs for a family of bodybuilders when Val showed up for work. Lucas, not known for his outward displays of emotion, was jumping up and down. "We had a girl—here—in our house!" He was pointing at the reinstated table four, for what reason Val couldn't tell. But Val picked Lucas up off the ground and hugged him and twirled him around like a dance partner.

"Congratulations, man." Val became serious. "Have you ever

seen anything so beautiful, man, as your own baby being born? So *emocional*, I couldn't hardly stand it. When the head came out—and then the placenta! Did you even know there was such a thing?"

Together they marched upstairs with the food. Val kissed Annie Lee gently on the forehead and then turned back to Lucas. "It's gonna change your life, dude," said Val with tears in his eyes. "It changed mine."

The atmosphere was festive at the Lodestone that morning, with free coffee and crumpets for everyone. The sisters had even suspended the jam-frugality rule for one day only and were spreading it on thick. Though Annie Lee did not go downstairs, she could hear the mayhem and feel the good wishes of people below as she wove in and out of sleep and nursing and people bringing food to her. Six inches of snow had fallen during the night. Outside, the world was big, and white, and felt like a lullaby.

When Val came up again later, with Jessica and Nico, his gaze rested on Gemma, whose eyes were open this time, jarringly pure in their calm absorption of the blurry world. After a good long look, he said, "*Cada cabeza es un mundo!*" He had his hands pressed together as if in thought, and then let them drop. "Put *that* in your gum-all machine, Annie Lee."

"Oh yeah? What does it mean?" She was staring at the baby in the same way Val was, pondering those deeply affecting questions of origin and family, connection and future, beginning and end. Their baby! She had fingernails the size of infant ladybugs. Her mouth was perfect. She looked so serious. What was she thinking, there, so near the edges of existence?

"It means," Val whispered reverently, "'Each head is a world of its own.' And in case you can't see it every day, especially in a place li' this where the world passes through the jingling-jangling doorway, you got it again ri' here in this little bundle of brand-new DNA. '*Cada cabeza es un mundo.*' My father used to say that."

Annie Lee wondered at the richness of life suggested in Val's proverb. Every person's brain contains a world within it, each world different from all the others. We are all—from the moment of birth—like aliens to each other, each from a different planet, wanting, without completely understanding why, to make contact with the rest of the universe. We try to understand, to fathom our coming together, but all we can really do is muddle through. If we are lucky, we marvel at what is before us.

If we are lucky, we marvel.

Appendix One

Winkleman Once Secret Roseberry Jam

Carefully pluck all the petals off a mature mountain rose bush (you should have at least six cups, not packed in). Place two cups of petals along with ¼ cup sugar in a jar—you'll need three jars—and put in the summer sunlight for at least one week, turning jars regularly. You should end up with a sweet and flowery-smelling paste.

Using a family recipe for raspberry jam (don't ask us for ours), incorporate the rose petals into the jam right before ladling into jars. Process jars. Let jam rest in a dark place for several weeks before use.

Do not use commercial roses or unripe berries. And if it doesn't turn out exactly like ours, why, don't blame us. We're old hands at it and we still have our secrets. If it does turn out, give thanks to the wild sweetness of nature, for it has always been our inspiration.

Beatrice and Eudora Winkleman
Pike, Colorado
1999

Appendix Two

Annie Lee's First Page of Her First Batch of Gum-ball Fortunes.

Take two aspirin, have a cup of tea, one cookie, and check in with yourself tomorrow morning. If you're still blue, why, scrub the floors. —Eudora Winkleman

Only dull people are brilliant at breakfast. —Oscar Wilde

When we were sweet and twenty / We never guessed that what we'd got / Though not a lot / Was plenty. —Noël Coward, *Bitter Sweet*

Everybody is ignorant, only on different subjects. —Will Rogers

He wrapped himself in quotations—as a beggar would enfold himself in the purple of Emperors. —Rudyard Kipling

It's like coming to a halting scratch. —Jimmy Doyle, age four, after learning a hockey stop on skates.

Rub the magic can of Niblets Brand whole kernel corn with a can opener. You'll get your wish, Mister, tonight or any night, any day of the year. —Green Giant ad, *Life* magazine, December 1, 1947

Everything is a miracle. It is a miracle that one does not dissolve in one's bath like a lump of sugar. —Pablo Picasso

Look at the camera and say "Cheese."

You only have to take the bitter with the sweet if you like bittersweet chocolate. —Ronny, from the Pike hardware store

To see the Summer Sky / Is poetry, though never in a Book it lie— / True Poems flee—Emily Dickinson

If you see life as a game, you play it. If you see life as a lesson, you learn it. My feeling is that it's somewhere between the two. —Bea Winkleman

"I can't help it," said Alice very meekly; "I'm growing." —Lewis Carroll

Where natural light alone isn't sufficient for plants to flourish, a boost from artificial lighting is often the best solution. —Houseplants care guide

Jell-O is like the princess in the fairy tale: it is as good as it is beautiful. —1928 Jell-O cookbook

Appendix Three

Grandma Salt and the Oatmeal Conspiracy

As aired on *From Hand to Mouth with Gabriel Salt*, National Public Radio

In the great legacy of rational thinking left to me by my grandmother, it was her take on oatmeal that stuck to my ribs the most. Over many years, you see, she had come to feel the world was being governed by pasty-faced persons lacking fiber in their diets. With continued observation, she resolved that only a full-on crusade with the Quaker Oats man imprinted on her hand-held flag could save the world from the sorry people in power. They were ruining things—and what's worse they were doing it irritably.

"It's easy to see, Gabe," she said on more than one occasion, shaking her head, "family life is breaking down. The breakfast ritual is gone. People simply aren't taking oatmeal anymore." A retired nurse, Gran used the word "taking" interchangeably with "eating," something I'd always found disquieting, especially in phrases like "Will you take some pudding, Gabe?" or "Your father's taking roast beef in the den." Come to think of it, it was probably Gran who stimulated my early interest in the alimentary canal, foods, poisons, and metaphors of ingestion.

Gran had a colloquial way with words. "It doesn't take a

genius," she said, "to see that intestines are directly related to disposition, and disposition governs not only the self but those in orbit around the self. Intestinally challenged men who sit behind desks and shake each others' hands all day—they don't have the benefit of regularity. They're cranky and they're powerful and the two just don't jibe. Not in my book they don't."

I had to take issue with the reasons for their peevishness. "You don't think politics has anything to do with it, Gran?" I queried. "It makes me cranky just thinking about it."

"Nonsense, Gabriel," she said. "Governance is not by nature an irksome task. No sir! Knowing cafeteria food, I guarantee you the majority of those men don't eat a raw vegetable more than once a week, unless it's iceberg lettuce or a carrot chip. The boys at the front are full of toxins, dear. We should be afraid for our country, our very lives. Look how many decisions are being made without the benefit of having had a good sit on the john!"

It was not enough for my grandmother—Valencia, but people called her Vee—to sit idly by, intestines supremely functional, while others, blockaded, obstructed, and cross, wrote legislation and pushed buttons. In her late seventies, she wrote to the Quaker Oats Company asking them to hire her as a lobbyist in Washington. In the letter, she certified herself as a lifelong lover of their product and swore that as a result she was hale, high-minded, and headstrong.

"Send me on a mission!" she wrote in her sensible script, throwing in an exclamation point even though she'd been told that such punctuation usually defeats the purpose. This time she could not help herself. "Yours in well-being," she signed it. "Valencia Salt LPN."

Three weeks later she received a form letter in the mail thanking her for her interest in the Quaker Oats Company and urging her to try some of the recipes in the booklet enclosed. Rather than feel slighted that no one had addressed her strategies for world betterment, she took it as a sign that the higher-ups at the company, who for obvious reasons could not condone such a campaign, could nevertheless give her the tools to do so on her own. She saw their meaning and got serious.

Granny Vee made thousands of copies of the recipe pamphlet, booked herself a flight to D.C., and spent two days at the Capitol handing out oatmeal formulas to legislators, judges, lawyers, and wannabes, and then, as an afterthought, sneaked over to the Pentagon, where she stood outside and did the very same thing there for another half day. She dressed conservatively in her gray wool suit and smiled at each person who took her handout. Occasionally, and only appropriately, she would say, "Have you had your oats today?"

When she returned home to Denver, every inch of her exhausted from so many hours pounding the hard pavement, she fully expected to see herself on the evening news, so great was her feeling that she'd finally made a difference in the world. Though careful not to reveal her firebrand activities, she penned a quick note to the Quaker Oats Company. "Thank you," it said, "for giving me the opportunity to prom-oat, spelled P-R-O-M-O-A-T, such a fine grain." Two weeks later she received another form letter, this one stamp-signed P. David Donahugh, kindly acknowledging her interest in the Quaker Oats Company and suggesting she try some of the recipes enclosed. It was the same booklet.

Little did P. David know of Valencia Salt. How could he? He was a new employee, a recent defector from the Kellogg Company . . . Overzealous in his first days in customer service, he'd forgotten the first rule of dealing with the public: Never sign your name, or even stamp-sign it. With his name at her disposal, Gran felt free to write to him weekly with her views on oats.

Kindly, he would acknowledge her ideas, stamp his signature, and send her nice little things. A Quaker Oats pen. A box of assorted flavored instant oats (which she gave to the birds). A stash of his personal Quaker Oats stationery. Soon enough, he started signing his name in ink and eventually felt compelled to tell her about himself. They became good friends. When he stopped hearing from her (she'd passed away), he wrote to me, extolling her virtues. I called him at work because I missed Grandma Vee and wanted to hear someone talk about her. No, he said, he'd never shown her letters to the higher-ups, they would have called her a crackpot. And he'd never known about the trip to the nation's capital. He just really liked her spirit.

"Guess where she got all her energy?" I asked him. "All that energy and good humor and snappiness?"

"I don't know," he said. "Good old-fashioned genes?"

"Nope," I said, feeling the force of Gran's ghost come over me. "Good old-fashioned oats." After I'd hung up, I felt sort of bad about lecturing the man. Then I figured it was just as well if he got fired up about the company—it would have been Gran's wish to influence the world just a little bit more from on high. So in tribute to a woman I loved so dearly—I have to say to everyone out there listening: Fiber up, folks, and get crackin'.